'*Meg, this is my s*

For a moment Meg thoug... wrong. But then, through ... disbelief, she realized that the boy had Joe's same angular jaw, his same heavy-lidded eyes. Meg had no idea how she reacted. She was dimly aware of Joe moving, reaching towards her.

All she could see was the boy. A nine-year-old version of Joe.

'Son, this is my wife.' Joe's words sounded strangely distant, but she saw the boy's eyes narrow in acknowledgement. Then Joe moved to take her numb hand in his.

'He's got nobody left,' he said softly, meeting her gaze with a mixture of apology, panic and love in his eyes. 'I don't have all the details, but we—' Joe faltered, then started again. 'I mean, we're going to—'

Meg drew a shaky breath, and smiled. 'We're going to take him home…'

C000010741

Dear Reader,

Seasons greetings from Silhouette Special Edition®. We are pleased to present you with some real gifts in this month's festive line-up.

Perennial favourite Cathy Gillen Thacker has come up with a real Christmas cracker—find out if mother-to-be Kate Montgomery and Dr Michael Sloane, the father of her unborn child, settle their differences in time for *Baby's First Christmas*. And a mail-order mix-up leaves the *wrong* brother marrying the *right* bride in Marie Ferrarella's *Wife in the Mail*.

Sexy sheriff Justin Adams breaks all his own rules by helping desperate single mother Patsy Langhorn in Sherryl Woods's *Natural Born Lawman*. And Joe McConnell wants to change all the rules when he discovers a son he never knew he had. Could he ask his wife to be a mother to his child? Don't miss *Unexpected Family* from Laurie Campbell.

College sweethearts meet up again, and Brent Morrison is about to discover *why* Blythe ran out on him all those years ago in Jackie Merritt's *The Secret Daughter*, the last part of THE BENNING LEGACY trilogy.

Finally, a passionate encounter and Caitlin's in trouble—the 6lb 12oz kind!—that's Lois Faye Dyer's *The Only Cowboy for Caitlin*.

Happy Christmas reading, and come back to us in 2000!

The Editors

Unexpected Family

LAURIE CAMPBELL

™ SILHOUETTE
SPECIAL EDITION®

DID YOU PURCHASE THIS BOOK WITHOUT A COVER?
If you did, you should be aware it is **stolen property** as it was reported
unsold and destroyed by a retailer. Neither the author nor the publisher
has received any payment for this book.

All the characters in this book have no existence outside the imagination
of the author, and have no relation whatsoever to anyone bearing the same
name or names. They are not even distantly inspired by any individual
known or unknown to the author, and all the incidents are pure invention.

All Rights Reserved including the right of reproduction in whole or in part
in any form. This edition is published by arrangement with Harlequin
Enterprises II B.V. The text of this publication or any part thereof may not
be reproduced or transmitted in any form or by any means, electronic or
mechanical, including photocopying, recording, storage in an
information retrieval system, or otherwise, without the written
permission of the publisher.

This book is sold subject to the condition that it shall not, by way of trade
or otherwise, be lent, resold, hired out or otherwise circulated without the
prior consent of the publisher in any form of binding or cover other than
that in which it is published and without a similar condition including
this condition being imposed on the subsequent purchaser.

Silhouette, Silhouette Special Edition and Colophon are
registered trademarks of Harlequin Books S.A., used under licence.

First published in Great Britain 1999
Silhouette Books, Eton House, 18-24 Paradise Road,
Richmond, Surrey TW9 1SR

© Laurie Schnebly Campbell 1999

ISBN 0 373 24230 1

23-9912

Printed and bound in Spain
by Litografia Rosés S.A., Barcelona

For Christopher,
Who asks every weekend between video games,
'So…you need any help with your book?'

LAURIE CAMPBELL

spends her weekdays writing brochures, videos and commercial scripts for an advertising agency. At five o'clock she turns off her computer, waits thirty seconds, turns it on again and starts writing romance. Her other favourite activities include playing with her husband and son, teaching catechism class, counselling at a Phoenix mental health clinic and working with other writers. 'People ask me how I find time to do all that,' Laurie says, 'and I tell them it's easy. I never clean my house!'

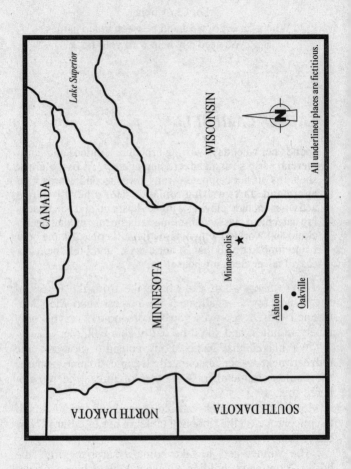

CANADA

Lake Superior

WISCONSIN

MINNESOTA

Minneapolis

Ashton

Oakville

NORTH DAKOTA

SOUTH DAKOTA

All underlined places are fictitious.

N

Chapter One

"How many words can you make from the letters of N E W B A B Y?" challenged the hostess, and Meg McConnell closed her eyes. Two more hours, maybe only ninety minutes, and she'd be out of this hellhole.

"We played that game at my cousin's shower!" the redhead next to her announced. Jeannie, Joanne, a name she couldn't remember. A mother of three, she remembered that.

Meg gripped her pink-and-blue pencil and forced herself to concentrate on the ribboned tablet in her lap. Baby. New baby. Baby...

"The winner gets to take home a surprise gift," the hostess continued, holding up what looked like a tissue-wrapped champagne bottle. "And I'll give you a hint—it has nothing to do with babies."

There was a chorus of laughter, and Meg hastily summoned up a smile. It felt frozen on her face, but no one seemed to notice anything wrong.

"You need to win that, Meg," her friend Susan called across the circle of women. Then, as if remembering that not everyone worked at the same school, she explained, "Meg and her husband are celebrating their fourth anniversary tonight."

A round of congratulations echoed through the room. This was a convivial group, Meg knew; she had always enjoyed the other secretaries and teachers at Oakville Country Day School.

It was just all this talk about babies that made her skin feel too tight.

"Has it really been four years?" asked the principal, a recent grandmother of twins. "My goodness, Meg, it seems like only yesterday we were at your wedding shower."

"Seeing how many words we could make out of B R I D E," Susan recalled, and everyone laughed. "Meg, where are you and Joe going for dinner?"

Thank God, a question she could answer. And an excuse to stop staring at the B A B Y letters on her pad.

"He made reservations at the Wayside Inn," she said, hoping no one would notice any strain in her voice. This was a sympathetic group of women, but there was nothing they could do…and it would be awful to spoil her co-worker's shower. "We thought about waiting for the weekend, but today's our anniversary date."

"Four years," the principal repeated, shaking her head in amazement. "Time goes by so fast, doesn't it?"

Oh, please, Meg thought, gripping her pencil so tightly that her shoulder started tingling. Please, somebody change the subject.

But the silence lingered for an agonizing pulse of time—during which she could almost hear the question forming on everyone's lips—before Susan leaped to the rescue.

"I hope as soon as we finish this game, Linda's going to start opening presents!"

There was a clamor of agreement, and Meg drew a shaky breath. No one was going to ask it now.

If she could just get through the next two hours…

But maintaining a smile was harder than she'd imagined. Not since her sister's baby shower two years ago had she sat through an afternoon of baby names, baby games, baby toys and baby gifts and baby plans—and two years ago, back when they'd barely started with the fertility specialist, there had still been hope.

She should have remembered, though, what it felt like to sit among a group of women exclaiming over babies. If she'd remembered, she would have made some excuse—any excuse—to skip this party.

And left everyone clucking with sympathy.

"Meg, how wonderful!"

With a start, she realized that Linda had just unwrapped her present: a yellow-rimmed bath set that she'd selected in Minneapolis rather than entering the Baby Emporium here in Oakville. She'd postponed wrapping it for as long as she could, yearning over the sweetly soft towel and nubby washcloth, the hooded robe and yellow rubber duck, and when she finally buried them in the yellow-flowered tissue paper she'd felt the familiar anguish twisting inside her.

"I hope you and the baby enjoy it," she managed to say over the tightness in her throat. She still sounded normal, didn't she? There was no way to tell, but at least no one looked at her strangely. She probably sounded just fine.

She'd had plenty of practice.

Most recently when the adoption social worker came to examine the McConnells. No one had put it in those words, of course, but she and Joe both knew they were on trial. It hadn't bothered him a bit, but then, her husband thrived on challenges.

"Oh, how darling!" she heard someone exclaim over Linda's next gift. "Pass that around, too."

Another white gown lavished with embroidery. Meg gritted her teeth, accepted the gown from the woman next to her and admired it for what felt like a decent interval before passing it along. To the mother of three.

Imagine having three babies. One at a time, probably, but even so—what incredible richness. Early on she and Joe had wondered how many children they should have, and decided on either three or four...a decision that now seemed wretchedly naive. But she had enjoyed planning for what she'd always viewed as her destiny. She had enjoyed picturing a houseful of daughters for whose dolls she would pour tea, and sons for Joe to take camping....

Elena would have given him children.

Before the thought could crystallize, Meg jerked her attention to the present in her lap. A handmade quilt, which all the mothers had just agreed was more a necessity than a luxury. She had nothing to contribute to the discussion, no experience to cite, but no one seemed to notice her reticence. She buried her hands under the satiny quilt, hoping she could clench her fists until the tension evaporated.

"Here, Meg, look at this."

She stared blindly at a pink-bordered blanket and felt another clutch of anguish twist inside her.

"Excuse me a minute," she murmured, escaping the offering as she rose from her chair and glanced down the hall toward the bathroom. "I'll be right back."

If she could just take five minutes alone....

Luckily there was no one in the bathroom. From force of habit she checked her reflection in the mirror and saw that her strawberry blond hair curled properly off her face, her wide collar lay straight and her plain silver earrings looked fine. Meg gripped the edge of the sink and took a long, steadying breath.

"You can do this," she said aloud. "You can do this, Meg McConnell."

She had made it this far, after all. They were on every waiting list in Minnesota, and one would surely yield a baby soon. Besides, there had to be more to life than just the quest for motherhood.

There was, she told the doubtful face in the mirror. After all, last year she had been selected to manage the Country Day alumni office. Her rose garden was one of the best in Oakville. And the church choir director swore they'd never had a better organist....

But until she could mother a baby, Meg knew, she would always be lacking something vital. She would never be a genius like her brother, nor a beauty queen like her sister, and she would never live up to Elena's daring, dazzling intensity. But as a mother—wholeheartedly loving, nurturing and sustaining a family—oh, then her ordinary life would shine.

If only this shower were for *her* baby...

A burst of applause came from the living room, and she tightened her grip on the counter.

She had to go back out there, Meg knew. She couldn't stay here all afternoon, aching for a baby and hoping the group wouldn't notice her absence. No, she was going to head back to the living room and admire the rest of the presents, take a piece of that pink-and-blue-flowered cake, exclaim over the decorations and keep from glancing too often at the grandfather clock by the door.

You can do this, she ordered herself. Just remember, one day you'll have a baby of your own.

She drew another deep breath, then another, and made her way back down the hall to the party.

The crowd was moving, she saw with a surge of relief. Linda must have unwrapped the last present, because people were congregating around the refreshment table. Thank God, she could hold onto a plastic cup of pink punch and make conversation with Susan, who wouldn't ask any agonizing questions. Susan knew the whole story.

Or at least most of it.

"Meg, would you like a corner piece?" the hostess called from the cake table. "Or one with a rose?"

"Meg adores roses, remember?" Susan teased. "She's the one who keeps our whole office smelling wonderful."

"Either one's fine," Meg answered, accepting a piece of white cake topped with a sugary rose. She wasn't going to eat it in any case, but maybe they could talk about roses for the next few minutes. For as long as it took to get herself geared up for the final hurdle, the last stretch of conversation before she could congratulate Linda and get out of here without looking anguished.

Roses were good. Gardening was always a good topic, and so was the unusually warm April weather. But no matter how doggedly she tried to ask about spring cleaning, Easter dinners, vacation plans and summer diets, the very air seemed to shimmer with images of babies. Baby pictures, baby sounds, baby scents...

"Just that new-baby smell," recalled the principal, "took me right back to when my daughter was born, and every night we'd do 'This Little Piggy.'"

"I can't wait to play that," Linda said. "And to start reading nursery rhymes."

"Speaking of reading," Susan interrupted, "did anybody see this morning's paper? Terrific story on the editorial page."

All eyes swung to Meg. "I'll tell Joe," she promised, hoping they hadn't seen her glancing at the clock. Although maybe they would simply assume she was anticipating her anniversary dinner.

"It *was* good," Linda agreed. "I don't read the *Herald*

every week—don't tell him that, Meg!—but whenever I read one of Joe's stories, I feel like I was right there.''

She felt a rush of pride—no one could ever view her husband as merely ordinary. ''Now I really can't wait to see him,'' she said, with a smile for Linda. ''He'll love hearing that.''

Then Susan, bless her heart, offered an even greater gift. ''Meg, you ought to be home getting ready for your big evening right now! You don't want Joe to come in and find you half-dressed, do you?''

''Maybe she does,'' Linda joked, and Meg felt herself starting to blush. It was silly—they'd been married four years, after all—but certain visions of Joe could still make her feel as giddy and trembling as she'd felt the first time she'd seen him.

That was half a lifetime ago, when her brother brought him home after football practice and she'd found them plotting tackles in the backyard.

Even then Joe had radiated more heat, more force, more intensity than anyone she'd ever known. She'd taken one look at his fierce, crackling energy, his rugged build and his rough-and-tumble, tousled dark hair and had fallen in love on the spot. And even now she knew if someone had told her, that afternoon in Larkwood, that one day she'd be planning an anniversary dinner with Joe Mc-Connell…she would have believed herself the luckiest girl in the world.

There had never been another man like Joe.

''Meg, you're blushing!'' Susan observed, putting an arm around her shoulders and guiding her toward the door. ''You'd better get home fast. And remember, tomorrow morning we're all going to come crowding your office asking about the Wayside Inn.''

''I'll give you every detail,'' Meg promised, ''about the food. But that's it!''

With a chorus of laughter lightening the farewells, it

was easy to escape the shower for the three-block walk home. She found herself smiling—not the forced smile she'd worn most of the afternoon, but one of pleasurable anticipation. In less than an hour, she'd be ready for an evening with Joe…and maybe tonight would be one of those special ones.

The kind she'd only dreamed of back in ninth grade. Back when she used to decorate her diary with hearts containing their initials. Back when Joe was still only fantasizing about a career as a globe-trotting reporter. Back when neither of them had ever heard of Milagua.

Of the prison camps.

Or of Elena.

"Story of the month!" Joe exulted. "You got it, Phil. This is it."

The rookie reporter looked almost as thrilled as Joe felt. "I thought when the deputy came in, he was gonna ticket my car or something. But when he dropped that list on my desk…"

"This is terrific." Joe scanned the list of phone numbers, halfway expecting the magic one to leap off the page. "Somewhere on here, we'll find hard-and-fast proof. Hey, Abby! Gloria! Come see what we've got."

The receptionist and typesetter joined him and Phil at the battered metal desk they had nicknamed the City Room. In an office this size, nearly every desk—not to mention every staffer—served double or triple duty.

"Sounds good," Abby agreed, handing him a sheaf of message slips. By now the entire staff knew not to forward his calls when he was hot on a story. "But, Joe, it's ten minutes till five."

He looked at her blankly for a moment before realizing what that meant. "Aw, damn!" The others could search the list without him, of course, but he hated to miss the thrill of the chase. "Well, let's see how far we can get."

"Since when does our fearless leader knock off at five?" Phil demanded. "Or did I miss something?"

"No, it's just…" Joe shoved the message slips in his back pocket and handed out the deputy's pages to everyone within reach, keeping a short stack for himself. "I'm taking my wife out to dinner tonight."

"Even with a story like this?" the reporter asked incredulously. "This is the kind of thing you ask Santa Claus for."

He was right. If the *Herald* could prove that the county sheriff was in league with a convicted drug dealer, they'd have newspapers all over Minnesota clamoring for the scoop. "I know," Joe muttered, scanning the top page and automatically grabbing a pencil off the desk. "It's a killer story."

Gloria glanced up from her own stack of pages. "So why don't you postpone your dinner?" the gray-haired typesetter suggested. "Meg'll understand."

She would, he knew. She was used to him coming home at midnight, working nonstop on weekends, calling to cancel plans whenever a story sprang up…and she always understood.

Which was why, at least on their anniversary, she deserved to come first.

"No," he said, resolutely ignoring the flutter of uneasiness in his chest. "You guys can handle it without me."

"Don't be too sure," the receptionist warned. "If this turns out as big as it sounds like, you're gonna be in here every morning at four. Proofing text, cropping photos and banging out editorials to beat the band."

Joe had to smile at that. She was right, and they all knew it—no one put more into this newspaper than its editor-in-chief.

"Let me know what you find, okay?" he asked, slashing his pencil across the completed page. "Leave a message on the machine."

"Oh, sure, and interrupt your anniversary celebration?" Abby protested. "You can take one night off, for heaven's sake."

One night off, Joe repeated to himself, crumpling the page for the discard pile. There was no reason to be nervous about one night off.

"Just don't forget your messages," she continued, "before you leave. The mayor insisted somebody has to cover his speech, and the social worker will be in tomorrow."

That sounded vaguely familiar, but he would have sworn he and Meg were safely through the home study. "Social worker?" he repeated, turning his attention to the next page. If he could just find something within the next few minutes...

"From Catholic Charities, remember? About helping the children of Milagua."

"Oh, right." He'd gotten some garbled message about that last week, and wondered how—even in Oakville, even four years after the book came out—his name could still be synonymous with Milagua. Although maybe they would have contacted any editor who could be counted on to promote fund-raising efforts. "I guess we can run an appeal over the next two weeks, while everybody's thinking about tax deductions."

"We just did one for the Children's Hospital," Gloria reminded him, adding another page to the discard pile. "It might be a little soon to start soliciting again, especially for some Latin American country that keeps killing its leaders."

Phil shot her a warning glance. "Gloria," he began, and Abby cut him off.

"Joe was there," she said. "For five years."

The typesetter looked up from the pages to him. "In *Milagua?*"

Gloria was new in town, but he was surprised—and a little gratified—that she hadn't heard anything. People in

Oakville tended to discuss each other's life histories as readily as the weather, and he'd lost count of the times someone had inquired in a low, confidential tone, "So... what was it *really* like?"

Joe stayed focused on the numbers in front of him, watching for the right combination to leap from the page. "It was a long time ago," he said flatly. "Back in the early days."

"But you were covering the rebellion? For the *Herald?*" Gloria sounded even more incredulous, and he could see why. No small-town newspaper could justify sending a reporter to Milagua. Not even the major dailies had bothered to cover the first few skirmishes.

"I was freelancing," he explained, crumpling the finished page and reaching for an untouched stack to add to his own. "Here, let me take some of those."

"You're not reading phone lists while you drive!" Abby protested.

He stood up, folding the pages into a vertical sheaf, and glanced around for his keys. "No, just at stoplights." There were at least five lights between here and home; he could easily—

"Forget it, Joe," the receptionist ordered, yanking the pages out of his hand. "I know you love living on the edge, but let somebody else do it for once. Go home."

Faced with an order like that, there wasn't much he could say. And he *had* made Abby promise to see that he left at five. "Okay, I'll see you guys tomorrow," Joe conceded. "But seriously, call me if you find something. Or if you need any backup."

"Right, chief," Phil said, giving him a mock salute. "Tell Meg happy anniversary from the *Herald* Angels."

Happy anniversary.

Right.

Joe grabbed his sport coat from the back of a chair, hurried to his car and tried to visualize where he might pick up some flowers on the way home. Most of the shops were closed for the day whenever he drove along Main Street...but then, today he was well ahead of his usual schedule. If he stopped at that Posy Place or whatever it was called, he could still make it home in time for a quick shower and shave before they set off for dinner.

And Meg's eyes would light up, he knew. Even though she would tell him "You shouldn't have," she'd be delighted with the gesture.

He let the clerk at the flower shop assemble a bouquet of yellow and white tulips, daisies and jasmine that looked like the sort of thing Meg would enjoy. Kind of sweet and traditional, but with enough spunk to brighten up the entire counter when the clerk placed it triumphantly in front of him.

"Terrific," Joe said. "This is just like her."

"Would you like a card to go with it?"

"Sure," he agreed recklessly. He could inscribe a card, no problem. He was, after all, a writer.

But with a blank card and a pen in his hand, he could feel the uneasiness rising in his chest again. Hastily, he scrawled "Happy Anniversary. Love, Joe," and jammed the card into the envelope. Then, slapping some money on the counter, he hurried outside without waiting for his change.

It didn't matter what the card said, anyway, he assured himself as he started the car. Besides, bringing home flowers was the kind of thing everyone did on an anniversary. It was a tradition, like champagne on New Year's Eve.

There was nothing to be nervous about.

He had everything under control.

It was unusual, Meg thought, to see Joe's car pulling into the driveway while there was still daylight outside. But it shouldn't come as a surprise. He'd promised to be home early, and she'd learned over the years—every time he refused another job offer which would take them out of Oakville—that he always kept his word.

"Happy anniversary," she greeted him at the kitchen door, then caught her breath as she saw the flowers. "Oh, Joe, you shouldn't have. But thank you!"

He responded with the crooked smile she loved, hugging her one-handed until she transferred the flowers out of his way. "Happy anniversary, Meggles. You look really good."

Whenever she worried about her husband's emotional distance, Meg reminded herself, she needed to remember that he always paid her the right compliments. "I've been looking forward to this all day," she admitted, raising her face for another kiss. Joe smelled good, with his usual sharp scent of newspaper ink and old smoke and masculine heat softened by the leftover sweetness of flowers. "Everybody at school was excited about us going to the Wayside Inn."

"Yeah? I figured that's the kind of place where I'd better shave again," he said, rubbing his cheek against hers as if seeking confirmation. The rasp of half-day whiskers felt curiously arousing, but she had to admit that a countryside resort wasn't the ideal place to sport the shadow of a beard.

"Go ahead," she told him. "I want to finish my makeup in the guest room mirror." In fact she had finished it half an hour ago, but she knew he'd rather have the bathroom to himself. Even though his body was as close to healed as it would ever be, Joe was still sensitive about the legion of scars.

He ran his finger slowly across her smudged lipstick, then touched it to his lips. "I'll just be a minute," he promised, dropping his coat over the back of a kitchen chair. "The reservation's for six-thirty, but it's kind of a drive out there."

The distant setting was part of what made the inn so

romantic, Meg knew. "Maybe we'll see a sunset on the way," she called after him, and heard his muffled agreement as he turned on the shower.

By the time she'd arranged her flowers in the tallest cutglass vase she could find and gone to retrieve her lipstick from the vanity tray, she found Joe already dressed and shaving in front of the bathroom mirror. "You take faster showers," she told him, "than anybody I know."

He smiled at her reflection in the mirror. "Speaking of showers," he asked, drawing the razor deliberately down the side of his chin, "how'd it go this afternoon? You get through it okay?"

She felt a tug of warmth at the realization that he understood how much she'd dreaded the experience. But it wasn't fair to make him listen to any more heartache, not on their anniversary. Not when he'd been so supportive already. "Just fine," Meg said brightly. "Linda got a lot of cute stuff."

She would have sworn her voice sounded normal, but Joe turned away from the mirror, holding her gaze with his, and gently touched her cheek.

Without a word.

For a moment they stood in silence, balanced in stillness...and then he drew a long breath. "You will, too," he said softly. "You'll see, Meggins. Soon as we get a baby, there'll be people lining up with all kinds of presents."

She had to swallow before she could reply. "I know," she murmured. But what she really meant was "thank you," and Joe seemed to understand that, too, because he rested his forehead atop hers in a gesture of acknowledgment.

This, Meg thought with a surge of gratitude, is why I love him. Never once, through all the turmoil and anguish of learning that her blocked Fallopian tubes meant she would never conceive a child, had Joe spoken a word of blame. Although he'd never once mentioned his own feelings, he had held her, comforted her through the months of grief and guilt, and agreed without reservation when she finally mentioned adoption.

Yet it had to be hard on him, knowing he would never have a child who shared his blood. Of course parenthood was more about love than biology, but still, didn't most men want to see their genes carried on?

Joe had insisted it didn't matter. That, having never met his own father, he couldn't really qualify as the founder of a dynasty. But even so—

"Hey," he murmured, evidently feeling the growing tightness in her shoulders. "Come on, Meggers. You don't want to show up at the resort all covered with shaving cream, do you?"

It was exactly the right question to break the tension, and Meg couldn't help smiling. "No," she said, dabbing a smear of lather off his chin. "I guess not."

With a quick caress of reassurance, he let her go and turned back to the mirror. "Good decision," he observed. "Do me a favor, will you, and pick me out a tie?"

She always enjoyed filling such requests. It gave her a feeling of being truly married, of sharing domestic comforts that only a husband and wife could enjoy. Meg selected a pink-and-gray stripe and a blue-on-blue paisley and held them both out for him to choose.

"Pink and blue, huh?" Joe rinsed his razor and left it on the edge of the sink, then rubbed a towel across his face. "I can tell you've got babies on the brain."

He was right, she realized, looking again at the choices. "But here you get to pick whichever you want."

Although the agency caseworker had warned that adoption was just like giving birth in that you couldn't specify a boy or a girl, Meg still secretly dreamed of a daughter. A daughter would enjoy the same Blue Willow teacups and Laura Ingalls Wilder books she'd always cherished,

would share the joyous satisfaction of watching her roses
bloom, would envision ruffled dresses that Meg could sew
for her. Although, of course, boys were probably just as
much fun in their own way…and all babies started out
equally adorable.

"This one, then," Joe said, selecting the pink tie and
making her wonder if he'd read her thoughts. Glancing
back at the mirror, he swiftly knotted it and then shrugged
into the suit coat he'd left on the bed. "So, Mrs. Mc-
Connell, you ready to go celebrate our four-year anniversary?"

Four years.

Four years of wishing. Of hoping for a child to work
the magic they needed.

Of reminding herself that nothing worth waiting for
happened overnight.

"More than ready," she agreed, waiting while he held
her coat for her. "I can't wait to see this Wayside Inn."

It was nestled in a grove of walnut trees at the end of
a quiet country road, and by the time they finished the
half-hour drive Meg felt as if the tranquility of the setting
had somehow seeped into them both. Joe was more relaxed than she'd seen him all week, although admittedly
she hadn't seen much of him. But she could tell the difference in his posture, even in his voice…the farther they
drove out of town, the more the pressures of the *Herald*
seemed to ease.

And when they arrived at the secluded inn just as twilight began settling over the tiny lights in the trees, Meg
thought of coming home to Cinderella's castle. White-
painted clapboard instead of stone turrets, and the moat
was replaced by a velvet green lawn, but even so the very
air seemed to sing of magic.

"All we need is a footman," she observed, and no
sooner had she spoken than a valet came forward with a
practiced welcome and held open her door.

Joe didn't seem unduly astonished, but then, he had seen a lot more of the world than she had. He nonchalantly left the keys in the car, offered her his arm and escorted her up the flagstone walk to a door that looked like something from Manderley.

She hadn't expected anything half so grand, and she felt a little uneasy when a doorman stepped forward to usher them inside.

"This," Meg whispered to her husband as she caught sight of the crystal chandelier in the foyer, "is a place for rich people."

"We're rich," Joe replied softly. Then, before she could wonder whether she'd made a mistake on their income tax return, he gave her a crooked smile. "Or at least *I* am," he amended. "I've got you."

She felt a thrill of warmth that had nothing to do with the fire crackling in the massive floor-to-ceiling fireplace. Joe was right—he'd captured her heart the very first time she saw him that afternoon in Larkwood, and he would have it forever.

Even without the blessing of a baby, she was definitely his.

It wasn't until they were seated at a white-draped table overlooking the starlit garden behind the inn that she remembered she couldn't really say the same thing about him. Joe had given her his wedding ring, yes. He had given her his name. And he had given her all the exuberant heat and passion of his body, but his heart...

No, his heart was still with Elena.

She'd come to suspect, whenever she saw that distant, yearning softness in his eyes, that she'd been far too optimistic about his first love eventually fading. That no matter how often Joe insisted "past is past," a part of his past would never die. That the woman whose memory had sustained him through those four lost years would survive in his heart far longer than she'd survived in the chaos of Milagua.

"Excuse me, sir, ma'am. Would you care for a drink, or some wine with dinner?" The waiter's voice jolted Meg back to the setting, back to the soothing grandeur of the Wayside Inn, and with a start she realized that she'd completely lost track of their reason for being here. They were celebrating their anniversary, for heaven's sake! No matter how much Joe might have loved Elena, he had married *her*.

"I don't think we could finish a whole bottle," Joe answered easily, glancing at the wine list the waiter held out. "Meg?"

"Oh, a…a glass of white Zinfandel." She ordered the same thing every time, but it was nice of Joe to act as if she had more varied tastes.

"And I'll have a Wild Turkey straight up," he ordered, handing back the wine list. "Thanks."

Never once since she'd known him had Joe ordered the same drink twice. But, to his credit, he had never once complained about her lack of imagination.

Nor about her insisting that a peaceful place like Oakville was the only place to raise a truly secure, happy child.

She saw his gaze following the waiter toward the bar, eyes narrowed with concentration. Then, with a visible shake of his head, he returned his attention to her.

"Sorry," he said. "I was just thinking I knew that guy from someplace."

The waiter didn't look familiar, but Joe met thousands of people every year. "You probably do," she observed. "A car fire story, a spring flood, a union strike…any of those getting close?"

He grinned, acknowledging her point. "Could've been a church picnic. I do those, too."

He did, but not with the same energy he devoted to periodic drug stories, arson investigations and search-and-rescue missions. For someone with every right to be uneasy about risks, he almost seemed to enjoy skating the edge of danger. "You can't live your whole life hiding from things you're afraid of," he explained whenever she urged him toward caution, and over the years she had grown accustomed to the niggling sense of worry that accompanied so many of his expeditions.

"And we all know you'd turn down whatever dangerous story came along for the chance to cover a church picnic," Meg said wryly. "When's the next one, anyway?"

He had a phenomenal memory; she knew he could recite practically the entire Calendar column from any first-of-the-month issue. But before he could run through the list of events for April, the waiter returned with their drinks and Joe touched his glass to hers.

"To four terrific years," he said. "And forty more."

That was sweet, Meg thought, taking a sip of her wine and enjoying the way Joe's eyes lingered on her. "This afternoon," she told him a little breathlessly, "I was remembering how you looked the first time I ever saw you."

Joe took a quick, startled gulp of his drink. "I looked like hell."

Oh, when he'd returned from Milagua weighing barely a hundred pounds.... "Well, but the *first* time I saw you," Meg reminded him, "was when you came home with Paul from football practice."

His hard expression softened slightly. "That's right. You were just a kid, though."

And at the time their three-year age difference had seemed like an impassable gap. But even a fourteen-year-old could feel those stirrings of fantasy, of hope, of longing for someone whose casual greeting would inevitably start her heart trembling.

Who could still set her quivering with a certain lazy smile, a certain caressing touch.

Whose heart she still wanted as much as she'd wanted it then. Not that she could very well say *that*.

"Anyway," Meg continued, "I was thinking this afternoon, if somebody had told me then that someday I'd be married to you—"

The lump in her throat caught her by surprise, and she had to stop before her voice gave way. Almost immediately, Joe reached across the table and caught both her hands in his.

"Aw, Meg," he murmured. "Meggers. I wish I could give you more."

"It's okay," she managed to answer, same as she'd answered his hesitant offer of marriage when he apologized that he couldn't give her all the love she deserved. Over the past four years she'd come to realize that she couldn't be everything *he* wanted, either...not that he'd ever voiced a comparison. Meg swallowed hard, lowering her eyes to avoid the piercing intensity of his gaze. "I wish *I* could be more—"

"And now," caroled the waiter, "are we ready to order?"

It took her a moment to recover, and Joe looked equally startled. Surely the waiter hadn't materialized from thin air, but neither one of them had noticed his approach.

"Oh," Meg mumbled, realizing that she hadn't even looked at the menu board propped against the windowsill. Although there was really no need for it, since a place like this would surely offer her usual petite filet.

And yet here she'd just been wishing she was more like Elena...

"The house special," she said firmly. Joe always ordered the special of the day wherever he was, insisting that the intrigue of the unknown more than made up for an occasional bad choice. And it wouldn't hurt her to exercise a little more spirit of adventure.

"Very good, madam," the waiter intoned. "Our soup

of the day is creamy lentil, and instead of the house salad I'd recommend the endive and radicchio medley. It goes very nicely with the frogs' legs.''

It took a moment for the realization to strike her, and she saw it strike Joe at the same time.

"I'll have that, too," he told the waiter, with a gesture for him not to leave just yet. "Meg, if you want to get something else instead, then we can both try each other's."

Oh, he knew. He knew what she'd blundered into. And he was offering her a remarkably graceful way out.

Meg swallowed. "I guess...the petite filet. Medium."

"Very good, madam," the waiter repeated. And bustled away, leaving her staring anywhere but at Joe.

Who, she saw when she finally raised her eyes to his, was watching her with a mixture of puzzlement and compassion.

"Meggins," he said gently, "you don't have to prove anything to me."

He'd never had to say that to Elena, she was certain. But Elena had never been what people would call ordinary. "I can be adventurous, too," she insisted.

Joe leaned forward, catching her gaze and holding it with his own. "Sure," he agreed, "if you want to be. But don't ever feel like you *have* to, okay? You're fine the way you are."

Even though he was only saying what any decent husband ought to say, he sounded remarkably convincing. "Okay," Meg murmured, remembering how he'd signed the card on her flowers with love. "Thanks."

He hesitated a moment, then gestured toward the dance floor. "Look, why don't we pretend I know how to dance?"

She knew he was still trying to comfort her, because ordinarily he would never suggest dancing, but at the moment she would take whatever comfort she could get. "I'd like that," she agreed. "Anyway, you dance fine."

The song was one she'd heard before, although she couldn't identify it, but the music didn't really matter. What mattered was Joe holding her, as carefully as the setting required but with the warmth of his body so reassuring that she wished she could bury her face against his chest. Wished she could stay this close to him for the rest of the evening, for the rest of the year—dear God, for the rest of their lives!

If she could just forget about Elena…

She had to stop comparing, Meg knew as his arms tightened around her. Aching over Joe's first love wasn't doing either of them any good. He had insisted that the past was past, and if she was smart she would focus all her attention on the future. On their family.

On the hope of a child.

She drew back so she could see his face, and found him watching her with a look of wistfulness.

"You know," she said resolutely, "this is just the beginning, really. Once we adopt our baby, then we'll be a real family."

For a moment he didn't answer, and she wondered if she'd felt a sudden flash of tension in his body, but his expression never changed as they continued moving slowly to the music.

"Yeah," Joe said finally, and in his voice she heard what almost sounded like a tremor of uneasiness. "I guess we will."

Chapter Two

There was nothing to be nervous about, Joe reminded himself as he drove to work the next morning with visions of Meg's prediction reeling in his brain.

He could handle a baby, no problem. He'd already agreed to that. It wasn't like a baby was a big risk, anyway, like someone who could tear up your whole world. As long as you kept them fed and warm and secure—tasks which would generally fall to Meg in any case—a baby couldn't send you spinning out of control.

And it would give Meg someone to love. Someone to care for other than himself.

Which was only fair.

He slammed the car door behind him and sprinted up the three steps to the *Herald* office door, only to find that someone had arrived already. Before five o'clock in the morning—which seemed a little compulsive, if you asked him. "Morning," Joe called, flicking on the master light switch.

"Hey," Phil responded from the file room at the other end of the office. "Joe, we found the number. It's Benny, all right."

"All right!" He felt a sweeping wave of relief—this would be a time-consuming story. Then he corrected himself, realizing that relief didn't make sense. Anticipation made sense. "Now we've got something to work with."

"Looks like," the reporter agreed. "I was gonna call you last night, but Abby swore she'd kill me."

Someday Abby would have to learn that editors had no such thing as a personal life, but right now all that mattered was the search. "Okay," Joe said, taking a county map from the cabinet and spreading it across the least-cluttered desk. "Let's see what we've got here."

By the time the office manager, copy editor, sales director and circulation manager arrived at the office, they were well into their plans. Phil would track down the deputy after hours, while Joe staked out the drug dealer's secluded house. There was no telling how long it would take to get results, but at least they had a strategy.

"Go ahead and run with it," Joe told the reporter. "Meanwhile, we need something on the mayor's speech. Can you stop by there, or is anybody else heading that way?"

"I'll take the mayor," offered Charlee, who handled social news as well as circulation.

"Okay, then Gloria can get back to the weekend edition. And I'll—"

"Joe," Abby called from the reception desk. "The Catholic Charities social worker's here."

He glanced at the front of the room, where the clock read nine on the dot. The woman was punctual, he had to give her that.

"Be right there," he called to her. He would handle her fund-raising appeal himself; he could write it while he waited outside the drug dealer's house. Meanwhile Charlee could do the mayor's speech, Mark was already writing up the high school basketball game between ad sales, and he could pull someone out of production if he had to.

Thursday was off and running.

The social worker looked a little harried, Joe noticed as he crossed the room, but she had a remarkably kind face. Whoever put her in charge of appeals knew what they were doing—this woman would be hard to turn down.

She accepted his handshake with a comforting smile, almost as if she thought he needed reassurance.

"I wasn't sure if you wanted to meet here," she said apologetically, "or if somewhere else would be—I saw a park just down the street. You know, away from all the…"

Her gesture encompassed all the hubbub of the office, which Joe considered his lifeblood. But he had to admit the setting could be a little overwhelming if someone wasn't used to newspaper work.

"Sure," he agreed. The city park was on the way to Benny's; he might as well get a head start on the drive east. And presumably the social worker had brought her own car. "You want to meet over there?"

She nodded, looking relieved. "I think that would be good."

It was too bad, Joe thought as he grabbed his coat from the rack by the door, that Randy was out this morning. This woman looked like the kind you'd trust with your last dollar, and a photo in the park—especially if they could get a couple of cute kids in the background—would help the pitch.

"I wish our photographer was here," he told her, opening the door so she could precede him down the steps. It wasn't until she shot him a startled glance that he realized not everyone thought in terms of newspaper layouts. "Fund-raising appeals always get a better response when we have photos," he explained.

"Fund-raising?" she repeated incredulously, as if she'd

never heard the term. "Mr. McConnell, that's not what I came for."

"It's not?" He didn't mind running an appeal for money, but an appeal for legislation was something else altogether.

She stopped short in the middle of the sidewalk and turned to look at him with an expression of growing dismay. "You didn't get my message."

He thought he'd told Abby to phone an affirmative response, but even a missed message couldn't explain this woman's distress. "Well," he began, "I—"

"Oh, Lord." Casting her eyes heavenward, she seemed to be fumbling for the right words. "How can…?" she murmured before she finally squared her shoulders and met his gaze. "Mr. McConnell," she said, "there's something you need to know."

"It *was* a surprise," Meg admitted, turning the glass dish of jasmine so it reflected the sun glancing off her desk. She'd left the arrangement pretty much intact this morning, but had taken a few yellow blossoms to brighten her office. "Joe's not much of a flower bringer."

"Well, you'd never know it," Susan observed in her faint Irish brogue, running her fingers across the side of the bowl and then examining the ceramic tulip paperweight next in line. "And dinner at the Wayside Inn, besides! Roxanne was saying she wished Joe had a twin brother."

"If he did, I'd introduce them." A few more inches, Meg realized, and Susan would be staring right at the notepad she'd covered with baby names. Trying to move nonchalantly, she stacked her newly addressed envelopes atop the page. "But he's an only child."

"Ah, the best husbands are always one of a kind," her friend said ruefully, crumpling her empty coffee cup and pitching it into the wastebasket. "You know what Dwight gave me for *our* anniversary? A bathroom rug!"

Susan's husband wasn't much on romance, but he'd never loved anyone more than his wife. "He probably thought you'd get a kick out of it."

"Oh, I know. I'm just jealous of your flowers." The teacher cast another glance at the bright yellow blossoms, then stood up as the lobby clock chimed ten. "So much for the morning break. I'll see you at lunch unless those sixth-graders mess up my lab."

The odds were in favor of a lab left decently tidy, Meg knew. Even though the whole staff agreed that this year's sixth-grade class was the most rambunctious they'd ever seen, Oakville Country Day students were generally a well-behaved group. Which made her job of maintaining alumni support all the easier…nearly everyone in southern Minnesota wanted their children placed on the waiting list.

She had no sooner retrieved her first draft of the scholarship letter and found her place on the page than she heard Joe's voice down the hall. Normally the sounds from the front office swept right past her, but even amidst the clamor of children waiting for passes and parent pickups, her husband's voice filtered through.

"Hi, is Meg in?"

Even as part of her wondered if something was wrong—Joe didn't sound quite like his usual self, and he'd never before visited in the middle of the morning—another part sympathized with the receptionist, who was probably dying to ask if he had a twin brother. With students in the office, though, Roxanne maintained a professional facade. "Yes, you can go right on back."

"Thanks. Can he wait out here?"

Joe definitely sounded frazzled, Meg thought as she moved the letter onto her typewriter. Admittedly, most of his morning stops didn't involve navigating through a cluster of children, but the note of tension in his voice was tighter than she'd heard in a long time.

Before she'd finished moving her tray of envelopes away from the desk, Joe appeared at her office door.

"Meg," he began, bracing both hands against the door-jamb as if he needed something to hold onto. "Uh…hi."

Good heavens, he looked awful. "Are you all right?" she asked, jumping up from her chair. There was no sign of a car accident, no sign of any bruises or blood, but not since he'd returned from Milagua had she seen Joe this obviously off balance.

"Yeah. I, uh—" He hesitated in the doorway, evidently at a loss for words. "I…I just had to see you."

But the sight of her didn't seem to be helping much. Even if he didn't realize it, his posture was so rigid, so defensive that she made no attempt to cross the space between them. Instead she stayed on her side of the desk, hoping she hadn't lost the soothing knack she'd developed during those months of his constant nightmares. "What's the matter?" she asked softly.

He took a long, shuddering breath. "Something… uh…something happened." And then, as if hearing the inadequacy of the statement, he dropped his hands from the doorjamb and gestured in frustration. "I don't know— I mean, it's—"

This wasn't another nightmare, she realized with a chill of dismay. This was real life, and already she could feel herself getting swept into the same baffled desperation that seemed to radiate from him. "Joe, you're scaring me."

"I'm sorry," he mumbled, then met her gaze for the first time. "God, I'm sorry. I just…it's— I don't know what to *do!*"

The words burst from him in such a torrent of anguish that she shoved back her chair and darted across the office, hoping to reach him before he exploded. But before she made it halfway there, he held out his hands as if to stop her flight.

"No, it's just—I can't—" he stammered, holding her at bay with the shattering intensity of his gaze. Almost as if he were pleading for her to leave him, and yet at the same time to come closer. "If you can—I mean, I know we wanted a baby and everything—"

More than anything she'd heard yet, the mention of a baby touched a core of fear in her heart. "What happened?" she began, but he kept on stuttering. Confusing her more, frightening her more with every halting phrase.

"Only I never knew—it never—Meg, I swear I didn't know until—"

"Know *what?*" she pleaded, and this time he stopped. Looking behind him, as if he'd just heard someone in the hall, he stiffened for a moment. Then a dark-haired boy she couldn't identify—maybe a fourth- or fifth-grader—poked his head around the doorjamb.

"Oh, God," Joe murmured. Then, before she could send the child back to the lobby, he rested his arm around the boy's shoulder and drew him into her office.

"Meg, this is my son."

For a moment she thought she'd heard him wrong. But then, through a dizzying cloud of disbelief, she realized that the boy had Joe's same angular jaw, his same heavy-lidded eyes. Her first sensation was that of a kaleidoscope, as if everything familiar had suddenly tilted in all directions—and it was followed by a raw, stabbing shock of pain that seemed to radiate from the very center of her body.

This was Elena's child.

She had no idea how she reacted. Whether she said anything or only stared. How she felt. Where she stood. She was dimly aware of Joe moving, reaching toward her, but she couldn't say whether he actually spoke.

All she could see was the boy. A younger version of

Joe. Looking so much like her husband—his defiant stare, his rigid posture—that she could almost believe she was looking at her husband a quarter century ago.

But his creamy bronze skin...his aquiline nose...his dark, curly hair—

Dear God, she must have been beautiful.

Meg heard herself gasp and felt a tremor of air running through her, then realized with sudden awareness that Joe was talking.

"Tony, this is my wife." His words sounded strangely distant, as if they were coming from light-years away, but she saw the boy's eyes narrow in acknowledgment. Before she could respond—what could she say? Nice to meet you?—Joe straightened up from his son's side and moved back to take her numb hands in his.

"He's got nobody left," he said softly, meeting her gaze with a mixture of apology and panic in his eyes. "Somehow, this social worker— I don't have all the details, but—"

But he had Elena's son.

"We—" Joe faltered, then started again. "I mean—"

Before he could finish the sentence, Tony muttered something in Spanish. Immediately Joe turned back to him, then squatted by his side and addressed him in English.

"Tony," he said tightly, "it's gonna be okay. I told you, remember, we're gonna—" He broke off, evidently at a loss, and she could see the frustration of helplessness in his gestures, hear it in his jumbled phrases. "It's— we're going to—"

Meg drew a shaky breath. "We're going to take him home."

She hadn't expected the statement until she heard herself speak, but she knew as soon as the words escaped that there was no other choice. And Joe must have known the same thing, because with his hands still on Tony's shoulders, he took one look at her and let out his breath in a rush of air.

"We have to," she murmured through a wave of dizziness. What else could they do? What else could they *do?*

"Well…" He hesitated. "I mean…"

None of this was the child's fault, no matter how it might be racking the adults. "Tony," she asked, feeling another kaleidoscopic sensation tumble through her as she met his sober gaze, "would you like to come live with your dad and me?" He looked so blank that she turned back to Joe. "How do I say it in Spanish?"

"He speaks English," Joe said encouragingly. "Don't you, Tony?"

Of course, Elena had spoken English as well as Spanish. Elena had studied medicine in the United States, and it made sense that she would pass both languages on to her son.

The boy stood silently for a moment before addressing his answer to the floor. "They said I would live with my father."

"Yeah," Joe agreed, still in that encouraging tone. Only Meg saw the tightness in his neck, the rigid tension in his shoulders.

But Tony wasn't finished. "With my *father,*" he repeated, then gestured stiffly toward Meg. "Not with her."

Joe moved so swiftly that the words had barely sunk in before he threw his arm around her shoulders and drew her close to him.

"You'll live with both of us," he told Tony in a voice she didn't quite recognize. Hard, yet pleading, and laced with both pride and pain. Dear God, Joe was as rattled as she was!

But he took hold of her hand and brought her a few steps forward toward the boy, as if trying to compensate both for startling his son and for shattering his wife.

"We don't have all the details worked out," Joe continued doggedly, "but we've got a room you can fix up however you want." Not the baby's room, she almost cried out before realizing that of course he hadn't meant that. They could make over the guest room for Tony. "And we'll get you a teacher who speaks Spanish in case you need help at school."

School. She hadn't even thought about bedrooms, and here he was—

"The public school," Joe specified, cutting off her protest just as she remembered the Country Day waiting list. "Nine-year-olds are in third grade, I think. But we'll see what the principal says."

The boy only nodded, looking a little uneasy.

"And if you want to get into Little League, that's—baseball? Do you play baseball? That's starting up pretty soon, if it hasn't already. I'll check on that."

"Joe," she began, noticing Tony's apprehensive expression, but her husband didn't seem to hear.

"We'll have to get you some clothes, too. I mean, what you've got is fine, but still we'll need to pick up some stuff."

There was no one better at details than Joe McConnell. But details weren't what anyone needed right now... especially not a frightened nine-year-old.

"You'll need books, I guess, and probably a backpack for school. We'll have to find someplace to organize your things. So," her husband concluded, "let's go show you the house where you'll be living, and maybe—"

"And maybe this weekend," Meg interrupted, laying her hand on Joe's shoulder and keeping her voice very slow, "you'd like to go on a picnic, since the weather's so nice. But there'll be plenty of time to get things figured out, Tony. You don't have to decide on anything right now."

The flicker of relief on his face was quickly replaced by a look of stoic indifference, but Meg knew her message had sunk in. What on earth must this child be going through, showing up in a strange country and meeting people who'd never heard of him? He had every right to feel edgy and withdrawn…just as she and Joe had every right to feel stunned.

But that was no excuse to make things any harder on Tony than they already were.

"Right," Joe agreed, evidently realizing what she meant. "You're right, Meggles. We'll just…uh, go home and see the house."

She could get fresh sheets on the guest bed in five minutes. Meg started to retrieve her purse from behind the desk, then saw the letter still waiting to be composed. "I'll try and find someone to finish this, or else come back—"

Joe cut her off.

"No, look, I've dumped enough on you. You don't need to mess up your whole schedule."

She couldn't sit here and write scholarship appeals, though, not with all this turmoil in her head.

But neither, Meg realized with a sudden wave of sickness, could she face spending the rest of the day with Joe and Tony.

And if she felt this way about only one day, how on earth was she going to manage…

You can do this, Meg McConnell.

You can do this.

She'd told herself that only yesterday, and it had gotten her through the baby shower. But never had she imagined it getting her through making a home for Joe's and Elena's son.

"We'll get out of your way," Joe continued, evidently taking her silence as confirmation that she didn't need to take on anything else. "I just wanted to—" For a moment he hesitated, as if unsure of what he'd wanted, then he quickly bent and kissed her. "I promise," he said in a low voice, "we'll get everything worked out."

"Sure," she said numbly, although she couldn't imagine how. "The sheets are on the third shelf of the linen closet."

The ghost of a smile flickered across Joe's face. "Right," he said. Then his expression grew sober again. "Megs... Thank you."

What was she supposed to say, you're welcome? She had no idea what they were getting into, and she suspected Joe didn't, either. But what else could they do?

"Sure," she said again, grasping the edge of the desk as they left her office...Tony impatiently, Joe heavily, as if he was only beginning to glimpse the magnitude of the task ahead. It would be enormous, she knew. A nine-year-old child wasn't like a baby, who could grow into the family. A nine-year-old was already a full-fledged person in his own right.

Of Joe's own, Meg corrected herself as she slowly lowered herself into her chair and fought back another wave of dizziness. After all, the boy was his son....

Which meant there was nothing left to hope for in their marriage. Nothing more she could offer her husband. Nothing she could contribute to their future.

Because he already had a child.

And the child was Elena's.

"I don't get it," Tony said for the third time, impressing Joe all over again with his easy grasp of American phrases. "How come you married *her* if you loved my mom?"

He had tried explaining twice already that there were different kinds of love, but somehow the boy didn't seem satisfied. Joe gulped the last of his coffee—always a bad choice at Buddy's Burgers, the red-and-yellow Main Street diner he'd figured would appeal to any kid—and launched another attempt.

"Because I didn't know about you, remember? Same way you didn't know about me until that birth-certificate lady saw my book. And all this time, I thought your mom was dead.''

Finally the explanation seemed to register. Or at least the last part of it did, because Tony looked suspicious.

"She *wasn't* until last summer."

"I know, the social worker told me." Apparently Elena had continued her practice in Milagua, treating hospital patients by day and rebels under cover of darkness, until suddenly she'd died of an aneurysm and left her son in the hands of Sister Maria at his school. "But back when I went looking for her, the people who knew her said she'd gotten killed in the fighting."

He could still remember the blackness of that night, although whether it was from the remote location or the utter loss of hope, he didn't know. He could still remember the soul-deep anguish of realizing he would never see or touch or laugh with Elena again. And to think she'd been in Milagua all along!

No, he told himself. You've got things under control. Joe took a long breath and continued with the story.

"I'm not sure if they thought it was true or if they were just trying to get rid of me, but I believed them." At the time he could think of no reason for the rebels to lie about one of their own, and the few who remembered him had seemed genuinely sorry for his loss. "I came back to America because I thought she was gone."

"She thought you were dead, too," Tony observed in a tone so matter-of-fact that Joe felt the coffee turn to acid in his stomach. Imagine growing up in a country that took such things for granted! But he should have known that nothing else would explain Elena raising their son alone.

"It makes sense," he acknowledged, crumpling the cardboard cup between his fists. "Somebody told me after I came back here that the prison guards had made a list of all the people they'd exec—uh, killed, and my name was on it.'' Even his mother had received word, which was one more memory that still left him raw with…

It's history. It's over.

''But they didn't kill you,'' Tony said, sounding a little smug as he dunked another French fry in the ketchup on his paper placemat.

''No.'' They'd done everything else, but somehow he'd survived it all…thanks to the single hope that kept him sane, kept him struggling, kept him alive. Even when he could no longer envision her face or feel her touch, he could still cry her name. ''I got through it.''

The boy evidently realized how unusual that was— everyone in Milagua must have heard of the prison camps—because he regarded Joe silently for a moment before asking, ''How come?''

There was only one answer, and his son deserved to hear it. ''Because,'' Joe told him, swallowing the unfamiliar hoarseness in his voice, ''I wanted to be with your mom again.''

The truth seemed to register with Tony, who gazed at him with narrowed eyes and then nodded in confirmation. ''You loved her,'' he announced.

He had loved Elena with an intensity he'd never thought possible. For the first time in his otherwise solitary, hard-driving life, he had joyfully surrendered his heart. And that decision, with all its giddy rapture and mindless emotion, had sent his entire life spinning wildly—and later, almost fatally—out of control.

Which was not something he wanted to admit to his son.

''Well, actually,'' Joe began, but the boy wasn't finished.

''You loved *her*,'' he declared triumphantly, ''more than this lady you married.''

Oh, God. He'd walked right into that one. ''Look, Tony, I don't want you saying that in front of Meg.''

His son dragged another French fry through the ketchup. "You understand me?" Joe demanded.

Still without looking at him, Tony nodded.

Damage control, Joe ordered himself. Meg didn't deserve to get smacked in the face with ancient history, and Tony needed to realize who kept his family alive. "She's a terrific person—I know you're gonna like her," he promised desperately. "She's really easy to be with."

Tony swallowed his French fry before issuing another challenge. "Is that why you married her?"

That was as close a reason as he could give, and yet it didn't begin to encompass the story. "Yeah," Joe said, closing his eyes for a moment as he remembered that first summer with Meg. "She was— Tony, she saved my life."

There was no other way to describe it. After four years of torture and starvation, followed by the devastating loss of Elena, he'd somehow struggled back to consciousness at a charity hospital in El Paso, where the desert heat reminded him far too vividly of those days spent chained under the merciless sun. Still weak with fever, he'd fled to Minnesota, where he knew his mother would offer sanctuary—only to find that she'd died two years before.

Except for the night he'd learned Elena was gone, it was the lowest moment of his life. Completely at a loss, he'd stumbled down the steps of the familiar house, now occupied by a painter, and come face-to-face with his best friend from high school...who'd taken one incredulous look at him and stammered, "Joe McConnell? My God, I thought you were dead!"

Paul had invited him home for dinner, pretended not to notice how shakily he handled a fork and suggested that if Joe didn't mind a lumpy mattress he was welcome to camp out in Stacie's room. Stacie was touring with a summer theater troupe, and Meg was helping their parents get settled in Sun City, while Paul was selling the house as soon as he finished his dissertation. "My folks offered us the house for as long as we wanted, but *I* sure don't need a place this big. And Meg's got a job in Oakville, so she's moving there before the school year starts.''

Meg. Even now, he could remember the indefinable comfort that had swept through the house when she'd returned from Arizona a few days later. She'd found him asleep and shivering on the living room couch, covered him with two quilts and let him sleep through the afternoon...then awakened him with a gentle touch and an offer of vegetable soup.

''She saved my life,'' Joe repeated, and Tony stuck his chin out.

''She wasn't a real doctor, was she?''

He should have known the child would resent any implication that Meg's accomplishments equaled his mother's. But at the same time, he couldn't let Tony go around devaluing Meg. ''Your mom was great at fixing people, and Meg is great at making them feel better. They're both special in different ways,'' he explained, sweeping the lunch trash onto their plastic tray and standing up from the red-and-yellow table. ''Come on, let's go look at where you'll be living.''

Tony seemed pleased with the idea of his own room. Joe could imagine how he'd been living since Elena died—even the best-run church orphanages were wretchedly crowded—and it was a relief to know that at least their *house* could accommodate a child.

He still wasn't sure about their life.

It was just the sheer unexpectedness that had him reeling, he reminded himself as he settled Tony in front of the TV set while he tried to come up with a plan of action. If he'd had time to prepare, time to get organized...

Except it wouldn't have made any difference, Joe admitted. He was out of his depth, and he knew it.

He had no idea what to *do* with a kid. Feed him a hamburger, okay. Get him signed up at school, sure. Then what, just park him by the TV? There had to be more to parenthood than that, yet he was utterly at a loss for what it might be.

Still, he couldn't very well turn the whole problem over to Meg. She would likely be far better at parenting than he was—after all, she'd been looking forward to a child for years—but there was no way he could pretend she'd been looking forward to a nine-year-old boy who would serve as a living reminder of the woman with whom Joe McConnell had lost control of his heart.

The woman for whom he'd virtually abandoned his freelance career. The woman he'd blithely planned to spend the rest of his life loving. The woman whose memory had prompted enough fruitless escape attempts to earn him fifty months in hell.

"Can I watch cartoons?" Tony asked, jolting Joe back to the situation at hand.

"Uh, sure." The social worker had mentioned that he'd already discovered the lure of television, so it would probably be okay. Joe scrolled through the channels until he came across a Disney cartoon that looked safe enough, and decided to phone the *Herald* while he had a free minute.

The sound of office clamor in the distance was sweet beyond all reason. "Where on earth have you *been?*" Abby demanded. "Phil can't reach the deputy until Monday, and he was scared to death you were already out at Benny's."

"No, I just—some stuff came up." He didn't want to go into details over the phone, especially when he still wasn't sure what might happen next. "Do me a favor, Abby, and tell everyone I'm out until Monday."

"You're what?"

"Have Gloria run the mayor's speech instead of the Milagua fund-raising story, and tell Charlee we'll need another six hundred words. Ask Randy for the cover shots, get Mark's copy into proofing and call me if there are any problems.''

He felt a little better hearing himself run through a day's work with such effortless precision. At the *Herald*, at least, he had everything under control.

But that still didn't take care of the problem at hand.

This whole business, Joe reflected as he hung up the phone and returned to the living room, wasn't fair to anyone. None of it was Meg's fault, nor Tony's, nor Elena's. Maybe not even his own...but still, he was the one who had to make things right.

Not only for his child, but also for his wife.

And he didn't know how to begin.

He did know he couldn't send Tony back to Milagua. Even if he wasn't feeling any of those stirrings of kinship that people were supposed to feel when presented with an unknown son, he knew the boy would have to stay with them. Nobody in a war zone would want to adopt a nine-year-old, especially one with an American father—and besides, the kid had been through enough already.

But damn it, so had Meg! And even though he suspected she was incapable of turning away a child in need, he wished the child could be someone other than his own. She'd wanted so badly to raise a family together, to give him a child, and now to confront her with another woman's son...

It wasn't until he heard her footsteps on the front walk that he realized he'd spent the past hour staring at Disney cartoons. Leaving Tony still engrossed in his show, Joe hurried to meet her and saw with dismay that her eyes were suspiciously red.

"Meggles," he said abruptly, surprising himself, "listen. I haven't told anybody he's here."

She cast a despairing glance at the house, almost as if she'd hoped Tony's presence was only a dream, and hunched her hands under her armpits the way she always did in the cold.

"Neither have I," she admitted. "I don't know why, but somehow I couldn't."

She didn't resist when Joe drew her back into the warmth of the house, where Tony barely glanced in their direction, but she pulled away from him and moved into the kitchen. "I just couldn't," she repeated. "It's stupid, I know, when he's going to be living here...."

Joe watched her peeling off her gloves. She was moving as clumsily, as jerkily as someone who'd just endured a beating. "Are you sure?" he asked softly.

Meg turned on him, her face flushed with anger. "Are you even *thinking,*" she demanded, "that I'd suggest sending him back to Milagua?"

"No, I know you wouldn't." He didn't even know why he'd asked, except that he hated to see her in such pain. "I just don't want to stick you with—"

She cut him off with a single, stark sentence. "It's already done, Joe," she said tightly, dropping her gloves on the counter and shrugging out of her coat. "We've got to keep him."

He knew she was right about that. What he didn't know was how they'd survive it. "Look," he offered, "we'll work it out somehow."

She gave him a level look, almost as if she suspected him of whitewashing the truth. "I've been thinking," she said, depositing her coat on the hook by the door and turning to face him again. "I took tomorrow off work...and if you can, too, it'll make things easier. Because we've got a lot to work out."

In a way he welcomed the challenge in her voice; he would far rather deal with demands than with helplessness. But then, Meg had never been the kind of woman to feel helpless for long. She might have given way to tears a few hours ago, but already she had mustered up the strength he'd always admired in her.

Even though Meg would never be a fighter, she had more grit than most soldiers he'd known.

"Sure," Joe agreed, straddling a kitchen chair back to front and turning another so she could sit across from him. "I told 'em I won't be in tomorrow."

She gripped the back of the chair so tightly her knuckles turned white, but she made no move to sit down. "I'm going to be a mother to him, Joe. You'll see." The passion in her voice, he realized, was even more intense than her grip on the chair. "I'm going to be the best mother—I mean stepmother—this boy could possibly have."

He had no doubt of that. When it came to nurturing, Meg was in a class by herself.

"But," she continued, "he needs a father, too. Somebody who'll listen to him. Teach him things. Be there for him."

Just because he had no personal experience with a father didn't mean he couldn't learn to be one, Joe reminded himself. Besides, he couldn't very well let Meg take on single-handedly the burdens of parenthood.

"I'm gonna do that," he said, flexing his hands together. "I already figured I'll take care of getting him to school, picking him up in the afternoon…"

She looked a little surprised, evidently remembering how they'd always planned on her being the full-time parent.

"That sounds great. But it'll cut up your day," she warned.

It would virtually cut his time at the *Herald* in half, but it wasn't like he had any choice. Tony was his son, and therefore his responsibility. Joe shrugged, trying to make the acknowledgment look easy. "Staff's always saying I spend too much time there, anyway."

No sooner had he spoken than he realized Meg's attention was half on him and half on the child behind him, who stood hesitating in the doorway. "Are we going on a picnic tomorrow?" Tony asked the air between them.

It was Meg who responded, sounding as relaxed and comforting as he remembered her sounding five summers ago whenever he woke from a nightmare—and for the first time he wondered what that effort had cost her. "Sure," she told the boy, "if you still want to."

Tony glanced from him to her and back again. "Okay," he said. Then, without another word, he returned to the living room and the sound of the TV show.

Meg stared after him for a moment, then looked at Joe with the barest hint of a smile. "Well," she said wryly, "I guess we're going on a picnic."

Chapter Three

It was happening again. He knew it was coming, knew it was about to strike, and all he could do was wait for the next blow, tensing his body in anticipation of the shattering pain—

And there it was, another wave of agony radiating through him, then another and yet another, sending him over the edge of reality, plummeting into madness, spinning out of control—

But he couldn't let go, he couldn't let himself break. Falling wildly toward the beckoning hell, he summoned up the last vestige of sanity and clung to it with every fiber of his soul.

"El-e-e-e-na!"

Meg jolted awake, startled by the cry. It sounded as if the plea had come from somewhere far beyond reach, somewhere she could never quite get to...no matter how much Joe needed her. But she scrambled to wake him, to offer whatever comfort she could give while he struggled free from the grip of the all-too-familiar nightmare.

It was happening again.

"Joe," she pleaded, shaking his shoulder. She didn't dare get too close until he came fully awake; otherwise he would strike out at her instead of the captors in his dream. "Joe, wake up. It's okay. It's all right."

He gave a hoarse cry and then gasped, cutting himself off in mid-shout, and she saw his body jerk as every muscle seemed to tighten all at once.

"Joe," she repeated, trying to keep her voice calm as he struggled to sit up, "it's okay. You're home. You're safe."

He shuddered convulsively, gave a harsh gasp, then raised himself on his elbows, opened his eyes and stared at her with a mixture of terror, hope and disbelief.

"It's all right," Meg said gently, cradling his face between her palms to prove there was nothing to fear. "You're okay now. It's all right."

She could almost see the moment when her words sunk in. The muscles in his neck quivered slightly, his eyes cleared and he drew a sharp breath, then grabbed hold of her and fell back onto the mattress with her clutched tightly against his chest.

"Meg?" he choked out, and she felt the wild pulse of his heartbeat beneath his sweat-soaked skin.

"I'm right here," she murmured, wrapping her arms around him and wishing she could surround him completely. "You're safe."

It took another minute for him to answer, but she thought she could feel his heartbeat slowing down a little by the time he spoke again. "God, I was—"

"I know." His memories of the prison camp, of Milagua, were enemies that would never fully fade. She brushed a hand across his forehead, automatically avoiding the ridge of scars at his temple. "Ah, Joe…"

"I'm sorry," he muttered, shifting so that she was positioned more comfortably across his chest...and so that his scars were beyond her reach. "I didn't mean to—"

"It's okay." She had told him countless times that she didn't mind waking him from a nightmare, but he never seemed to remember. And he probably didn't even know he'd been crying out for Elena, which meant there was no reason for him to apologize. "Don't worry about it."

He sighed, and in the faint glow of moonlight she could see the look of shame in his eyes. "I...I kind of thought I was all over that by now. I guess it was just, you know, Tony and everything."

"Sure," Meg said gently, trying not to sound surprised at his belief that the nightmares might vanish. Even though they were far less frequent now, they always returned during times of stress. But she knew how Joe hated any sign of weakness in himself. "Here, let me just get the blanket."

He moved his hands with her as she restored the tangled bedclothes, never breaking the contact between their bodies. Then, with the blanket draped over them both and with her cradled comfortably against his chest, she began to feel the rhythm of his breathing gradually settling back to normal.

It was relaxing, lying here in his arms and feeling the warmth of his skin on hers, knowing they were safe from whatever terrors had woken him. Knowing there were still a few hours until dawn, and that they could fall asleep at their leisure. There would be nothing but companionship tonight, Meg knew—Joe would never make love to her with the scent of fear still on his skin—but still she treasured those nights when just holding each other could send them both softly, pleasurably back to sleep.

For a long few minutes there was nothing but silence, darkness and warmth. Then, just as she felt herself sliding toward a deeper level of ease, he spoke again.

"Megs, I'm really sorry."

His voice was so low that she had to repeat the phrase in her mind before it fully registered. This wasn't an apology for waking her, she knew. This sounded far more painful, far more intense. And with a sudden wrench of her heart, she recognized what he meant. "You mean, about having a son?"

The silence answered for him. Of course he would be sorry, Meg realized with a mixture of appreciation and regret. As much as Joe had loved Elena, as much as he would welcome a son of his own, he certainly wasn't insensitive. He had to know how she felt.

Still, there was nothing either one of them could do about it. He had loved another woman long before he married Meg, the woman had given him a child, and now that child was asleep in the guest room.

"Look," she said, leaning up on one elbow to face him, "it's not what I would've chosen. But none of this is your fault, Joe."

It took him a while to respond, and when he did he neither denied nor accepted her reassurance. "I was thinking the same thing about you this afternoon," he answered. "None of this is *your* fault, either."

She supposed that was true, although it didn't really make any difference. Even if she'd been able to give him children, they would still need to make a home for Tony.

There was no other choice.

Meg took a long breath. "So," she said resolutely, "we've just been handed a surprise, that's all. And I'm going to be a great mom, Joe. You'll see."

"Yeah, I know you will." She could hear both relief and gratitude in his voice as, with another sigh, Joe drew her back against him. For a while they lay snuggled together, easing toward sleep, then he drowsily drew a finger down the side of her cheek.

It was a touch she remembered vividly from their first

summer together. Back in Larkwood, with Paul asleep at the other end of the house, when nearly every night she would hear Joe crying out in terror, anger or pain. She would stumble into his room and sit with him until he relaxed, trying to sound as reassuring as possible, trying not to let the warmth of comfort simmer into the heat of desire…and yet, as the summer nights progressed, feeling it happen in spite of herself.

She wasn't sure when Joe had finally touched her cheek that way, but she knew it was during the daytime. On the porch swing, where they'd taken a lemonade break as they usually did during afternoons of him typing the notes that became a book. He'd been watching her, listening as she described the summer's roses, then he reached forward and very slowly, very gently, drew his finger down the side of her face.

At that moment, she had known. Not in her mind, which still saw all the problems of hospitality and embarrassment and guilt and hesitation…but her heart and her body saw beyond all that, responding with an immediate quickening of pulse, a sudden weakness, a tantalizing rush of hope.

Yes, I want you. And you want me.

It had taken a few more weeks of uncertainty, of trembling anticipation, before Joe came to accept what she already knew. It had taken days of repeating that Paul didn't care what his friend and his sister did with their nights, that she understood things between them might not be ideal right now, if ever, and that it simply didn't matter. Because she secretly knew that once he let himself go, things *would* be ideal—that love would make everything right, that the damage of Milagua would magically disappear and that Joe's appalling scars would fade as quickly as the memories of the woman he'd loved.

Nearly five years later, she was still waiting.

Still believing, with an ever-diminishing portion of her

soul, that one day Joe would love her the way he had loved Elena.

At first she had assumed it was just a matter of time until he lowered the barriers around his heart. Then, a matter of marriage. Of building a family. Of him settling into a job that kept him excited, kept him vital, kept him strong and focused and intense.

But the magic hadn't happened yet. They'd had time, they had a marriage, he had a job he loved....

The only thing left was a family.

Which Joe himself had agreed would make all the difference, she remembered as she settled more comfortably into his drowsy embrace. The other night during their anniversary dance at the Wayside Inn—a dance that now seemed like a very long time ago—he had confirmed that a baby would make them "a real family."

Tomorrow, Meg resolved, she would begin showing him the joys of a family. Tomorrow Joe would finally start to appreciate that while his wife might not have Elena's vivid courage, at least she would excel as a mother...not only of his son, but also of a child they could share. And tomorrow, just to be safe, she would confirm with the adoption caseworker that in spite of this unexpected son, the McConnells were still ready and waiting for a baby.

Yes, tomorrow—before Tony's picnic—she would confirm that they still had reason for hope.

Tony's picnic got off to a good start. While the entire winter had been unusually mild, today's weather was almost picturesque, as though Mother Nature had decided to create the perfect climate for a family outing. The basket they'd used for the past few years was filled with turkey-and-Dolfino sandwiches, apples and Joe's favorite deviled eggs. And the oak-lined field an hour west of town, Meg decided when they finally unloaded the car, was nothing short of splendid.

The only flaw in the picture was Tony himself. He couldn't help it, she knew; he'd been through too much upheaval for any nine-year-old to feel at ease among strangers. Although he didn't seem to consider Joe a stranger, and in fact had already started calling him Papá...pronouncing it the Spanish way, with the second syllable accented. But whenever he spoke to Meg, there was a definite coolness in his tone.

"Papá says to bring the soccer ball he got this morning. But we'll probably play by ourselves."

She could tell Joe had noticed that surliness, but she'd asked him not to say anything. Even though it was annoying to find herself cast in the role of a wicked stepmother, she knew it would be wiser to ignore Tony's attitude. Once he saw for himself that his father's wife was no threat—that in fact she wanted to give him all the security she could—surely the boy would relax. Maybe he would never call her by the coveted name of Mommy, but surely he would take the suggestion Joe had offered.

"I know Meg isn't technically your aunt, but there's nobody else you call Tía, is there?"

Tony had mumbled an agreement, although he had yet to address her directly. Whenever he had a comment, he offered it to Joe.

"Papá, I kicked four goals one time."

"Can you and I make a campfire?"

"Look, there's a river down there!"

The Minnesota countryside was obviously a source of fascination; from what she'd heard of Milagua Meg could imagine how Tony must be marveling at the grassy hillsides dotted with wildflowers. She sent him and Joe off to explore while she set out their picnic, enjoying the scent of springtime herself.

When they came back across the field, Joe was carrying a heart-shaped yellow wildflower, which he deftly tucked in her hair. "There you go, Meggins."

She felt herself growing warm at the gesture, and he must have sensed it, because as soon as she looked up at him, he drew her into his arms for a kiss. It wasn't a long kiss, it was more friendly than passionate, but when she turned back to the picnic basket she saw Tony watching them both with dark suspicion in his eyes.

"Tony," she asked, trying to sound perfectly matter-of-fact, "are you ready for lunch?"

He only shrugged, which she took as answer enough. Wondering whether the three of them would ever sit down to lunch with the same easiness her family had always taken for granted, Meg handed out sandwiches and water bottles and passed the container of deviled eggs across the blanket to Joe.

"Terrific," he said, giving her an appreciative smile. "You didn't have to go to this much trouble, but I'm glad you did."

Making deviled eggs wasn't what she considered trouble. Making conversation with a sullen nine-year-old was far more difficult. But Joe seemed to have a knack for drawing people out—part of what made him a good reporter, she supposed—and the three of them made it through lunch without any awkward silences. It wasn't until she brought out the brownies she'd made as a special surprise and Joe kissed her again that Tony turned surly.

"I don't like those things," he announced.

"That's okay," Joe told him, taking another one. "I'll eat your share. Tía makes the best brownies in the world."

The boy couldn't very well contradict such a statement, having already refused a taste. Instead, he fixed his gaze on the air between them and announced, "My mother did more important things than make brownies. She was a doctor. She saved people's lives."

Meg saw Joe caught with a mouthful of chocolate and hastily stepped in to answer.

"I'll bet you're proud of her, Tony."

"She saved my father's life," he continued, this time directly to Meg. "He had a bullet in him and she got it out."

If not for Joe momentarily closing his eyes, she would have assumed Tony was making up stories. But her husband's uncomfortable expression confirmed the truth. Elena *had* saved his life.

"I didn't know that," she managed to say.

Joe swallowed the last bite of his brownie. "That was how I met her," he said abruptly, and stood up. "Come on, let's go take a look at the creek."

The creek was barely half a mile away, and Meg decided a walk might be a good idea. It would give her an excuse to move around, to avert her gaze from her husband while she tried to regain her composure. Because for all Joe's glowing talk about Elena, he had never once mentioned her saving his life.

Joe let Tony lead the way, then silently took her hand—almost as if he knew she needed reassurance, which was humiliating for her to admit. Even so, she couldn't help appreciating his solid presence at her side.

"Look at this!" Tony called. "Papá, can we go across?"

A fallen oak tree spanned the width of the sun-sparkled water, which splashed in the creek bed twenty feet below them. Meg could see how the haphazard bridge would appeal to a nine-year-old boy and decided it would be smarter to let Joe explain the danger. Tony would take a refusal better if it came from his father.

But Joe surprised her by looking at the deadfall, testing it with his foot and then nodding.

"Sure, let's see what's over there."

"What?" she protested. "You're not walking on that!"

"It's okay," he assured her. "It's solid enough. You wanna go across?"

"Yeah!" Tony cried before Meg could answer, and Joe clapped a hand on his shoulder.

"Come on, then." And as she caught her breath, he grinned at her. "What do you say?"

If anyone fell from a height like that— She couldn't even find the right words, but Tony seemed to read her thoughts. "She's scared," he announced.

Joe glanced at the water one more time, as if confirming his original appraisal. "She's scared for *us,* Tony," he told his son. Then, taking Tony's hand and stepping onto the makeshift bridge, he gave her a reassuring smile. "We'll be okay."

Oh, great. Risking his life for a news report was bad enough, but for a picnic outing? She could just imagine the tree giving way and all the search-and-rescue people Joe assisted racing out here to haul him and Tony back to safety. Meg watched them make their way forward, unable to turn away, and heard the boy's smug voice.

"My mother wasn't scared of anything."

She felt a sudden rush of anger—Tony had no business comparing her to Elena when all she wanted was to protect him—but caught herself before calling a protest across the creek. And when she heard Joe's response, she felt a mixture of vindication and dismay.

"Everybody," he answered Tony, "gets scared for the people they love. Come on, let's see what's over there."

She wasn't scared for Tony because she loved him, Meg knew. She would care for him, yes, because it was a chance at motherhood…but it was hard to imagine truly *loving* Elena's child.

And yet she would love some other woman's child with all her heart, once they adopted a baby. But that child wouldn't serve as a constant reminder of a woman she could never live up to…of everything she could never give Joe.

It took no more than ten minutes before he and Tony

returned, during which time she packaged up the remains of their picnic and tried to arrange her thoughts as deftly as the apples, brownies and trash. She had made a decision yesterday, and she was going to see it through. She was going to love Joe's son, no matter how hard it might be at first...because while she might be ordinary in every other respect, caring and nurturing were what Meg Mc-Connell did best.

Joe and Tony looked surprisingly relaxed as they came sauntering back across the field, as if they hadn't just risked a bone-breaking fall and emerged unharmed. But even without their shared nonchalance, she realized as she watched them together, there was something very similar about the way they moved. The same crackling energy she had always admired in Joe seemed to be reflected with equal intensity in his son.

"I'm glad you got across the creek okay," she said, making a point of addressing them both. "Anybody feel like playing catch?"

She was pretty decent at throwing, she knew, and nobody could accuse her of being scared of the ball. Joe retrieved the new soccer ball from the car while Tony helped pack up the water bottles they'd carried across the creek, seeming a little friendlier than before.

"You're not supposed to touch the ball in soccer," he told her, "but if we're just playing catch I guess it's okay."

Joe positioned himself facing into the sun, with her and Tony forming the other points of the triangle, and sent her a smooth, easy ball. Feeling a little smug at her perfect catch, she threw it to Tony, who leaped dramatically into the air like a prime-time sports star.

The boy was good, she realized, as he hurled the ball toward her with dazzling showmanship. She managed to catch that one as well, hurting her thumb in the process—a bad move, Meg realized, if she was going to play that new Alleluia on Sunday. So after throwing the ball to Joe, she backed up to indicate that the two of them could continue without her.

There was nothing Joe McConnell couldn't do well, she decided as she watched him play to Tony's exaggerated catches and retrieve what looked like impossible, grandstanding throws. He started issuing challenges, which Tony seemed to love—"Let's see you get this one!" "Look out, here comes a high ball!"—and she enjoyed the boyish happiness on her husband's face as they continued showing off catch after catch after catch.

"Okay, this one's gonna be the toughest ball of the year!" Joe called, sending it high into the air. She found herself drawn to his side of the field, warmed by the pleasure in his voice as Tony backed up, watching the ball soar higher, moving into position underneath it and finally executing a triumphant catch.

The boy whooped with exhilaration, whirling around with the sun lighting him from behind, laughing in sheer exultation. And as she moved toward Joe, who was watching with an expression of mingled wonder and pain, she heard him whisper, "*God,* you look like her."

Meg stopped. He was talking to Tony, she knew; he didn't even know she was there. And staring at the child, who seemed almost aglow with excitement, she saw for the first time how Elena must have looked to Joe.

"Was that the greatest catch of the year?" Tony yelled, and Joe jerked out of his reverie.

"All-time greatest," he called back, then glanced around and saw her. "What do you say, Megs, shall we leave on a note of triumph?"

Her smile evidently didn't strike him as off-key, even though her skin felt as tight as it had at the baby shower. "Might as well," she agreed as Tony came running toward them with the ball. "We probably could've sold tickets to this."

"You were terrific," Joe told the child, ruffling his hair. It was the first spontaneous gesture of affection she'd seen him make toward his son, and she had the sense that the two of them had just crossed some hurdle far deeper than the creek. That image of a sentimental moment had to be why her throat felt so tight.

But the hollow ache in her chest didn't fade, even while they drove back home with Tony asleep in the back seat. Which meant, Meg knew, that there was more behind this sensation than simply seeing a father and son play catch.

She didn't especially want to admit that to Joe, but neither could she hush the persistent whisper of inferiority inside her as she remembered how rapturous and how stricken he'd looked at the memory of Elena. Meg cleared her throat.

"I didn't know," she said in what she hoped sounded like an ordinary, conversational tone, "that Elena got a bullet out of you."

Joe shot her a startled look, but apparently saw nothing strange in her expression. "Well, it was ten years ago."

He probably remembered it vividly, though. She swallowed, avoiding his gaze. "What happened?"

This time it took him a while to answer; she knew he hated talking about Milagua. Once his series of articles covering the rebellion had been published as a book, he seemed to feel the entire episode was finished. "I was out scouting with the rebels, my first summer there," he said finally, "and we ran into a patrol. Took off running through the jungle and I got hit in the shoulder." He paused, then shrugged off the rest of the story. "It turned out okay."

"Because of Elena," she concluded.

He must have heard the tension in her voice, because he turned to face her as if hoping to smooth things over. "Meg, that's all in the past, okay? There's no reason to talk about it."

But no matter how much he might insist that past was past, the wonder and pain she'd seen on his face while watching Tony proved that Elena was a bigger part of the present than she had ever guessed. "I just want to know," she muttered, "what she was like."

Joe reflexively glanced at the road, then back at her. "I already told you, remember?"

He'd talked about little else during those first few weeks of healing. But that was before either of them suspected that their relationship would grow into something more than casual housemates. "I know she was extraordinary," Meg acknowledged, recalling the fragmented memories she'd heard on those summer nights in Larkwood. "Dedicated and really smart and beautiful. And full of courage…and grit and…and you would've married her in a minute if it wasn't for the war."

Her words tumbled out in a rush, and when she finished she saw Joe looking a little stunned. "Well, yeah," he admitted, then reached for her hand as if to soften the truth. "But that was a long time ago. Now I'm glad I'm married to you."

He had to say that, she supposed, but the obligation nullified the spirit of the words. Meg leaned her head back against the seat and closed her eyes against a wave of despair.

Joe lifted her hand and squeezed it, maybe trying to reassure her with his touch. "You're not feeling jealous or anything, are you?" he asked awkwardly. "Because there's nothing to be jealous of. Elena's dead."

"But you loved her." Her voice sounded so thick, she didn't even finish the statement. In her mind, though, she could hear it very clearly: *And maybe you don't realize it, but you still do.*

"I did, yeah," Joe said, keeping hold of her hand and looking at her curiously, as if he couldn't imagine why it mattered. "But that's all in the past. The past doesn't have anything to do with now."

Not unless you counted all the things he'd loved about Elena that Meg could never match. Her striking beauty. Her indomitable courage. Her dazzling sense of adventure.

"Do you ever wish," Meg managed to whisper, "that I was more like Elena? Less…less ordinary?"

He shook his head and let out his breath in a rush of impatience. "You're *you,* Meggins," he said simply. Then, raising her hand to his lips, he kissed her fingers and gave her a quick smile. "You're terrific the way you are."

Apparently she believed him, which was a relief. Joe didn't know what other assurance he could have offered, but he had seen her press the yellow wildflower in the pages of her journal, which must have meant she'd enjoyed the picnic as much as he had. And now, watching her smile at Tony as they poured whole-wheat flour into a measuring cup, he was glad to see that Meg seemed completely recovered. She looked like her usual, cheerful self.

"We want seven cups," she told the boy, who appeared fascinated by the process of making bread from scratch. "You keep count, and tell me when we have enough."

"Can I eat it when it's cooked?"

"You sure can," Meg told him. "Tomorrow morning we'll make sandwiches for your lunch at school."

Filling out the school forms was a task he'd postponed until tonight, and Joe knew he wasn't giving it his full attention. He was still basking in the glow of the past three days, which had been more invigorating and yet somehow more relaxing than any in recent memory. His decision to stay away from the *Herald* until Monday was probably part of the reason…but a lot of it, he suspected, was from spending all this time with Tony and Meg.

"That's four cups," the boy announced.

"Okay, let's keep going."

With an effort, Joe turned his attention back to the page in front of him. The very first question reminded him of why he'd postponed this job—because it raised the perplexing issue of his son's name.

"Wait," Tony ordered, "that cup's too full."

"All right, we'll make the next one a little shorter."

He could, of course, fill in "Antonio Carlos Montoya" and be done with it. But sooner or later, they would switch from Montoya to McConnell, and it seemed simpler not to wait for the obligatory three months until they could begin adoption procedures. Unless the boy preferred to keep his mother's name...

Let the question wait, Joe decided, and wrote "Tony Montoya" on the first line.

"Papá, you said you'd help make bread."

He glanced at the kitchen counter, where Meg and Tony were surrounded by baking paraphernalia. "In a minute," he promised, and saw her eyes crinkle with amusement.

"Why," she asked the room at large, "does this remind me of 'The Little Red Hen'?"

Joe laughed in recognition, turning back to his forms as proof that he had everything under control. Address, home phone, parents' daytime phones...

"What's the little red hen?" he heard Tony ask.

"It's a story," Meg explained. "The hen bakes some bread and none of the other animals want to help, but when the bread's finished they all want to eat it."

"Do they get to?"

"I guess it depends on who's telling the story," she answered, and Joe's gaze drifted back to the kitchen as she set the empty measuring cup in the sink. "Okay, now for the fun part. We get to mix this up with our hands."

He had always enjoyed the smell of fresh bread when he came home to find Meg baking, but he couldn't remember ever watching the process before. Joe found himself absorbed in the sight of his wife and son up to their elbows in fragrant dough until a cramp in his fingers reminded him that the pen was still poised on the address line.

Focus, he ordered himself.

It was just the past few days of leisure that had thrown him off his stride. After Friday's picnic, they had taken Tony shopping for school clothes, then out for ice cream that night. Saturday had brought a drive north in search of enough snow to build a snowman, and Meg had proven herself a master at snowmen as well as snow women and children…a talent, he told her, that he'd never known she possessed.

"I guess it never came up," she admitted, her face rosy with cold. "But Paul and Stacie and I used to fill our whole yard with them."

"We'll have to bring your family up here after Easter dinner next weekend," Joe teased, "to work off all those chocolate bunnies." And then he'd ducked as she aimed a snowball at his face.

Tony had been enamored with the snow, clamoring to repeat the experience this morning. But Meg had insisted that Sunday was for church.

He had never set foot in St. Cecilia's before, but he'd promised Catholic Charities that Tony's religious heritage would be respected…even though the morning Mass conflicted with their usual ten o'clock service. Joe noticed during the sermon that his son was attracting a lot of attention from the congregation, but he supposed the same thing would have happened in their own Valley Cathedral, where Meg had driven alone with her new Alleluia music. All of Oakville must know by now—or at least they would within half an hour after church—that the McConnells were adopting a boy from Milagua.

A boy Joe had never heard of until a few days ago. A

boy who reminded him far too much of Elena, especially when their conversation drifted into Spanish and he found himself remembering again those heady, exultant months when he'd neglected to file any stories. A boy for whom he was going to have to learn virtually overnight all the parental skills he'd never practiced before.

Meg, on the other hand, seemed to have been born with hers already in place. All weekend long, she'd been doing a terrific job with this kid. Gently directing, reassuring, coaxing, instructing him—and although she might not realize it, instructing Joe as well—on what it meant to be part of a family.

"How come this doesn't look like bread?" he heard Tony ask, and absently turned the pen in his hand while he waited for her soft-voiced answer.

"We have to bake it first. But all this mixing is what makes the yeast work. You're doing a good job."

Focus, Joe reminded himself, forcing his attention back to the forms. There were a few spaces he regretted having to leave blank—preschool activities, allergy records, teacher comments—but he finished signing all the pages and folded them into a vertical sheaf. Tomorrow he would drop them off when he took Tony to Oakville Elementary, and maybe stop by the *Herald* on the way in, just long enough to check his messages....

"I like how this smells," he heard Meg tell Tony. "But it'll be even better once we get it in the oven."

He wasn't going to think about the *Herald* tonight, Joe decided, leaning his elbows on the desk and watching the activity in the kitchen. Tonight was for enjoying the last few hours of the weekend. Tonight was for remembering Tony's excitement over the snow...Meg's rapt expression when he described the St. Cecilia's choir...the way they'd dived into their ice cream with such vigor that it seemed impossible the dish could turn out too big....

The song of sparrows in the picnic field. Her pleasure

over the gift of a simple wildflower. Tucking Tony into bed last night. The way they'd handed clothes back and forth in the store as if they'd done this a hundred times before.

"There, we've got it." He saw Meg brush the last sticky bits of dough from Tony's hands into the mixing bowl and point him toward the sink. "Now we'll let the dough rise and when your hands are clean, you can punch it down as soon as it's ready."

The boy scrubbed industriously while she brushed her own hands free of dough. There was still flour up to her elbows, and when Tony turned away from the sink he remarked, "You look like the little *white* hen."

Meg laughed. She brushed a strand of hair off her forehead, leaving another white smudge, lifted the mixing bowl and set it down on the counter—and all of a sudden Joe felt himself swept with a rush of feeling so intense it seemed as if every cell of his body had halted except for his heart.

Meg…!

Control, he ordered himself sharply. He had everything under control. But for some reason it took him a fraction of a second longer than usual to push his chair back from the desk, drop the school papers by his car keys in the living room and grab the phone to call Phil at the *Herald.*

The reporter was still at work, and he didn't sound at all surprised to hear from his editor on a Sunday evening. "That drug dealer hasn't made a move all weekend," Phil announced. "I'm betting something will happen tomorrow."

"Bound to," Joe agreed. His hands were still shaking, and he tensed his fingers against the phone, waiting for the sensation to subside. "So you cover the sheriff, and I'll take Benny's house."

Phil sounded a little uncertain. "Thing is," he said awkwardly, "I don't know if…I mean, Gloria's neighbor said you and Meg are adopting a kid? With a family and everything…I mean, if you wanted somebody else to cover the house, that'd be okay.''

Joe closed his eyes for a moment, gripping the phone even tighter. ''No,'' he said, ''it wouldn't. You know damn well I don't ask any of my reporters to take a story I wouldn't take.''

''Well, I know, but with a kid… I mean, Charlee was kind of afraid someone might get hurt.''

''Afraid,'' he snapped, ''isn't an option! Tell Charlee—hell, I'll tell her myself—you can't stay afraid and get things done.''

He must have spoken more severely than he intended, because Phil sounded startled. ''Okay, sure,'' the reporter agreed. ''So are we still having the staff meeting tomorrow?''

There were too many unfinished stories to let the staff meeting wait, Joe knew. He never should have taken the past three days off, but all he could do about it now was damage control.

''We sure are,'' he said abruptly. ''Tomorrow we're back to business as usual.''

Chapter Four

"So how's business?" her brother greeted Joe, and Meg flinched. She'd hoped that at least during Easter weekend, Joe would slow down a little. But let Paul start asking about the *Herald,* and they might as well forget about a relaxing lunch.

"Wait!" Stacie protested, leading her daughter into the living room. She and Paul had no sooner emerged from his car than she'd hurried Becca off to the bathroom, and now the toddler looked remarkably shiny. "Thanks for inviting us and everything, but Beck and I didn't get our hugs yet."

Joe turned away from Paul, looking genuinely pleased to see Stacie and Rebecca. In three broad strides he crossed the room and swept them both into an exuberant hug.

"Stace, you look great!"

Meg scooped Becca from between them, wholeheartedly enjoying the feel of a child in her arms. As much as she'd been looking forward to seeing her brother and sister, she had to admit that holding her niece was the biggest attraction of the visit.

Joe was right, though; Stacie did look good. Even as a teenager she had always dressed with dramatic flair, turning Meg's hand-me-downs into striking ensembles, but since her divorce last year she'd added a few streaks of gold to her dark blond hair and lost just enough weight to pass for a runway model.

"Thanks," Stacie answered, laughing as she turned to hug Meg and found Becca already in her arms. Without missing a beat, she returned her gaze to Joe. *"You,"* she observed dryly, "are looking overworked. As usual."

Paul snorted, the way he always did when their sister started extolling the virtues of playtime. But it didn't faze Stacie a bit. "Meghan," she demanded, "when was the last time you two had a nice quiet evening together?"

It took her a moment to remember, she was so wrapped up in the feel of Becca's soft hair and warm, silky hands against her cheek. "We went to the Wayside Inn for our anniversary," she recalled. "A week ago Wednesday."

"Happy anniversary," Paul offered. "What's it been, four years?"

"And eleven days," Joe confirmed. "Meg, look out, she's got—"

Before he could finish the warning, Rebecca yanked Meg's hair so hard she felt the shock all the way to her scalp. Stacie jumped to her rescue, freeing the snarled curls from the child's fingers, and handed Becca over to Paul.

"You're going bald anyway, *you* take her," she ordered. "Besides, I didn't get to hug Meg."

Her younger sister's embrace wasn't quite as heartwarming as Rebecca's, but she welcomed it nonetheless. It wasn't fair to neglect the rest of the family, Meg knew, just because she wanted to play with her niece. And Becca seemed perfectly happy to sit with her uncle Paul, who looked more like a caricature of an absent-minded professor with every passing year.

It was hard to believe, Meg thought again as she watched him talking to Joe, that the two had played high school football together. Paul looked a good ten years older than her husband...even though Stacie was right about Joe looking overworked. He'd been driving himself harder than usual for the past week, leaving the house at four in the morning to complete a few hours at the *Herald* before returning to take Tony to school and going back to the office late at night. It was only until they finished the drug dealer story, he'd said, but Meg wondered how long he could keep functioning as a full-time father and a full-time journalist.

Although if anyone could manage such an impossible feat for months on end, it was Joe McConnell.

"So," Stacie asked, pushing Becca's toy bag under the coffee table with her foot and glancing around the room, "where's Tony? I've been looking forward to meeting him."

That was probably an understatement, Meg thought. Stacie had been frankly intrigued at the prospect of an unexpected son arriving on her sister's doorstep and had asked if she should brush up on her Spanish. She'd sounded almost disappointed when Meg assured her that although Joe had insisted on maintaining his son's native language, Tony spoke English almost as well as his classmates and was already coming home with questions about the Easter Bunny.

Questions he addressed solely to Joe.

"He's busy hiding eggs," Joe answered Stacie. "Meg thought Becca'd get a kick out of finding jelly beans in the garden."

"Oh, how sweet! I guess we can let her try."

"I told him he'd better remember where they are," Joe said, "in case she needs some help."

Tony had agreed with only the faintest hint of truculence, but Meg knew that was because the request came from his father. Over the past week he had skated the fine edge of defiance, always improving his behavior whenever Joe appeared. Yesterday, though, he had been openly surly when she enlisted his help in putting away groceries, and she had the feeling that today only his father's presence was keeping Tony civil.

But she wasn't going to make a fuss with company in the house. She was going to win Tony over, no matter how long it took.

"Worst-case scenario is," Paul predicted blithely, "you'll be finding rock-hard jelly beans in the garden for the next five years. Speaking of which, Meg, Fiona said to tell you again she'll definitely make it next year."

Paul's longtime girlfriend rarely attended family events, with her schedule as a flight attendant requiring frequent weekend work. "Sure," Meg said, forcing her thoughts away from how to reach Tony. Today was supposed to be a holiday, after all. "She's welcome anytime."

The mention of welcome must have registered with Joe, because he suddenly snapped to attention as a host. "Paul, Stacie, anybody want a drink? Coffee? Chocolate bunnies?"

Becca's eyes lit up, and Stacie giggled. "You just said the forbidden word. What he meant, Beck, was apple juice. And yes, we'd love some."

"Same kind the Easter Bunny drinks," Joe said solemnly, heading for the kitchen. "Paul, you doing okay?"

Joe could take care of drink duty, Meg decided, while she checked on dinner. She tested the ham in the oven, started the asparagus simmering, set the butter in her mother's leaf-shaped plate and returned to the living room to find everyone comfortably settled in conversation and

Becca just finishing her apple juice. With a pang of pleasure, she sat down across from the child and watched her
slurp the last few drops with her straw.

Becca toddled toward her, juice carton in hand, and Stacie grinned at them both. "No more hair pulling, Beck, if
Auntie Meg is nice enough to let you sit in her lap. Is
there anything I can help with?"

It was such a joy to lift Becca into her lap, to feel her
wriggle into place. "It's all ready," Meg answered her
sister. "I figure we can sit down to lunch in about fifteen
minutes."

"Bless your heart," Stacie said fervently. "No way
would I invite people over for Easter dinner unless I had
a team of caterers lined up, and here you make it look
easy!"

Dinner for a group this size *was* easy, Meg thought. Far
easier than dinner for the three of them, which over the
past week had become a battleground with Tony doggedly
addressing his father in Spanish and Joe insisting on the
courtesy of English.

"It's just cooking," she protested.

Paul raised his eyebrows. "Right, like anybody could
cook. Did you hear about Fiona setting the microwave on
fire?"

She wouldn't have believed such a thing was possible,
but Paul told the story well. So well, in fact, that Meg
found herself laughing and saw Joe regard her with an
expression of mingled pleasure and relief.

Had he been worried about *her* stress level this past
week, when all the time she'd been worrying about his?

Which reminded her...

Meg jumped up, still holding Becca. "I'm just going to
check on Tony," she told the group.

Joe lifted his hand to stop her flight. "He's fine," he
said softly, evidently sensing her uneasiness that fifteen
minutes was a long time for a nine-year-old to spend hid-

ing plastic eggs in a garden. "I looked at him a minute ago. But I'll tell you, Beck's gonna have a hell of a time finding anything."

Stacie set down her apple juice beside Becca's. "That's okay. She doesn't get the whole idea yet, anyway."

"Maybe that's what Tony was hoping," Paul observed wryly. Even though he was sitting closer to Joe, he addressed his next question to Meg. "How's it been?"

For a moment she wondered if word had already spread from Oakville to the Twin Cities that Tony Montoya was trouble. He had come home from his first day of school simmering with resentment over the teacher who'd referred to Meg as his mother, and her cautious hope of him someday addressing her as Tía had been withering ever since. But her brother didn't need a laundry list of complaints, not during a holiday celebration.

And regardless of how long it took, she was going to win Tony over.

"Pretty good," Meg lied, keeping her gaze on Becca. "He brought home an A on his spelling test Friday. Joe's been helping him with homework every night."

Almost as if he could see her desire to slip out of the limelight, Joe stepped in. "Third-grade math," he announced plaintively, "is more than I can handle. I figured, hey, essays on summer vacation, no problem, I'm a writer. But math…"

Stacie laughed, but Paul rolled his eyes in disbelief.

"Says Mr. King-of-the-Algebra-Class!"

"That was a long time ago," Joe protested. Which didn't seem to carry much weight with Paul, who turned to Meg and Stacie for support.

"He aced the SATs, can you believe it?"

Meg didn't remember recording that in her ninth-grade diary, although she supposed it was entirely possible that her brother had never mentioned Joe McConnell's SAT scores. "You did?" she asked.

"I'm jealous," Stacie pouted. "How come you're not running a bank someplace?"

Joe shrugged off the question with a quick smile. "I'd rather be running a newspaper."

That seemed to jog Paul's memory. "Say, have you gotten any more job offers?"

"Not since Christmas," Joe answered, surprising her again. He hadn't even mentioned a job offer at Christmas…maybe because he'd known there was no point in discussing the issue again. "Anyway, we're staying here."

It was what they'd agreed on before their wedding, and she knew her husband would keep his word. He might feel occasional flashes of yearning for the excitement of a metro daily, but there was no way Meg would raise a child in some frenzied city. On that one point, she was standing firm.

"I still can't believe you turned down the *Journal*," Paul marveled. "I thought for sure that'd get you out of Oakville."

The *Chicago Journal*? Meg wondered. She knew Joe had sold them stories in the past, impressing enough editors that he'd been invited to speak at an upcoming newspaper conference, but a job offer was something she would have expected him to brag about.

"I think that's so sweet," Stacie said. "If Andy had cared half as much about where *I* wanted to live, we'd still be married."

It wasn't just *her* wanting to live in Oakville, though. "We both agreed," Meg told the group, "that this is a better place to raise a family." And surely, with the caseworker's assurance that a ready-made brother might be an advantage rather than a drawback, it wouldn't be too much longer before they welcomed their baby.

"Speaking of family," her brother observed, "it looks like Tony's finished with the Easter Bunny detail."

She barely had time to hope that the boy would be on

his best behavior for Paul and Stacie before Joe beckoned him in from the side door.

"Tony, come meet your cousin Becca."

That was apparently the right invitation, because Tony's sullen expression softened as he regarded the child on Meg's lap.

"She's pretty little," he remarked.

"And that's your aunt Stacie and uncle Paul," Joe concluded just as the timer in the kitchen rang. Meg excused herself from the group exchanging greetings and went to take the ham from the oven. It would be simple to get dinner on the table for this group, she knew; she and Stacie had performed the same routine so many times—although always with their mother on hand until three years ago—that it was almost automatic. And when her sister joined her a minute later, she proved that even without Mom's direction and with a toddler underfoot, they were still a good team.

"Let Becca sit on my lap at lunch, okay?" Meg asked, pouring milk into her niece's lidded cup and setting it at her own place.

Stacie shot her an incredulous glance as she headed for the living room to summon the rest of the group. "We brought the high chair, but, if you want her she's all yours."

There was nothing like holding a child and sharing bites of ham, raisins from the carrot-raisin salad and tiny corners of homemade bread. She would do this with her own baby every night, Meg decided during lunch, even though they would probably have a high chair at the table...but there was nothing quite so wonderful as feeling a child this warm and soft and solid in her lap.

She was distantly aware of conversation around the table and even managed to take part in it, but she felt as if the person who answered questions and laughed at stories and suggested second helpings was only a cordial shell. Her real self was solely focused on Becca, on the sheer pleasure of feeding a child, and Meg let herself drift in the sweet tranquility of it as the dinner progressed all around her.

This, she knew, was her reward for having made it through the past week. There had been times when she wanted to scream, when she had to remind herself through gritted teeth that Tony was only a child, that Joe was doing the best he could, that eventually her mothering skills would bear fruit. But Tony's unpredictable surliness was getting harder and harder to endure, especially when she remembered the hope she'd felt last weekend.

Last weekend, while the three of them had spent nearly every minute together, she'd started entertaining visions of what life could be like once they added a baby to the family. Joe would spend more time at home, Tony would blossom as they enjoyed new activities together, and she would bake bread with the children every Sunday night.

But this week she'd realized that her fantasy was sadly premature. While Joe had kept his word about shortening his work hours, his attention stayed focused on the *Herald*. Either that or on Tony, with whom he had developed a casual intimacy she couldn't help but envy. Whenever she arrived home she would hear them chatting in Spanish, and even after they switched to English she was aware of Joe sharing stories with his son that he'd never shared with her.

But still, to keep things in perspective, Joe was certainly doing his part in helping with Easter dinner. He had promised to spend the entire day at home, and he hadn't phoned the newspaper even once. He was as entertaining a host as anyone could possibly ask for, keeping the conversation flowing so she could devote herself to Rebecca. He even enlisted Paul's help in clearing the table when dinner was finished and waved away her offer of assistance, suggesting instead that she and Stacie take it easy.

"He's so sweet," Stacie declared, leaning back in her chair as the men began rattling dishes in the kitchen.

"Uh-huh," Meg murmured, burying her face in her niece's silky hair. She ought to appreciate Joe's help instead of yearning over what she might never have. "Aren't you precious, Becca?"

Becca gurgled, and Stacie shook her head in amazement. "I swear, she wouldn't stay nice this long for anyone else in the world. Your mom," she told Tony, who was just finishing his milk, "is terrific with kids."

Tony responded with a glower, and Meg hastily corrected her sister. "Tony's *own* mother," she said pointedly, "was terrific, too."

"Oh, sure." Stacie sounded a little bewildered, but then she hadn't seen how fiercely Tony resented any hint that Elena had been supplanted by another woman. "I just meant—"

Tony didn't even let her finish the sentence. Scrambling out of his chair, he muttered, "I have to go do my homework," and stalked from the room.

"Well," Stacie said, staring after him. "Pardon *me*."

"He's having a hard time, that's all," Meg apologized, wondering how much longer the excuse would hold water. "Once he feels more secure here, things will be better." She had to cling to that hope, anyway, because it was hard to imagine bringing the baby she still coveted into a household filled with such turmoil. "So," she asked by way of distraction, "what's happening with the theater?"

The distraction worked. Stacie immediately sat up straighter in her chair, her eyes lighting with enthusiasm. "We had the greatest workshop last week. We—" She broke off, evidently realizing the audience could be bigger. "Hey, guys," she called toward the kitchen, "come listen to this!"

Joe stuck his head in the door that separated the kitchen from the dining room. "Anybody want coffee?"

"No, just come listen," Stacie ordered. "Paul, here's your chance to get out of cleanup!"

The summons worked like magic, because Paul joined Joe at the door. "I don't know…"

"Don't worry about it," Meg told them both. It was sweet of them to help, but visiting was what made holidays special. "Come on, Paul, Joe, we can get that later. Stacie's got a story to tell."

Without waiting for further introduction, her sister plunged into the narration as the men returned to the nearly cleared table. "All right, it's workshop night at the theater, okay? And they bring in this psychologist who's talking about how there's only three kinds of people."

"Three kinds?" Joe repeated, sounding as fascinated as he always did when presented with a new concept. "What are we talking—red, white and blue?"

Paul grinned. "Yes, no and maybe?"

The two of them had always been quick together, Meg remembered. But once Stacie embarked on a story, nothing could throw her off stride.

"No, it's people who are governed by their mind, their body and their heart," she announced. "You're supposed to be in touch with all three, but hardly anyone is—most of us hang out in just one or two."

"Mind, heart and body," Joe mused. "Covers all the bases, I guess."

"Mind people," Stacie continued, "are big on thinking, figuring things out, living in their head. Paul, that's you."

"Why am I not surprised?" their brother muttered. Even before earning his Ph.D., he had always been considered the brain of the family. Or, as their father often bragged, of all Minnesota and then some.

But Joe was equally smart, Meg thought. "Doesn't acing the SATs make Joe a Mind person?"

"I'm betting he's part Mind and part Body," Stacie answered. "Body people are always focused on the here and now. And they like *doing* things more than getting emotional or intellectual."

Joe nodded, looking intrigued. "You got that right," he agreed.

"I'm pretty much all Body," her sister concluded, evidently recalling her tenure as the beauty queen of Larkwood High. "And, Meg, obviously, you're a Heart."

Paul chuckled, probably remembering how their parents had always introduced Meg as the kindhearted one. "No argument there."

"Hearts are the people who care about feelings," Stacie explained. "The interesting part is, like we were saying afterward, you're probably supposed to marry someone who's got whatever you don't. So you see, Paul, you make up for Fiona's not having a mind."

Only Stacie could get away with saying something like that, Meg knew. Their younger sister said whatever came into her head with such cheerful ease that people never seemed to take offense. And Paul was no exception.

"Finally, the real reason we belong together," he said. "I'll tell her you said so."

"And as for Meg," Stacie began, but she never finished the sentence. Down the length of the table, Joe caught Meg's gaze with his own and looked straight into her eyes.

"Meg," he said quietly, "is my heart."

She swallowed, caught by surprise with a sudden tightness in her throat, and clutched Becca a little closer. "You've got a heart, too," she whispered.

Joe's gaze never faltered, but she saw his eyes grow slightly darker. "Not anymore," he said.

There was a sudden hush. They might have stayed frozen around the table, with no one quite able to break the unexpected silence, if Tony hadn't called from his room upstairs.

"Papá, I need help with this."

Joe seemed to snap back to attention with an almost visible jerk of his body. "S'cuse me," he murmured to the party, and headed out of the room.

Stacie cleared her throat. "Speaking of help," she said brightly, "Paul, can you get Becca's travel crib put together someplace? It's the one you got her, Meghan, and I don't know what I'd do without it. She even naps in it at home."

Her lips felt numb when she answered, and Becca must have sensed the tension in her body because the child began squirming as she protested that she didn't need a nap. "Use our room," Meg managed to say. "Tony's in the guest room now."

Her brother and sister didn't ask any questions, but instead proceeded to unload the crib from the car and get Becca settled upstairs. Meg moved blindly into the kitchen and began mechanically rinsing dishes, still hearing the echo of Joe's stark statement.

Not anymore.

Had his heart died with Elena? Was that what he'd meant?

She stacked the plates in the dishwasher, noticing with abstract detachment that Paul had arranged all the glassware in order of size. That seemed like a Mind person, all right....

Elena, she realized with a twisting sensation in her chest, had been all three. And Joe had loved her for it. Her body, her mind and her heart were all exactly what he'd wanted, what he'd needed...and what he'd loved.

With Elena, he had given his heart.

And never recovered it.

Meg closed her eyes, drew a deep breath, then jolted herself back to awareness as she heard Paul walk in.

"You okay, sis?"

Trust Paul to come right out with it. While Stacie could

chatter brightly through the most awkward moments, and Joe could simply withdraw, her brother—with all his lack of social grace—had a way of cutting right to the core of things.

"I'm fine," Meg told him, straightening up from the dishwasher and giving him a cheerful smile. "Really, I'm fine."

Paul didn't seem convinced. He emptied a few more glasses into the sink, then turned to face her again.

"Joe loves you, you know," he said.

That was probably true, in a way. He had certainly promised to love her at their wedding ceremony. He signed all her birthday cards "with love." He definitely made love to her with all the soaring passion of a devoted lover.

But never once had he said, "I love you."

Paul must have seen the doubt in her eyes, because he continued his reassurance. "He does, Meg. Okay, maybe in Milagua he shut down his heart to stay sane, but if it was still missing I wouldn't have let him marry you."

She had to smile at the idea of her brother thundering into church to stop their wedding. "I don't know how you would've stopped us," she observed.

To her surprise, he took the challenge seriously. "By telling him you deserved somebody better," Paul said simply. "He would've listened, because he loves you."

She could imagine all too clearly Joe's reaction if Paul had insisted that his sister deserved someone better. Joe would have agreed with him, no questions asked. In fact, he had warned her before she accepted his proposal that he couldn't give her all the love she deserved. So if her brother had tried to intervene...

"If you'd told him that," Meg realized, "I wouldn't have let him listen. I would've married him no matter what—because I *wanted* him, Paul." No matter what happened, she was sure of that. "I still do."

It seemed as if her words had barely finished echoing through the kitchen when Joe came in with Tony and Stacie behind him.

"Well, the homework's done," he announced. "Tony, you want to show Beck her Easter eggs?"

"Oh, no," Stacie said regretfully. "I just put her down for a nap."

The disappointment on Tony's face showed he must have been looking forward to gathering bright-colored eggs full of jelly beans. Which meant she had been right, Meg decided, in preparing a separate basket just for him. Pretending it had been hidden by the Easter Bunny seemed too juvenile for a nine-year-old, but she had stashed it in the back of the pantry for presentation at an opportune moment.

"Well, as long as Becca's sleeping," she said, "Tony, you can get a head start on the Easter candy."

He looked genuinely amazed when she handed him the woven straw basket filled with a few choice treats. "For me?" he asked, staring at it in wonder.

Joe turned from his son to her with the same look of wonder in his eyes. "You're terrific," he murmured, and drew her into his arms for a long, appreciative kiss.

Only after she looked up from his embrace did she see Tony take his basket to the cupboard under the sink. Deliberately emptying the candy into the trash, he dropped the basket on top of it and shut the cupboard door. "My *mother*," he announced to the room at large, "never acted like I was a baby."

Stacie gasped, Paul's jaw dropped, and Meg felt as if she'd just been converted into stone. Only Joe moved, and he moved fast. Grabbing Tony by the shoulder, he marched the boy out the back door and slammed it behind them.

"My word," Stacie breathed, staring after the child. "Is he always like that?"

It seemed to take her longer than usual to find her voice. "Pretty much," Meg answered slowly. "I keep thinking he'll come around, but—I'm starting to wonder."

Paul immediately crossed the room to her side and hugged her, reassuring her with his familiar presence. "I'll bet you're knocking yourself out for him, too," he said. "Meg, it isn't fair."

No, it wasn't. Right now, with her brother and sister here, she could afford to admit that. Could afford to wish that Tony Montoya had never been born. But she couldn't let herself give in to the anger, the desperation, the hot turmoil of rage—because what good would it do?

"It isn't fair," Meg agreed, swallowing a knot of frustration. "But I've always wanted to be a mother, and now—"

"And now you feel like you should be *grateful?*" Stacie protested, squeezing in beside Paul so they could both hold her even tighter. "For a brat like him? He's lucky you don't throw him out on his ear!"

It was hard to laugh with her sister's and brother's arms around her, but the image struck her as just true enough to be funny. She gulped back a laugh, which somehow turned into a choke—and then, as Stacie held her even tighter, the choke emerged as a sob.

"It's okay," Paul murmured. "You can cry in front of *us.*"

She had never before fallen apart in front of her brother and sister—Stacie was the one with the dramatic tantrums—but right now she couldn't stop herself. Right now she couldn't hold back anymore. With a sudden burst of despair, she let the next sob escape, then the next, and by then she was past counting. Surrounded by Paul's and Stacie's solid support, she let herself go. Let herself cry out the frustration, the disappointment, the bitter dread that things might not ever improve.

It was jarring. It was embarrassing. But it was also a

tremendous relief to let go of the strong facade she'd maintained for the past ten days, and to know that Paul and Stacie understood. She could feel herself drawing strength from their support as they stood locked in a three-way embrace until her sobs finally gave way to sniffles…and Meg realized with a surge of gratitude that no matter how dismally she might have failed with Tony, at least she had her family on her side.

Which made it easier to look at the situation realistically when she finally stepped back from their comforting, sustaining hug.

"I've got you guys and Dad," she explained a little shakily, knowing they appreciated how much it meant, "but Tony hasn't got anyone except Joe. The only times he gets really worked up are when—"

The door banged open, and Stacie broke off as Joe ushered in his son. "Tony has something to say," he announced grimly.

Tony didn't look any happier than Joe, but he faced Meg squarely and recited all in one breath, "I'm-sorry-and-thank-you-for-the-Easter-basket."

Before she could respond, Joe put his hands on Tony's shoulders and pointed him toward the stairs. "If you decide you want it, you can get it later. Now go on."

Tony, without meeting anyone's gaze, headed out of the kitchen. He was immediately followed by Paul and Stacie, who murmured something about checking the car.

Which left Meg alone with her husband.

Joe turned away from watching Tony ascend the stairs, his posture rigid, and as he moved toward her she saw the grim lines of discouragement on his face. "God, Meg, I'm sorry."

"It wasn't your fault," she said automatically, then jumped as he slammed his fist on the counter.

"Damn it, we keep saying that!" When he spoke again his voice was more tightly controlled, but she could still see the tension in his body. "I'll tell you, though, I'm not putting up with any more of those digs from Tony. He's got to get off this thing about his mom."

Knowing that Joe was as firmly on her side as Paul and Stacie made it easier to feel a twinge of compassion for the boy who'd lost his mother. "Well," Meg acknowledged, "he loved her. And when you love somebody—" Joe of all people should understand this "—it's not so easy to let them go."

"He'll have to," Joe said bluntly. "She's gone."

From the way he sounded right now, so stark, so unsympathetic, it seemed entirely possible that Elena had truly taken his heart with her. "You didn't say that to Tony, did you?" she protested.

To her relief he shook his head. At least he had that much heart left, to realize you couldn't make a child forget his mother. "I told him," Joe said flatly, "that in this house, people respect each other. Not only does he respect me, but we respect him, and he and I *both* respect you. That's all there is to it."

Right there, she realized with a sinking sensation in her chest, was the difference between herself and Elena. Joe and Tony would both respect Meg, and would probably do a decent job of it. But respect wasn't what they'd felt for Elena.

Elena, they had loved.

"All right," she murmured. She had to appreciate Joe's doing what he could, even if respect wasn't quite what she wanted. "I guess that's that."

Even though respect wasn't love, it did make things somewhat easier over the next few weeks. Tony stayed scrupulously correct about performing his chores and maintaining a show of courtesy, although he still never addressed Meg directly, and stiffened whenever she touched him. Joe made a point of thanking her for dinner every evening, although he raced back to work as soon as he finished, and Meg did her best to show she appreciated their efforts.

But the forced goodwill felt stiff and uncomfortable, and when Joe came home exulting that the drug dealer had been indicted because of the *Herald*'s story, she knew the time had come to initiate a change.

"Congratulations," she told him, glancing toward the basement steps and seeing no sign that Tony had finished his daily pastime of exploring for hidden treasure. "Now, let's take a look at the home front."

To his credit, Joe didn't hesitate. "I know you've been pulling more than your share lately," he said. "And it's not fair. Listen, why don't you come with me to Chicago?"

Of all the responses he might have made, she hadn't expected that one. "Chicago?" Meg repeated, pausing in the midst of her salad preparation and staring at him in surprise. "What for?"

He reached across the table and helped himself to a cherry tomato. "Well, I've got that conference next weekend. But I was thinking if we *all* went…it could be like a family vacation."

"Don't you have to work, though?" As much as she liked the idea of creating some family memories, she didn't especially want to compete with a hotel full of journalists for Joe's attention.

"All I'm booked for is the speech and that panel Sunday afternoon," he explained, his eyes already lighting with the energy that seemed to radiate from inside him whenever a new idea sprang up. "The rest of the time we can spend having fun."

It *would* be fun, she thought, if they could somehow break through the stiff cordiality of the past few weeks and recapture the excitement of Tony's first weekend.

Maybe a trip to Chicago would be exactly the kind of family outing they needed.

"You're doing your workshop Friday, right?" She brushed her hands free of moisture from the lettuce and moved to the kitchen calendar, where she had jotted his conference schedule and flight times. "And checking in early that morning?"

"Yeah, but there won't be many people on the seven-thirty flight. We can still get tickets for you and Tony."

He sounded so confident that she wondered whether he'd forgotten or simply dismissed the only flaw in the plan. "You mean," Meg asked, "we'd take him out of school?"

She saw the realization strike him—Tony's teacher had sent home repeated warnings about daydreaming in class, and a note last week about picking fights on the playground. "Maybe skipping a day isn't so good," Joe muttered, retrieving another cherry tomato and staring at her calendar as if it might provide a solution. "Could you bring him Friday after school?"

"I guess that'd work," she agreed. Maybe getting Tony out of town next week would give him something to look forward to...some reason to watch his behavior on the playground.

"Great, then I'll meet you at the airport," he promised, and she saw a flash of pleasure on his face. "It's only twenty minutes from the hotel. And we can have dinner at the—remember that place?"

They had visited Chicago together only once, but she remembered the lakeside restaurant vividly. It was one serene highlight in a city whose frantic rhythm had seemed to captivate Joe and overwhelm her. But things would be different this time. With a child along, they would move at a slower pace.

"Of course I do," Meg said, recalling again the shimmer of lights on the water and the relief that after what felt like a year of nonstop sight-seeing, her husband was finally concentrating his fierce, rapt attention on her. "That night on our honeymoon."

"We can call next weekend a second honeymoon," he suggested just as they heard the basement door creak open and Tony heading up the stairs.

"It won't be quite the same thing with a nine-year-old," she reminded Joe, and he raised his eyebrows.

"Maybe not," he said softly. "But I'll call the hotel and see if they've got some kind of suite." For a moment, when his gaze met hers across the room, she saw in his coiled energy a warmth that made her catch her breath. "Maybe we can get a room to ourselves."

Maybe they could, she thought, and felt a curl of antic-ipation inside her.

It was silly to look forward so wholeheartedly to a weekend in Chicago, Meg knew, but the chance to com-bine a night of romance with a potentially healing family vacation was too appealing to resist. She changed her mind three times about what to pack in her lingerie bag—the white silk nightdress, the lavender tap pants, the dusty rose gown—but she finally decided to bring them all and began counting down the days until departure.

On Monday she arranged for Susan to water the flower beds. On Tuesday she phoned the hotel to ask about a sitter for Saturday night. On Wednesday she bought a Lego set to entertain Tony on the plane. On Thursday night she packed bags for all three of them before shaving her legs with extra care. And on Friday she spent far more time glancing at her watch than matching names on the yearbook order list. Susan stopped by her office during the morning break to wish her a wonderful weekend, and laughed when Meg admitted she hadn't gotten past the Gs.

"I'm not surprised. I think it's great that you're getting away."

Susan was the only friend who knew about the stresses of the past few weeks, and even she didn't know the whole story. While anyone who observed Tony and Joe together could see that another woman had given her husband a son, there was no point in revealing—not even to her best friend—that the son's forced politeness was a constant reminder of the love Meg still hadn't measured up to.

"I hope it'll help," she admitted. "Joe was right, we need a break." Even if a weekend out of town didn't completely lift the formal barriers that had prevailed since Easter, it would at least provide some family memories of their own.

"And Chicago, of all places!" Susan set her cardboard cup of coffee on Meg's desk and settled into the chair across from her. "You haven't been there since your honeymoon, have you?"

It seemed silly to admit that she'd deliberately avoided the city. That its pulse seemed too vibrant, too demanding—which, of course, was exactly what Joe loved about it. Still, now that she knew he was committed to staying in Oakville, there was no reason to worry about the lure of a fast-paced metropolis seducing her husband away.

"I'm looking forward to it," Meg said. "It'll be fun showing Tony around, but the best part will be getting some time with Joe."

Susan nodded, as if that went without saying. "This is your big Saturday night date, right? Did the hotel find a sitter?"

Word had trickled through the Oakville Country Day School office that the McConnells were indulging in a second honeymoon, and it seemed as if everyone knew the details. Roxanne had offered her a *Victoria's Secret* catalog, Linda had recommended a touch of perfume behind each knee, and even the principal had hinted that if Meg came in late on Monday, no one would be upset.

"They found a great sitter. I talked to her yesterday."

"I hope," Susan observed, "she told you to stay out as late as you want."

Staying out late wasn't exactly what she'd been looking forward to. But once they returned to the hotel...

Meg felt a blush creeping up her face, and her friend evidently saw it too. "I don't believe this!" Susan teased. "Married four years, and you're still fantasizing like a bride?"

The ring of the phone saved her from a useless denial. Picking up the receiver, Meg used her free hand to try and cover her blush. "Alumni office," she murmured.

"Mrs. McConnell?" The caller's voice snapped her from the warmth of fantasy back to reality. "I already tried your husband but they said he's out of town. This is Anna Hagen, the nurse at Tony's school."

Dear God, was Tony hurt? Had a playground fight gotten out of hand? "Yes," she answered faintly. "Is everything all right?"

Susan looked startled; her voice must have sounded more frightened than she knew. But the nurse sounded remarkably matter-of-fact.

"Well, he keeps insisting he's fine. But I think that's because he doesn't want to miss going on vacation this weekend. I can understand that, of course, but I don't think the doctor will let him—"

The doctor? This sounded worse than an ordinary scuffle; this sounded more like a broken arm or a damaged eye. "What *happened?*" Meg interrupted.

Even before she heard the answer, she felt the premonition of warning. This vacation wasn't going to come off the way they'd planned.

With a sigh, the nurse confirmed it. "Mrs. McConnell, you'd better get here as soon as you can. Tony's coming down with chicken pox."

Chapter Five

"Chicken pox," Joe repeated hollowly. Saying it again didn't seem to lessen the impact of the blow. "Are you sure?"

Meg didn't sound nearly as devastated as he felt—although he didn't feel devastated, Joe corrected himself as he crumpled the phone message into the wastebasket by the bedside table. Startled, that was all. Maybe just a little disappointed. After all, he'd been looking forward to having his family with him. But *devastated* was too strong a word.

"Dr. Brandt says to keep him inside until Sunday," Meg confirmed. "I'd gotten him some toys for the plane trip, so we're okay there. But I feel awful about missing this weekend!"

So did he. Well, maybe that was a little strong. But the whole conference seemed suddenly flatter, duller, and the two-bedroom suite he'd admired a few hours ago now seemed ridiculously big. "Look," he said, turning away from the silver-framed mirror above the dresser, "I could skip the panel Sunday and leave right after my workshop this afternoon."

"Bless your heart." Meg and her mother were the only people he'd ever heard use that phrase, and he had always liked it. "Tony's not that sick, really, and I know they're counting on you for both presentations."

If his wife and son needed him, though, the Society of Professional Journalists could lump it. "You sure?" he asked, aware of an unfamiliar emptiness somewhere inside his chest. "Because I don't mind coming home tonight."

"It's okay, Joe, really. I just wanted to let you know why we weren't coming...and to wish you good luck with your speech."

"Yeah, thanks." The speech seemed like a minor afterthought right now, although by two o'clock he would surely have himself back on track. By two o'clock he would be completely rid of this empty feeling, completely absorbed in the reason for his trip to Chicago. "I'll let you know how it goes."

The speech went fine, according to half a dozen people who congratulated Joe during the next few workshops. Even though he appreciated hearing their comments, he forced himself to stay focused on the issues, to concentrate his attention on the programs. This, after all, was why he had come—this chance to analyze and celebrate and debate the business of news.

This chance to mix with other journalists.

He ought to be pleased at not having to miss the keynote dinner for an airport pickup, rather than a little let down. He *was* pleased, Joe told himself as he joined the group at his table that night. How often did he get the opportunity to talk shop with editors and reporters and publishers like these? With people who understood the rush, the compulsion, the endless fascination and challenge and promise of news?

This endless challenge was what mattered. This was what he'd chosen long ago when, as the annual newcomer without any roots or network in whatever small town could offer his mother a waitressing job, he'd discovered the advantage of observing from the edge. The ability to land in the thick of things without having to be invited. The chance to belong at the heart of the action while asking, never answering, questions.

And the people around him knew exactly what that was like. Sure, there were a few hangers-on who viewed journalism as no different from teaching or preaching or providing entertainment, but the real news people were a community of their own. These were the people who stayed moving, who wandered from boardroom to boiler room to battlefield armed with nothing but the need to observe. To record. To show the realities of life to all those other people who belonged in the shelter and comfort and richness of home, but who would never truly belong in the world of news.

He was glad he had come, Joe thought again when the dinner gave way to a late-night exploration of the smoky jazz bars never mentioned by the hotel concierge. This group of people knew what mattered, knew how to keep moving, knew how to get the most out of a beer at one place, a saxophone solo at another, a search for cigarettes at the next. A few of them trickled back to the hotel as the hour grew later, but most of the group stayed out enjoying the rare camaraderie until the last bar closed.

Yes, he was glad he had come. It wasn't until he concluded the convivial good-nights and returned to the luxurious suite alone that he felt another echo of the fierce disappointment that had crashed through him this afternoon when Meg said she was staying home.

"She had to," Joe said aloud, startling himself with the

sound of his voice. Talking to himself was probably a bad sign. At home, of course, he'd be talking to her—but she and Tony must have gone to bed hours ago. Calling home now would be stupid.

He emptied the change and keys from his pockets, dumping everything on the vast, marble-topped dresser. It was probably just the size of the suite that had him missing Meg, because he sure hadn't felt this way at other conferences. Not that he'd ever expected her to join him before.

Not that he'd ever spent the night in a king-size bedroom where her absence seemed to infiltrate his soul.

Well, tomorrow he would switch back to a regular room—and save some money while he was at it. He should have thought of that earlier, Joe realized, dropping a half-empty book of matches into the wastebasket from which some housekeeper had already removed his crumpled message slip. In a normal room, the kind he'd always occupied alone, Meg wouldn't seem nearly so essential. So necessary. So very far away.

Impatient with himself, he kicked his shoes toward the corner and dropped the rest of his clothes in a haphazard pile on the chair. All he needed was a shower, and then he could go to sleep without another thought.

But the shower didn't help. Neither did the conference notes he'd deposited on the sofa before dinner. Neither did the late-late movie, although he managed to drift off before the final credits filled the screen.

It was just, he decided the next morning, a lack of sleep that had him so far off base. Normally when he stayed away from home for two or three days at a time, he could get by with only a few hours here and there. But this empty sensation, this feeling of something lacking, had to be from missing too much sleep.

Joe ordered a pot of coffee from room service, figuring that would get him back on track. He started to dial the front desk and ask for another room before catching himself and slamming down the phone. "Bad idea," he muttered aloud. Even though he might attribute it to saving money, asking for another room would be like running away...and running away was a sign of fear.

Which was something he refused to accept.

Besides, there was really nothing to run away from. Nothing to feel uneasy about. Sure, he might have missed Meg something fierce last night, but that was only because he hadn't spent any time alone with her since Tony arrived last month. Under those circumstances, anybody would miss their wife.

It wouldn't hurt to call her before the morning session, though, just to see how Tony was doing. But even though there was clearly nothing wrong with missing his wife, he made himself wait until he'd read the condensed *Chicago Journal* that accompanied his coffee before he dialed the number of home.

Meg sounded exactly the way he'd imagined. Calm, cheerful, as relaxed as ever...traits that she never seemed to realize set her apart from everyone else he knew. "Tony had a pretty good night," she reported. "He's doing his best not to scratch, but I'm slathering that pink lotion on him every half hour."

Joe closed his eyes. "Yeah," he said. "I can imagine."

"How did your speech go? I was thinking about you all day yesterday."

"Were you?" He didn't know why that should make his heart feel lighter, his body more aware. "It went better than I expected. Couple of people said they liked it."

"Of course they did!" Her utter confidence in his abilities was something he'd always appreciated. "I wish I could've heard it."

"Well, I'll do it for you at home if you want. Although it's not quite the same without the podium."

"I know, everything's better in Chicago." He could almost hear the smile in her voice. "Seems like I've heard that before."

She probably had; he'd spent a lot of effort trying to convince her that kids could be happy growing up someplace besides a small town. "I'll prove it to you some weekend this summer," he offered, hoping Tony wouldn't mind revisiting some sites from their honeymoon. "Although if I remember right, you weren't all that crazy about the big city, anyway."

"I would be now," she answered, surprising him. "I'm looking forward to it already."

So was he. Joe finished the conversation and his coffee, deciding that people who insisted caffeine couldn't improve your mood didn't know what they were talking about. He felt ready to take on the world this morning, and the sense of competence lasted throughout the workshops and into his scheduled lunch with the *Journal* editor.

"Great piece on that drug dealer," Warren congratulated him while they waited for a table at the deli behind the hotel. "And I see they've already handed down an indictment."

It was gratifying to know that an editor he'd always admired was keeping up with his work. Joe hadn't even attempted to sell the *Journal* his series on Benny and the sheriff, figuring it was basically Minnesota news, but he was pleased at the acknowledgment.

"Yeah, they'll probably do the trial this summer," he said, nodding at the hostess who beckoned them from across the room. "There's a new guy who wants to cover it, so I'll let him finish the story on his own."

"Not much danger in covering a trial," Warren agreed, following him to a circular wooden table set with three flavors of mustard. "Might as well stay open for something else."

Joe had to give the editor credit. Not many people saw his preference for high-risk stories so quickly and so clearly. But then, Warren had bought that piece on the firefighters as well as the mine cave-in and the strikebreakers last fall. He must have recognized the common thread.

"We don't get a lot of stories I'd sell my soul for," Joe admitted, taking a menu from the hostess. "But you never know what'll come up."

It wasn't until they'd started their pastrami sandwiches that Warren brought up his reason for the lunch invitation. "Am I right," he asked, "in thinking you'd rather be doing the kind of work we feature in Focus than in Metro?"

Joe gulped on a bite of sandwich that seemed suddenly much too large. "No contest," he managed to answer. The Focus section came out whenever a compelling story warranted it...sometimes daily, sometimes only twice a month. "But that's staff work, not freelance."

The editor nodded. "I know you have a commitment to the *Herald,*" he said, citing Joe's reason for refusing the Metro job offer last year. "If there's any chance of your reconsidering, though, I'd like to recommend you next time there's an opening in Focus."

There was nothing he wanted more. Nothing he'd rather take on. Except he couldn't forget the promise he'd made Meg before they were married...that they would raise their children in Oakville.

Still, Joe remembered with a sudden lurch of hope, she had said only this morning that she wouldn't mind Chicago now. Of course she'd been talking about a vacation rather than a life, but the fact that she'd been willing to bring Tony for the weekend might indicate a subtle shift in her attitude. Maybe Meg was beginning to realize, like he was, that there was a huge difference between raising a fragile baby and a streetwise nine-year-old.

"We probably won't need anyone for another year or two," Warren continued, "but I try and keep a list of people to call. So...any possibility you might be interested?"

Joe flexed his fingers, thinking wildly of promises and changes and hope, then rapped his knuckles together. "Yeah," he answered the editor abruptly. "I might."

"This itches," Tony complained, rubbing the calamine lotion on his arm.

"Don't scratch, remember?" Meg reminded him, watch-ing as he spooned up the last of his brown-sugared oat-meal. "It'll feel better sooner if you leave it alone."

He gave her a dubious look. "Promise?"

Tony seemed to have a very clear notion of what a promise involved, she and Joe had discovered over the past few weeks, and it was ironclad. A promise could never be retracted or amended, no matter what the circum-stances.

"Well, no," Meg admitted. She couldn't stake her in-tegrity on a notion as frail as untouched chicken pox feel-ing better sooner. "But if you scratch off those spots it'll leave scars."

He gave her an appraising glance from across the kitchen table, as if considering his options. "Like Papá's?"

She almost dropped her spoon into the oatmeal bowl. Joe was so careful about keeping his back and shoulders covered, it surprised her that Tony would have seen any-thing. "No," she answered hastily, realizing what the boy must be planning. "Smaller. But Papá wouldn't want you to have scars."

"How do you know?"

The edge of challenge was back in his voice, a sure sign that Tony was feeling more like his usual self. Still, this was a challenge she could easily face—because no one in the world, Meg felt certain, knew Joe McConnell better than she did. "I know," she told the child, "because he doesn't like looking at his."

Tony hesitated a moment, evidently weighing the truth

of her answer, then nodded in acknowledgment. "Okay. It still itches, though."

She took both their bowls to rinse in the sink. "Well, we need to keep your mind off it. Why don't we play Old Maid?"

They'd played countless games of Old Maid this weekend, and it was getting progressively harder to keep Tony amused as his fever wore off. By ten o'clock, Meg thought, she'd be tempted to stuff him in the car and haul him off to church for an hour of peace and quiet...even though she knew it would be flat-out wrong.

The music director had already arranged for a substitute organist this morning, and she couldn't justify infecting a whole churchful of people with chicken pox just to get a break from Tony.

But it was tempting. Even though he was still being as respectful as Joe had ordered, she knew his cooperation was strictly on the surface. What she'd hoped would be her chance to finally win him over had turned into a weekend of frustration.

Although, Friday night hadn't been so bad, Meg reminded herself as she watched Tony laboriously counting out two piles of cards. Friday night he had been feverish, hungry for comfort, and she had been glad to provide it. He'd even asked her to rub his back, a request so childlike that she'd felt her heart enlarge, and when he murmured sleepily that "Mamá used to do this," she'd been touched rather than hurt.

At least in this one area, she could live up to Elena's memory.

But yesterday, which had started out so bright with Joe's suggestion of a Chicago getaway, had turned into a steady grind of annoyance. Tony was petulant, fretful—probably the same as any child with chicken pox, she admitted—but last night when she'd put him to bed and asked if he'd like another back rub, he had fixed her with a cool stare and replied, "No, thank you."

"Are you sure?" Meg had asked him. "It might help you sleep, and I'll be glad to do it."

Tony clutched his pillow against his chest and turned away from her. "No," he told the wall. "Mamá did it better."

It was pointless, Meg reminded herself again this morning as she gulped down the last of her coffee, to take such a statement personally. Tony would have rejected anyone Joe married; millions of children over the ages had resented their stepmothers. But did every stepmother wind up comparing herself with her husband's first love?

And wondering whether she could ever measure up?

She needed time to regroup, Meg told herself, that was all. With Tony napping yesterday there had been no chance to play the piano—using the mute pedal was worse than no music at all—and Dr. Brandt had warned that he might spend most of today asleep, as well. But as soon as they finished their twenty-fifth game of Old Maid, she was going to escape to the garden.

To the seedlings waiting for transplant.

To a world where she could turn every problem into something beautiful.

No sooner had she gotten Tony dressed in jeans and sweatshirt over a layer of calamine lotion, dosed him with the recommended brand of nonaspirin and settled him in his room with his Legos, than she hurried out to the backyard. She had already moved her seedlings into the cold frame on Friday afternoon, so for the next few hours she could lose herself in the rapture of planning, planting and watching the color of her garden take shape.

It was a calculated risk, but never before had a winter stayed this warm. So if ever there was a time when she could plant so early without risking a frost, this was the year...and today, she had decided, she was going to start her annuals. Sweet peas and snapdragons around the edges, pansies and peonies along the side, and the petunias wherever she needed an extra splash of pink.

Here she could create order. Here she could lavish all the care and attention she had to give, and see it returned in full measure as flower after flower responded with glorious bursts of fragrance and color and light. Here, she could coax dreams into reality.

Already she could feel the earth responding to her hands, could feel the fresh hope of the tender seedlings in her fingers. In June, in July, there would be scent and sensation and sweetness beyond compare as her vision bloomed in this oasis of birth and abundance and growth.

Here, Meg vowed as she eased the next seedling into place, here she would teach her daughter the joys of bringing beauty to life.

"Can I help?"

The question startled her, she had been so completely lost in her own world. She looked up from her bed of sweet peas and saw Tony standing a few feet away, with calamine lotion still on his face and with a garden spade in his hands.

At least he was holding the right tool, not that she'd left many beside the cold frame. "Sure," Meg said reluctantly. She didn't especially want to share this experience with Tony, but she couldn't in good conscience turn down an offer of help. "Why don't you start getting these out of the containers?"

He must have been watching her longer than she'd realized, because he followed her process exactly. Loosening the dirt around the edges of the first plant, he carefully lifted the fragile green leaves from their resting place, then gently deposited the seedling into a hole just big enough to accommodate its roots.

She should have expected him to be good at this, Meg reminded herself as they worked their way silently through the tray of seedlings. The boy was Joe McConnell's son, after all. There was likely nothing he couldn't pick up after only a few minutes of study.

And she had to admit he was helpful. They made an efficient team, with her scooping the holes at just the right distance apart and him pressing the earth back into place around the newly transferred plants until they'd finished the last of the sweet peas.

"Thank you, Tony," she told him, looking over what they'd accomplished in barely ten minutes of work and noticing how neatly the flowers were tucked in place. "You're good at this."

He wiped his hands against his jeans. "Yeah," he began, "I—" Then he broke off, evidently realizing that whatever he'd been about to say might not qualify as polite. "Thanks," he muttered without meeting her gaze. "Which ones are next?"

He was obviously in this for the long haul, Meg decided. And for the first time she regretted Joe's insistence on respect...she wouldn't have minded Tony crowing about his newfound skill. Better, though, to stay focused on the garden. "Next we'll do the snapdragons. The pink ones over there."

Without a word he set to work loosening the dirt around the edges, and she started arranging the pale pink ones in front, with the rosy ones behind, and the deep pink in the very back. Yes, there was the look she wanted....

This wasn't like she'd envisioned planting with her daughter would be, Meg thought as she and Tony proceeded through the various colors, but it was kind of nice to have company. She set out a row of pansies, and Tony nestled them in place.

She moved on to the peonies, and Tony kept pace.

"This," he observed when they had finished the edges, "is looking good."

"It is, isn't it?" She could see on his face the same

feeling of pride and pleasure that fluttered inside her, and a sudden rush of awareness made her catch her breath. Maybe, finally, she and Tony had found a common meeting ground.

Even though it might be a little soon to start imagining they'd turned a corner, she felt a rush of hope as bright as the late April sun. It lasted as they transplanted the phlox, the petunias and the English daisies, and by the time they'd emptied the last trays she felt like caroling thanks to the heavens. Creating a garden could be their own activity, one they could enjoy together...a shared source of wonder that would finally establish her in Tony's mind as something more than a poor substitute for Elena.

She only wished she had thought of it sooner.

He set to work stacking the empty trays, and Meg gave him an impulsive hug. "Tony, I really appreciate your help."

For once he didn't stiffen at her touch, but neither did he respond. Instead he took a step back and turned his gaze toward the garden.

"When all those pink flowers come up," he said briefly, "it'll look like a picture somebody painted."

Even though the coolness in his voice reminded her not to assume the distance between them had magically vanished, she knew from his words that he understood exactly what she loved about gardening. In fact, he sounded as though he'd experienced it before. "Did you see any gardens in Milagua?" she asked him.

"My mother had one with all the colors in the world," Tony answered, and Meg felt a lurch in her stomach. "Sister Maria said it was the most beautiful place she'd ever seen, because Mamá could make anything grow."

A wave of dismay rose dully through her chest.

Even in gardening, Elena had outshone her.

Moving mechanically, she gathered up the cold-frame coverings and folded the plastic into neat squares. All this

time while she'd been envisioning a new hobby for herself
and Joe's son, he'd been remembering how his mother
could make anything grow.

Tony brought the trays over to her stack of supplies and
started back toward the house. Then, halfway to the door,
he turned and addressed Meg over his shoulder without
ever meeting her gaze.

"But of course," he said, "it was a lot warmer in Milagua."

It was too damned cold to justify jumping into bed beside Meg. He'd freeze her with his touch, and she looked
so blissfully peaceful right now. Joe watched her in the
faint glow of light from the hallway as he shed his coat
and gloves, wishing for the fiftieth time that his plane had
stayed on schedule.

Midnight was no time for a homecoming welcome.

But then, it wasn't like he needed her welcome in order
to feel complete. Fine, maybe he'd missed her more than
usual, but that was only because the suite was so big. And
because he hadn't seen much of her lately, what with Tony
always around.

It had nothing to do with needing this woman. Wanting,
okay, he'd admit to that. And maybe even needing her in
a practical sense—after all, he'd be hard-pressed to manage a house and a son and a newspaper without her on his
side. But that kind of need wasn't dangerous. That kind
of need didn't send you spinning over the edge of control.

He had everything under control, Joe reminded himself
as he watched the light on her skin. After all, there was
nothing wrong with wanting your wife. He'd just have to
wait for tomorrow night before he could do anything about
it.

Tomorrow morning would be even better, but he already
knew she was due at work early. She needed to make up
for missing Friday, and he'd agreed to take care of Tony

tomorrow—fair was fair, and Meg had handled the past three days alone. But tomorrow night...

It might take some effort, he admitted as he went through the newly familiar routine of checking on his son, turning off the porch light and observing all the other rituals of getting settled for the night. It might take some finagling, some phone calls, some swapping of favors owed. But he had all day to get things ready.

As it turned out, he needed most of the day. By the time Meg came home from work, though, he'd accomplished everything he set out to do. The pediatrician had predicted that Tony could return to school on Thursday, Abby had dropped off his VIP passes and taken a load of notes back to the *Herald* staff, and the grandmother who ran their church's child care center had agreed to baby-sit for the evening.

"So all you need to do," Joe told Meg while he cleared Tony's homework from the kitchen table, "is get dressed up. Helen will be here at six, and we can have the date we missed this weekend."

She looked astonished. Delighted, but disbelieving. "Tonight?" she asked, reflexively checking the shape of her hair with her fingers. "Joe, how did you—"

"I had all day," he reminded her, not realizing until he saw her look of amazement that she knew firsthand how difficult it was to accomplish anything with a sick child at home. "Now, Tony and I are going to stay out of your way so you can get ready. Okay?"

She stared at him for a moment longer, then broke into a smile. "Okay," she said.

Half an hour later it was Joe's turn to stare. Somehow this woman had transformed herself from an alumni manager into the kind of lady who would draw covetous glances from any man lucky enough to get within fifty feet of her. He didn't know what she'd done, exactly—her hair was still blond, her jewelry was still quiet—but she wore some kind of sparkly black dress that matched the sparkle in her eyes, and there was something about her face that made him want to kiss her far more thoroughly than he could do with Tony and Helen standing right behind him.

"You look great," he said, knowing even as he spoke that *great* didn't begin to cover it. Why couldn't he, as a writer, come up with something more descriptive? But Meg seemed to understand what he meant…she gave him a teasing smile, then turned to exchange greetings with the baby-sitter.

"Don't you look lovely!" Helen exclaimed. "Now, where are you off to?"

"It's a surprise," Joe answered, and everyone looked at him curiously. "But you've got my pager if anything comes up."

"Tony and I will be fine," the baby-sitter assured him while he helped Meg into her coat—the nice one, he was pleased to see, because they'd be spending most of the evening outdoors. "Now, you two have a wonderful time!"

No sooner had they backed out of the garage than Meg wriggled in her seat to face him. "All right," she coaxed, "where *are* we off to?"

He was still basking in the scent of her, something floral and tantalizing and warmly feminine that he hadn't noticed until they were closed in the car. "Can't tell you," Joe said. "That'd spoil the surprise."

If she noticed the huskiness in his voice, she gave no sign of being warned off. Instead, she leaned even closer to him. "Come on, you can tell *me*."

All right, if she wanted to play tease, he could keep it up as long as she could. "Nope," he said. "You'll see in about twenty minutes."

"Just a hint?"

Did she realize what she was doing to him—leaning so close, looking the way she did, smelling the way she did?

He couldn't tell whether it was deliberate or not, and that made it all the more intriguing.

"Not even a hint," Joe said gruffly. "Sorry, Megs. You'll have to wait and see."

With a petulant flounce, she settled back in her seat. He was glad the scenery between Oakville and Ashton was among the best in southern Minnesota, because it gave them both something to look at besides each other. Even so, he was keenly aware of Meg at his side...stealing an occasional glance in his direction...feeling the heat slowly building between them....

By the time they arrived at the Ashton Festival of Arts, he was almost wishing he'd booked a motel room instead of passes to the music festival. But one look at Meg's face convinced him he'd guessed right about an evening she would treasure. She looked absolutely thrilled.

"Joe, this is wonderful!"

"I thought you'd like it." The ten-day festival hadn't gotten any publicity in Oakville, but as soon as he saw it on Gloria's calendar notes he'd suspected it was something Meg would enjoy. And the fact that tonight featured piano music rather than cowboy guitarists or marching bands was a stroke of luck. "We've got passes for the VIP section in front."

She threw her arms around him, confirming his hunch with even more enthusiasm than he'd expected. "Oh, I love it! Joe, you couldn't have thought of anything more perfect."

He wished they could stay this close together for another few hours, but already an usher was approaching to request their tickets. Still, the feel of her body against his lasted while they made their way to the front of the park, found their seats and listened to the speaker introduce the first musicians in tonight's competition.

They were good, Joe had to admit. Good enough that he actually found himself listening and enjoying the music, rather than wondering how long it would take for the performance to end. Still, after the first round of applause, he was pleased at the chance to actually spend a few minutes talking to his wife.

She was exhilarated, he could tell. Wrapped up in the pleasure of the music, almost floating on the magic of the night. He could spend the next few hours just watching her, Joe thought, but he wanted more than just the sight of this woman. He wanted her laughter. He wanted her attention. He wanted the feel of her, the taste of her lips, the scent of her skin and the sound of her breath coming faster and faster....

He wanted all of her. And she must have sensed it, because she turned from the stage to him and leaned a little closer to make sure he could hear her murmured question.

"So," she asked softly, "how was your weekend?"

All he could remember of it now was having missed her with an ache that reverberated through his body and into his soul. "I'll tell you about it later," Joe offered, feeling hungry for even more of her voice. "How was yours?"

She smiled at a memory, and he felt his heart warming at the way her face lit up. "The best part," she told him, "was when Tony helped me with the garden. When we were finished, and he—I don't know, it was like for the first time, he might care about how I felt."

He wasn't sure what had convinced her of that, but she seemed encouraged by the possibility. "That's great," he said. It was a relief to think that Tony had actually been some help, because when his son had bragged this morning about planting the garden, Joe had wondered what a nine-year-old could actually accomplish. "He didn't get in your way?"

"No, actually he was a big help. Apparently Elena taught him a lot about gardening," Meg added, and in her voice he heard what sounded like a note of wistfulness. "He said hers was beautiful."

Right now, though, it was impossible to think of anything more beautiful than a garden created by the woman beside him. "That's because he hasn't seen yours yet," Joe observed, and her eyes widened as if the compliment meant far more than he realized. "Anyway, I'm glad you had some help."

Before she could reply, the opening chords of the next piece came thundering from the stage. Meg gave him a smile and settled back in her seat, leaving him to divide his attention between the music and the fun of speculating on whether she knew what he was imagining.

What he was planning for later tonight.

Maybe she did, because it seemed like she was sitting a little closer to him than she'd been sitting a few minutes ago. Or maybe she was just trying to stay warm. He felt warm enough for both of them, but he didn't want to start running his hands over that sparkly black dress here amidst a bunch of music lovers. And he damn sure wasn't going to rush Meg home during the middle of the concert when this was supposed to be their big night out.

Still, he could fantasize....

Another round of applause jerked him out of his reverie, and he saw that people were standing up, moving out of their seats. It must be intermission, Joe realized, which meant they were halfway through the show.

And with at least another hour to go, a drink might be a good idea.

He found them a quiet table on the lawn and made his way through the crowd to order a glass of Meg's favorite wine and another for himself, then rejoined her and offered a toast.

"To the lady who put music in my life."

She blushed almost the same color as her wine, he saw in the soft glow of lights strung through the trees overhead.

"Thank you," she murmured. "Joe, this was such a great idea."

He felt a swell of pride at knowing he'd guessed right, and that he could use his press contacts for something she so obviously enjoyed. "I'm glad you like it."

"And getting Helen! I can't think of anybody better to stay with Tony."

Maybe it was just the pleasure of the evening, but she didn't sound nearly as careful as she usually did when she mentioned the child's name. But then, Joe remembered, there had evidently been some kind of breakthrough during the weekend. "So," he asked, taking a sip of his wine and wishing he'd thought to share a single glass with her, "when did Tony start calling you Tía?"

Meg gave him a bewildered look. "He hasn't."

He didn't think she would have forgotten such a tribute, but he wished she could have heard Tony this morning. "First thing today, when he showed me the garden," Joe told her, "he said, 'Tía and I planted this.'"

The sudden radiance on her face sent a rush of warmth through him. "Really?" Meg asked, sounding genuinely touched. "I guess there's hope for us, after all."

It saddened him to think she'd stayed worried about his son's acceptance, and he wished she could see herself as clearly as he did. As a woman with so much heart and so much grace that no one could resist her for long. "He'll come around," Joe assured her, enjoying the way her long-lashed, smoky blue eyes stayed focused on his. "Pretty soon he'll be crazy about you. Anybody would be."

She must have heard the huskiness in his voice, because she lowered her eyelashes and tilted her gaze. "I don't know," she murmured.

His wife was flirting with him, he realized with a quick thrill of anticipation. This woman in the sparkly dress, sitting right across from him, smelling better than flowers and caressing the stem of her wineglass, was actually flirting with him.

And doing a damned good job of it, too.

"*I* would be," Joe said, and suddenly the flirtation seemed too gamelike. Not real enough. He reached across the table and lifted the wineglass from her hand so he could take both her hands in his. "I missed you, Meg."

"I missed you, too," she said softly, and he could see the honesty of that written all over her face. "How was Chicago?"

Chicago seemed like a distant memory, although he'd been there less than twenty-four hours ago. "Pretty good," he answered slowly. The narrative of events didn't matter, but talking to her mattered a lot. Meg was a better listener than anyone he'd ever met, and there was an almost physical pleasure in telling her about the workshops, the jazz bars, the sense of camaraderie. "It was kind of like a family or something, like I belonged there... Oh, and I got another job offer."

Her smile was filled with appreciation, with understanding, with feminine pride. "That's nice," she told him, "that everyone wants you."

"I don't know about *everyone,*" Joe began, but then he saw the color rising on her cheeks.

"Well," she murmured, twisting the wineglass in her hands, "*I* do."

He felt a jolt of energy shoot through his veins, a heady rush of awareness. Recognition. Heat. There was no mistaking it. This woman wanted exactly what he'd been imagining all evening, and when he saw the flush of arousal spreading across her face, he knew with fierce, impassioned certainty that she wanted it as intensely as he wanted it. Right away. Right now.

Moving with deliberate care to control the unsteady force inside him, Joe took her wineglass, set it on the table, stood up and helped her from her chair.

"Let's go," he said.

Chapter Six

His hands. For some reason all she could focus on was his hands. She'd known the man for years, but never before had she been quite so aware of his hands.

The way they rested on the steering wheel. Just the slightest touch of pressure right now, with the road this smooth. The way his fingers tightened during the curves, flexing with such deliberate control.

What he could do with those hands...

What he *would* do as soon as they got home.

Meg shifted in her seat, wishing Oakville weren't quite so far away. This was too long to wait, too long to stay on her side of the car and watch Joe's hands and imagine them pulling down the zipper of her dress...sliding over her shoulders...peeling off the silk...

She drew a sharp breath, caught by a wave of longing, and saw Joe tighten his grip on the steering wheel.

"Ten minutes," he muttered. "Almost there."

Ten minutes seemed like an eternity. Especially with

the car as hot as it was. She had already shaken off her coat, but the heater must be kicking into overdrive. Meg reached to turn it down, then saw it was already off.

Joe glanced at her in acknowledgment. "It's not the car, Megs. It's us."

First his hands, now his voice. What he could do with just his voice! Ever since he'd murmured those words tonight about her garden outshining Elena's, she had been aware of a growing warmth, a sweet anticipation blossoming within her. And now the sound of her name on his lips made her feel both tighter and looser inside, as if he were already touching the very core of her.

But he was still on his side of the car. With his hands still controlling the smooth leather grip of the steering wheel. Firmly. Deftly. Oh, what she'd *give* to feel those hands on her....

Ten minutes to wait. Meg wriggled in her seat, knowing even as she tried that there was no comfortable position to be found. Ten minutes didn't sound like much, but ten minutes of watching Joe's hands and hearing the rasp of his voice in her mind was going to send her right over the edge.

"This is driving me crazy," she said aloud.

He gave a quick, sharp sigh. "Same here. You want to try reciting the multiplication tables?"

"The what?"

"You know, six times seven is forty-two. Seven times eight is fifty-six."

Nobody else in the world, Meg thought, could make the multiplication tables sound sexy. But tonight, every word he spoke seemed to shimmer with promise. "It won't help," she murmured. "Joe, just your *voice* is making me crazy!"

"Yeah?" He shifted in his seat, flexing his shoulders as if to relieve the tension from his body. "All right, then, forget distraction. Why don't I make you really crazy and tell you what's going to happen when we get home?''

This was masochistic, she decided, watching his hands and longing for more of his voice. But it was also too arousing to resist. ''Tell me,'' she invited, undoing her seat belt and sliding as close to him as she could.

''Well…'' He sounded hoarser than ever, although she couldn't trust any of her senses right now. ''As soon as we're inside—'' Then he broke off, and she felt the dismal realization strike her at the same time. As soon as they got home, there would be the baby-sitter to deal with.

Which meant that ten minutes would turn into twenty.

Meg closed her eyes against a wave of frustration. Twenty more minutes! ''Couldn't we just pull off to the side of the road?'' she moaned.

She didn't realize that her question could be taken seriously until she saw Joe give her a speculative glance. But there were no houses or lights within view, and they hadn't seen another car since leaving Ashton.…

His hands tightened on the steering wheel. ''We could do that,'' he said in a gravelly voice, ''if you want.''

This was bizarre, the idea of pulling over to the side of the road like teenagers at a drive-in movie. But to have his hands on her right now, to hear the hunger in his voice grow hotter, to feel the fierce soaring heat between them begin spiraling right here—

''It's dark out,'' she answered in a rush, and with a confirming growl Joe swerved the car into a roadside field. In one swift move he extinguished the motor, released his seat belt and yanked her into his arms.

''Aw, Meggers,'' he muttered hoarsely. ''Meg…''

''Yes,'' she whispered in a swell of exhilaration. Yes to his body against hers, yes to his voice murmuring her name. He couldn't sound like this, he couldn't feel like this, unless he felt the same way she did. ''Oh, yes.''

With a groan, he pulled her closer to him and lowered

his lips to hers—so intensely, so thoroughly that she felt herself reeling under a wave of sensation. All she could do was hold on to this man, whose hands were finally where they belonged. Finally, finally he was stroking her, surrounding her, shielding her from the sudden rush of dizziness that invaded her senses at his touch.

Oh, his touch... His hungry hands caressing the sides of her face, the back of her neck, the silk against her shoulders. His skin growing warmer against her fingers as she explored his face and neck, running her hands through his close-cropped hair. His mouth moving so roughly, so sweetly over hers that she wanted to cry out in pleasure, moan with longing, shout for joy.

Joe...!

This was happening unbelievably fast, she knew, yet nothing mattered right now but the feel of him against her. The pressure of his hands against her back. The roughness of his hair against her fingers. The welcome invasion of his tongue, teasing and promising and coaxing her even farther out of herself, farther into the heights of sensation, until she felt a slow, hot shudder radiate from within her.

At that exact moment, he drew back. "Meg," he murmured. "If we don't stop now, we're gonna—I mean—" In the faint glow of starlight through the foggy window, she could see in his eyes a mixture of exultation and disbelief. "Damn it, you deserve someplace better than this!"

Better? she wondered dizzily. Satin sheets, a hotel suite? The car might be a little cramped, but she was beyond caring. "I just want *you*," she gasped.

He stared at her for a moment...a single, pulsing moment that seemed to last for an age. And then, with a muffled groan, he invaded her mouth again. So desperately, so thoroughly that she felt herself growing wildly dizzy. A kiss was one thing, but this was beyond kissing. This was primal. This was raw. This was passion soaring past the bounds of reason and into sheer, staggering need.

She needed him now. Fiercely, feverishly, with such aching desire that every obstruction—her panty hose, the seat-reclining lever, the belt buckle Joe had to help her undo—seemed to vanish under its force. Another time she could wait and savor the anticipation, but right now all she wanted was Joe and the hot, hungry passion of him filling her to the very depths.

Now, right now. But he was still struggling with his clothes, as if he couldn't dishonor her with such frantic haste. As if she *cared* how he took her, if only he would hurry!

She heard herself moan as he hesitated above her, still not right where she wanted him, but so close, so very close.... "Joe, yes," she pleaded, and then with a sudden, savage thrust he was inside her and she cried out in wonder, in joy—to have him with her finally—"Oh, yes!"

Finally, finally he was with her, filling her, and she gasped with the shock of it, gloried in the absolute wild rightness of it, taking him in, inviting him deeper, slowly deeper, until she whimpered with pleasure, and he hesitated, then gently ran his finger down her cheek.

"Meg..."

Oh, she wanted him, she wanted him! And he must have seen it in her eyes, because he took a long, slow breath...and then he began to roll his hips.

Oh, yes. Now, Joe, yes, Joe—

She murmured his name over and over, a litany of wonder—Joe, yes, oh, do it, now, Joe, yes—and as the rhythm grew hotter, more intense, her words tumbled faster and faster. Joe, yes, there, oh, now, please, yes—until suddenly she was beyond words, beyond all reason, suspended for a moment in a wild, rich darkness where there was nothing but sensation, nothing but sparkles and stars and this sweet, soaring—

Oh!

She felt her back arch, felt a sudden flood of heat surging through her, and Joe cried out—a harsh, guttural cry of joy—and then he was holding her close against him, still shaking, with his skin moist and slick against hers as he collapsed beside her in the passenger seat.

With her eyes still closed, she felt him shift his body so she could pillow her head on his shoulder, and she settled into a more comfortable position against him. It might have been hours, it might have been years that they lay there together, glorying in the languorous return to reality, but the moon hadn't vanished by the time she finally opened her eyes.

And saw Joe watching her.

"When we get home," he said softly, "I bet you're going to taste salty."

Of all the things he might have said, she hadn't expected that. "What?" she stammered.

He leaned up on one elbow, regarding her appreciatively. "We're not finished yet," he promised. "I still haven't gotten to kiss you everywhere."

Without warning, she felt another tremor of longing radiate from the very core of her. The core she'd believed he had satisfied only moments ago, except that already her heartbeat was speeding up again. As if they hadn't just gorged themselves beyond all reason.

What on earth was this man doing to her? And how could she want him again already?

"Joe!" she gasped.

He must have heard the astonishment in her voice, because he sat up straighter and put a modicum of distance between their bodies. Then, as if realizing those few inches weren't really enough, he moved back to the driver's seat so they could both arrange their disheveled clothes. It wasn't until she'd crumpled her panty hose into her coat pocket and fastened her seat belt that he kissed her again and started the car.

"When we get home," he announced, "*then* I'm going to kiss you everywhere. But not until then."

"I don't believe this," she breathed, feeling the coil of anticipation resume its dance inside her. They had never shared an evening like this before...but it seemed as if what he'd said about her garden outshining Elena's had started something magical fluttering between them. Something she'd been dreaming of for years. "Joe, this is crazy."

He gave her a crooked smile as he turned on the headlights and drove slowly back onto the road. "All night, listening to the music, I was thinking about how you'd taste," he murmured, and in his voice she heard the same ragged wonder that echoed within her. "But still, I guess we can wait another ten minutes."

The way he was driving, as if every movement required more thought than usual, it took them a little longer than ten minutes to get home. She felt as unsteady as Joe looked by the time he pulled into their garage and came around to open her car door; and it took an effort to adjust her expression into pleasant nonchalance as they went inside to greet the baby-sitter.

"Tony's sound asleep," Helen reported. "I gave him chicken pie for dinner, and we watched *Bambi* on TV."

Chicken pie and TV sounded as incomprehensible as nuclear physics right now, but Meg was pretty sure they managed to say all the appropriate things before the sitter departed. At least Helen hadn't looked as if she noticed anything strange, like the balled-up panty hose in her coat pocket or the scent of sex that must be clinging to them both.

Joe was still disheveled, she realized, with his collar slightly crooked and his hair a little mussed, but she had never seen him looking more appealing than he did right now. And he evidently felt the same way about her, because no sooner had he locked the door than he returned to her side and cupped her face in his hands.

"Longest ten minutes of my life," he murmured, gazing at her for a moment as if to fix her image in his memory before he took the first taste and then gobbled her up. "You smell so good...."

He was going to do it, she realized with a shiver of pleasure as he smoothed his hands down her cheeks, across her shoulders and around to the back of her dress. He was going to do exactly what he'd promised, and already she could feel the heat shimmering between them again as he ran his tongue across her lips.

"Joe," she whispered, and suddenly the night was split with a scream.

"*Mamá! No!*"

They both jerked back, as if someone had just tossed a flamethrower between them, and she felt the realization strike them both with horrifying force.

Tony had seen Bambi's mother die.

Together they ran upstairs, and Joe turned on the bedside light while Meg gathered Tony into her arms. "*Mamá!*" he cried again, and she felt her heart twist as she rocked him against her, trying to shelter him from the shattering grief.

"Hey, Tony," she heard Joe command. "Come on, guy. Wake up."

That didn't seem like the right way to wake a screaming child, but to her surprise Tony's eyes opened and he stared at her in confusion.

"It's all right," she whispered, still holding him. He felt so small right now, so defenseless that she wished she could somehow restore his customary truculence. Right now she could even wish he had Elena back, she felt so sure of Joe's love. "It's okay, sweetheart."

He blinked and turned his gaze on Joe, who knelt beside her and brushed his hand across Tony's forehead.

"You're okay, guy," he said softly. "Bad dream, that's all. Go back to sleep."

She only wished it were that easy to soothe someone waking from a nightmare. "It's all right," she repeated, cradling him gently as she murmured a string of soothing reassurances, and to her amazement Tony's eyes closed before she even finished the litany. Surely he couldn't have drifted back to sleep so quickly.

But apparently he had. Either children were considerably easier to reassure than adults, or Joe had some sort of magic in his hands and voice.

Which was exactly what she'd been thinking in the car tonight…

"He's fine," Joe said softly, resting his hand on her shoulder. "Come on, Meggers. Let's just let him sleep."

It seemed odd that he could be so certain, but maybe he'd seen his share of nightmare victims in Milagua. The way he'd dealt with Tony, so easily, so matter-of-factly, spoke of experience she'd never even suspected.

"You really think he'll stay asleep?" she asked, watching the child's steady breathing.

He nodded, stepping back so she could adjust Tony's blankets before turning off the bedside light. "I've never seen that happen to anybody more than once in a night," he answered, letting her precede him across the hall into their room, where he closed the door before turning on the light. "And you're great at getting people calmed down."

She supposed she was, after all this time. "It's the story of my life," Meg said, realizing with a flicker of astonishment that she could actually joke about it. "Everyone wakes up crying for Elena."

He gave her a startled glance, as if she had just revealed some appalling secret. "I don't still do that, do I?"

"It's okay," she assured him, wishing she'd kept quiet. He looked genuinely disturbed, as if he might have hurt her without ever realizing it. "I know it doesn't mean anything."

Joe flexed his fingers together, evidently searching for the right words. "It's just," he explained haltingly, "in the nightmares, it's like I'm back there. And when I...I needed something to hold on to...Elena was all I had."

"I know. It's okay," Meg repeated. Someday she would probably feel nothing but gratitude for the woman whose memory had sustained him through four years of hell, but her newfound confidence wasn't quite that strong yet. "I know she got you through a lot."

He moved closer to her and took her hands in his, as if to make sure his message came through. "But Elena isn't—" He stopped and started over. "I mean," he said softly, "it's *you* who I'm making love to."

She felt a rush of love so strong that it nearly toppled her into his arms. He couldn't have offered any sweeter confirmation, any greater reassurance than that. "So," she asked, swallowing a lump in her throat and trying for a breezy tone, "when you say you're making love to me, are you talking about anytime soon?"

Joe's earnest expression gave way to the crooked smile she loved. "Matter of fact," he answered, drawing her into his arms, "I'm talking about right now."

With a surge of joy, she raised her face for his kiss. This man was so dear, so precious, so intriguing and enticing and vital that it felt as if her heart might overflow. "I'm glad you're home," Meg whispered, and he drew his finger gently down the side of her cheek.

"So am I, Meggles. So am I."

He'd never spent this much time dreaming about his wife before, Joe thought with a twinge of embarrassment as Abby slammed the photos down on his desk. He had a paper to run, and here he was off on some cloud of marital bliss.

"Sorry," he said, jerking his attention back to the prints in front of him. "Tell Randy to get me a blowup of the scout leader, and I'll run it with the sidebar."

He had to focus. There were too many loose ends left dangling from last weekend in Chicago, followed by three days at home with Tony, but now that his son was back in school he needed to turn his full attention on the *Herald.*

"Okay," Abby said, taking the photo he handed her. "And Mark just phoned to say he's got a new angle on that car dealer story. Can you remember what we said about the highway bill two years ago?"

Joe closed his eyes, trying to envision the editorial he'd written on highway funding. This wasn't like him, he knew; it shouldn't take this long to recall a two-year-old article. He needed to sharpen his focus, to remember that an editor had no such thing as a personal life...at least not during a workday.

"I'll call Mark," he promised, pushing back his chair and heading for the archive cabinet. "Thanks, Abby."

The highway editorial appeared in the first paper he pulled, which reassured him that he hadn't entirely lost his professional competence. For that matter, yesterday's paper had looked decent enough, but he knew there were signs of his having spent so few hours at work. A misaligned caption, an oversize headline, a typo on the editorial page...maybe nothing the average reader would notice, but still, it was obvious that he'd done less than his best.

Next issue, though, he'd have everything back in shape. Joe typed up a summary of the highway article and phoned it to Mark, started the first draft of his weekly column and sent Charlee off to cover a quilt show at the heritage center. He went back to work on his editorial, resized Randy's photo for the front page sidebar, finished half a paragraph of his column and took three phone calls from subscribers with suggestions for editorials about a new grandchild, a new litter of puppies and a spelling bee in Wyoming.

"Abby, come on," he pleaded when she gestured another phone call. "Tell 'em if they want an editorial column, they've got to let me write it."

"Okay, but this is your son's teacher. You want to call her back?"

"No, I'll take it." Tony had returned to school yesterday with no apparent ill effects, but the amount of homework he'd incurred during his absence had been staggering. Joe had dropped him off this morning with a note for Mrs. O'Donoghue requesting an extension on the book report project, so the least he could do was talk to the woman.

Who, he realized with a glance at his watch, must be giving up her lunch break to offer advice on covering *Horton Hears A Who*.

"Mr. McConnell?" She sounded slightly apologetic, which struck him as odd. "I don't normally call parents in the middle of the day, but something happened this morning that you need to know about. Tony brought a knife to school."

"He did?" Joe felt a cold twist of alarm in his gut before he realized that on the streets of Milagua, such a weapon was normal. Still, if Tony had appropriated his Swiss Army knife—which a quick search of his pocket confirmed—there was clearly something Joe had failed to explain about life in America. "What happened?"

"He was showing some of the other children on the playground, and the monitor took him to the office. Now, no one got hurt, but we can't just let this go."

"No, right," he muttered. Damn it, why hadn't he seen this coming? "I'll have a talk with Tony tonight. Or should I come by there now?"

"What worries me, Mr. McConnell, is that he honestly doesn't seem to understand that he's done anything wrong.

I know he's only been here a short time, but I have to tell you, he doesn't seem to be adjusting as well as we might hope.''

So what the hell am I supposed to do about it? Joe wanted to ask. Instead he promised to have a talk with his son and meet with the teacher first thing Monday morning.

He could make that right after he dropped Tony off at school, although it might not be the most convenient timing for Meg. In a way he hated to get her involved with the whole sordid business—this was his son, which made it his problem—but if she knew about it, she'd want to help.

She wanted to make their family work. And she was knocking herself out to give Tony all the nurturance he'd missed during his months at the orphanage, even though the kid made a show of not needing any. But Joe knew he did, and he also knew that Meg was the glue holding their family together. Without her, Tony and he would be completely at a loss.

Because parenting still didn't feel natural to him. It had sounded easy enough in theory, back when he'd agreed they should have a few kids, and it looked easy enough on TV. You played ball, shared popcorn at the movies, brought home toys at Christmas and everybody stayed happy.

Well, and there were times when the reality lived up to the image. Last night he and Tony had had a lot of fun playing one-on-one soccer in the street, and when they came in for dinner Meg had observed, ''You look happy.''

Realizing that she was right, he had given her a quick kiss and ruffled Tony's hair. ''I am, Meggers,'' he'd told her. ''I've got a great son.''

But his son obviously needed more fathering than he was getting. And Joe had no idea how to provide it. He would have to come up with something—a child psychologist, maybe, or maybe just more time and attention.

Although it was hard to imagine where the time would come from.

Still, he would manage it somehow. Get things under control at the *Herald* this afternoon, since Meg had already offered to pick Tony up at school, and then turn his attention to the home front. Plan some kind of family activity for tomorrow. Call the plumber about the basement sink. Stop by the bank with the deposit he should have made last week, because Meg had discovered last night while balancing the checkbook that they were skating on the edge of disaster.

It was his own fault for forgetting the deposit, Joe knew, but he wished they had a bigger safety net. Money hadn't been a problem until recently, and it still amazed him how much an extra person in the family cost.

"Joe," Abby called across the room, "Charlee says she needs a photographer out there. And Mark wants another column on the highway story."

Everybody needed something, he thought, ripping the editorial text out of his typewriter. Everyone except Meg, who would be waiting for him tonight with her usual soothing calm. They hadn't had much time together all week, and maybe they wouldn't this weekend...but even so, just thinking about her made him feel good.

Four hours later he was still feeling good. Still thinking about Meg. The bank record matched the total she'd printed in his checkbook, the editorial was finally off to typesetting and the *Herald* Angels had already begun their weekend kickoff party. Normally he would stick around for that—it was his nickname the group had adopted, and he always enjoyed their Friday night festivities—but tonight he felt like heading home.

It felt pleasantly nostalgic following his old route without the detour to pick up Tony. Not that he minded swinging by the school, but driving through the heart of Oakville had its own appeal. The brick-front grocery on the corner. The real estate office where he'd signed the papers for their house. The Posy Place where he'd stopped to get Meg flowers on their anniversary.

On an impulse, Joe parked at the corner and went back inside the Posy Place. With her garden underway, Meg wouldn't likely need any flowers for the rest of the summer...but for some reason he felt like surprising her tonight. And he could imagine her pleasure at an unexpected bouquet.

The flower shop was more fragrant than he remembered from his last visit, but maybe things always smelled better in May. There were two boys chasing each other around the waiting area up front while their mother conferred with the new florist, and he felt a twinge of sympathy for them—they looked as if they'd rather be anywhere else in the world. Whereas their mother and the girl waiting on her looked absolutely content in this haven of pink and lavender and lace.

Basic difference between men and women, Joe decided, realizing with a sudden flash of understanding why Meg was so eager for a daughter. Being the only girl in the house must be kind of lonely, especially when he and Tony started wrestling over the soccer ball. Not that she'd ever complained about it...but still, she had to be feeling outnumbered.

Not that he could do much about it. Except hope for a girl if they ever reached the top of the adoption waiting list—but he had to admit he wasn't in any hurry for that. The child they already had was more than he'd bargained for, and even though he would never be sorry they'd taken in Tony, he had never realized how much it cost to be a father. Not as much in terms of money, or even time, as in emotional involvement. With a child, it was harder to keep your feelings at a distance.

But there was nothing to worry about, Joe reminded himself. He had everything under control.

"I said, can I help you?"

It was his turn, he realized with a start. The woman before him was shepherding her sons out the door, and he had lost himself in some kind of half-baked philosophical musing. "Yeah," he said hastily. "I wanted to get some flowers."

The clerk seemed to recognize that he was out of his element, because she assumed a professorial air. "For a hostess or for someone in the family? And if it's your wife, is this an apology or a special occasion?"

"Neither one," Joe said. "I mean…it's just, you know, giving her flowers."

Apparently that was all the guidance he needed to offer, because the florist gave him a delighted smile. "Oh, how lovely! I know just what you want." Within moments she had assembled a profusion of red and white blooms which he couldn't identify, but which seemed to glow with vibrant promise. "Now, if you're giving her these yourself, you won't want a card."

"Uh, no." He hadn't even thought about a card, and it was a relief to know he wouldn't have to think of what to say. All he wanted was to make her smile, and it looked like this bouquet would do the job. "This is great, thanks."

He'd never bought flowers for no reason before, and it surprised him how exhilarated he felt as he returned to the car. Just imagining Meg's face…the way her eyes would widen…the way she smiled with her whole heart in it…

He loved that smile.

Joe positioned the flowers carefully on the passenger seat and started for home, enjoying the anticipation that seemed to be dancing in his veins. It was almost like the feeling of embarking on a blockbuster story, or the inkling that preceded great sex. Like riding on the crest of a wave, or soaring above the stars, or floating in a world of warmth and wonder, only there was more to it than that. More exultation, somehow. More passion. More joy.

He almost laughed aloud, glorying in the sheer high spirits of feeling this way, until it occurred to him that this wasn't an entirely new sensation. No, as shining and new as it seemed, he knew he had experienced this giddy rapture before.

Not in a long time, though, he realized with a sudden thud of apprehension. Not in at least ten years. Not since he'd discovered what could happen when you lost control of your heart.

He'd felt this way before, all right.

When he loved Elena.

Chapter Seven

Never before had she seen such a glorious abundance of roses, daisies, carnations and lily of the valley spilling over a cluster of ferns. "Oh, how beautiful!" Meg marveled, accepting the bouquet Joe handed her with a thrill of amazement. He must have already heard the good news, although she hadn't expected him to respond this lavishly. "Joe, how did you know?"

He shrugged, not quite meeting her gaze as he deposited his briefcase behind the desk. "The clerk thought these'd be good," he muttered. "I just wanted to thank you for balancing the checkbook."

"The checkbook?" she repeated in disbelief, spreading the spectacular red and white blooms into the glass pitcher on the dining room table and wondering if she'd heard him right. Straightening out their bank statement hadn't taken nearly as much work as these flowers implied.

"Yeah," he said, giving her the same impersonal smile

he might have given the CPA who did the *Herald*'s books.
"I appreciated it."

"Well, you're welcome." At least that answered the
question of whether he'd already heard the news, although
such an unexpected gift would still be a nice celebration.
She was relieved that Tony hadn't came downstairs yet,
because this moment should be for just the two of them.
"Joe, guess what happened today."

For the first time he met her gaze, and she saw his
posture tense as if he expected bad news. Maybe she
should have phoned him at work, brightening what must
have been an unusually tough day, but she'd wanted to
share the excitement in person. "We got a call," Meg
announced.

"Huh?"

It was the call she'd been hoping for every time the
phone rang for the past eighteen months. The call that
would make her into what she'd dreamed of for most of
her life. The call that would finally give them a baby…a
child she could mother from the very beginning.

"It's finally happening," she told him, waiting for the
realization to dawn on his face. "Joe, we're getting our
baby."

He stared at her blankly. As if the news hadn't quite
sunk in yet. She must have looked the same way when
Rita first phoned her with the announcement, Meg realized—it was too much to take in all at once. And he hadn't
even heard the best part.

"It's a girl!" she continued, and saw his start of recognition. "I would've been happy enough with a boy, but
they did an ultrasound and they know this baby's a girl."

"Ah," he said slowly, sounding almost dazed. "Yeah."

"She's due in about two weeks." Two weeks would be
barely enough time to prepare the nursery, but already it
seemed like an eternity. "Rita said the couple who was
supposed to get her just backed out because the wife got

pregnant, so the agency's looking for a new family. And we're next, Joe. This could be our daughter!''

"No kidding,'' he murmured, drawing a deep breath. "We're next, huh?''

"Normally we'd get a lot more notice—well, you remember all that preparation stuff. But I told them we'd take her on a minute's notice. And our paperwork's already done, we just have to go see the social worker.''

"Ah,'' he said again, sounding even more dazed than before. "Yeah. Okay.''

He didn't seem as happy as she'd expected, though. Unless he was simply too overwhelmed to show any reaction. "You…you still *want* a baby, don't you?'' Meg asked.

Joe flexed his fingers together. "I—yeah, sure,'' he answered slowly, then met her gaze with a look of resolve. "Sure. Just caught me by surprise, that's all. So what do we have to do?''

"Rita wants to meet with us in person to go over the details.'' She had to admire the adoption agency's dedication to finding each baby the best possible parents, and it was a relief to know that the McConnells had already made a good impression. "Anytime Tuesday, she said, so I'm supposed to call and say when.''

"Tuesday,'' he repeated, staring into the distance. "Okay, sure. Whenever you want to do it is fine.''

She had never expected him to be so flat, so listless—but then, she realized, he hadn't felt the same spark of intuitive certainty she'd felt as soon as Rita mentioned a baby girl. Without that confirmation, no wonder he was afraid to get his hopes up.

And maybe he wouldn't fully let himself hope until the baby was safely in their hands. But she could at least reassure him that some ancient core of belief inside her had recognized that their child was coming.

"It's going to work out, Joe,'' she promised, crossing

the room to where he stood watching her guardedly, then sliding her arms around his waist and resting her head against his chest until she could feel his silent tension start to relax. "You'll see. In another two weeks, we're going to have a daughter."

It would take a little longer than two weeks, Joe learned on Tuesday. The baby would have to wait in a foster home until the birth mother signed all the necessary papers, and they would likely have to wait another six weeks before actually taking the infant home.

And they still needed the approval of what sounded like half a dozen people from here to Minneapolis.

"Not a problem," he assured the social worker, Rita Kroeger, an energetic blonde who looked like she weighed about ninety pounds soaking wet. He'd seen her around the courthouse every now and then, probably processing other people's adoptions, and she seemed as if she knew what she was doing. "We'll be in town the whole time, anyway."

Meg shot him a quick glance, as if wondering whether he'd forgotten the possibility of an out-of-town story. He hadn't forgotten, Joe wanted to tell her, but he knew how much this baby meant. He wasn't going to jeopardize his wife's most cherished dream for a story someone else could cover in his place.

Although he hoped no one would have to.

"Now," Rita concluded, "we just need to go over a few more things." She closed her file folder and leaned back in her seat, indicating that the formal part of the interview was over. "You've got the baby's room ready?"

"Not yet," Meg answered eagerly. "But everything's ordered, and this weekend I'm going to start wallpapering. I didn't want to pick out colors until we knew if it would be a boy or a girl."

He'd thought all they needed was a crib and a car seat,

but if Meg wanted wallpaper then he'd make sure she got it. Pink flowers, pink bunnies, pink flamingos, whatever she wanted.

"And a girl is fine with both of you?" the social worker asked.

"Oh, yes." There was no mistaking the happiness in his wife's voice. "I've always wanted a daughter. And we already have a son."

A son who, according to the school counselor, still had a lot of adjusting to do. But there was no way Joe was going to mention that to a social worker. He hadn't even told Meg yet, figuring it would be safer to wait until after the adoption interview.

She didn't need anything distracting her now.

"That's right, his forms are down the hall," Rita said. "The international adoptions go through a different office."

"And everybody's told us," Meg reminded her, "that adopting Tony won't make any difference to us getting a baby."

"Right, because that's Immigration. Now, how does your son feel about the baby?"

He'd better answer a few questions, Joe decided, before it looked like he wasn't involved with the process. "I don't think he quite believes it yet," he said, relieved that at least this much was the truth. "It was kind of a shock for all of us."

Meg hurried to add her own reassurance. "But Tony will be a wonderful big brother," she announced. "When he met my little niece, he was really sweet to her."

Really sweet? Hiding eggs the kid couldn't possibly find? Joe shifted in his seat, trying to look like one of those fathers on TV commercials whose kids always behaved right, and tried to imagine Tony admiring a baby.

"And of course we'll make sure he doesn't feel left out or anything," Meg continued. "As soon as we can travel,

I want to have their picture taken together to send to my dad. Tony's getting a new suit for his First Communion, and we've been saving my mother's christening gown for the baby.''

This woman could run a newsroom, Joe thought with a flash of amazement. He had no idea she'd been planning in such intense detail. But then, considering how deftly she'd arranged a replacement for the alumni office so she could be a full-time mom once the baby arrived, he shouldn't be too surprised about a simple portrait.

''And, if it's okay with his teacher, I was thinking he could bring in cupcakes when we get her,'' Meg concluded in a rush. ''You know, like how men hand out cigars?''

''That sounds cute,'' Rita agreed, then turned to Joe. ''Have you been stocking up on cigars?''

''Uh, no,'' he answered, hoping that was the right response. For some reason, even though the social worker seemed perfectly cordial, this interview had him a lot more nervous than any they'd been through before. Maybe because they were right on the edge of parenthood. ''I guess I could, though. Sure.''

She gave him a compassionate smile. ''I get the feeling this is all a little overwhelming for you.''

Overwhelming was a good word, all right. But he wasn't about to admit that. ''It's okay,'' Joe said hastily. ''It's not a problem.''

He must have spoken too quickly, he realized, because Rita gazed at him thoughtfully for a moment. ''If you had any doubts about adding a baby to your family,'' she asked gently, ''what would they be?''

''Uh—'' Careful, he warned himself. This was a trick question. ''I don't have any doubts,'' he answered, hoping his voice sounded relaxed but not defensive. Comfortable. Confident. ''I think it's great.''

Apparently that wasn't enough, because she seemed to

be waiting for something more. "Really," he added, turning his gaze from the social worker to his wife. Meg, at
least, looked like she believed him. "I think it's great."

That must have been the right answer, because Rita returned her attention to Meg. "And how about you?"

"Do I have any *doubts?*" she repeated, sounding almost
bewildered by such a question. "No. I mean, I know everything won't be perfect all the time. But to finally have
our own baby…!" In her voice was all the wonder, all
the joy of a dream come true. "I can't wait to hold her."

"Same here," Joe agreed. Better establish right up front
that he was prepared for this baby. "Holding her and…and
everything…that'll be great."

He should have kept quiet, he realized, because the social worker was looking at him again. "And you're sure
that, even without much warning," she asked, "this is a
good time for a baby?"

"Oh, yeah," he said immediately. "Yeah, of course. It
is. Absolutely." He was babbling, Joe realized with a pang
of embarrassment, same as a witness trying to hide evi-
dence. Which wasn't the case at all. Maybe there was no
such thing as an ideal time for a new baby, but he would
make sure they got through this just fine. "I mean," he
corrected himself, "it kind of caught me by surprise, but—
yeah, no question. We want this baby."

Meg gave a soft sigh of anticipation that answered the
question better than anything he could have said. "We'd
take her home right now if we could."

The social worker smiled at them both and stood up,
which he realized meant they were finished. "Well," Rita
concluded as Joe hastily rose from his seat, "there's still
a ways to go. We need to compile the evaluations and all
the paperwork, but you'll definitely be hearing from us
within the week."

"That's wonderful," Meg said, and Joe reached forward to offer a handshake.

"Yeah, thanks a lot."

"You've got our phone numbers at work *and* home, right?" Meg asked, picking up her purse. "Anytime is okay to call. Three in the morning. Whenever."

"We pretty much stick to business hours," the social worker told them, nodding in acknowledgment as Joe opened the office door for both women. He must have done all right, he realized with a surge of relief, because she didn't look as though she had any lingering doubts about the McConnells. "But we'll definitely be in touch. And I hope it'll be with good news."

She should have known, Meg realized through another wave of nausea. She should have realized that Rita was trying to warn them it might not happen the way they'd planned.

But how could anyone expect a blow like this?

The sudden beeping from the phone startled her, a reminder that she hadn't yet replaced the receiver. She must have been sitting here staring at it ever since the social worker said goodbye—what, two minutes ago? An hour? A lifetime?

A lifetime and then some, it seemed, considering how fatigued she felt right now. But there had to be a mistake, Meg told herself as she hung up the phone with shaky hands. She was still in shock, that's all, same as when Paul had phoned about their mother's heart attack three years ago. Sitting at this very same kitchen table listening to her brother, she'd felt this same numb disbelief, this same queasy certainty that someone, somewhere, must have made a mistake.

This couldn't really be happening.

Joe ought to be home any minute, she thought dizzily, noticing the clock above the sink. He'd stayed later at the *Herald* today, since Tony wouldn't be dropped off by the school field-trip leader until five-thirty. Rita had timed her call carefully, trying to catch them both at home—but Meg had managed to coax the news out of her without waiting for her husband's return.

Which she now regretted. Maybe Joe could have explained better, asked the right questions, done something to convince the social worker that the McConnells were absolutely ready for a baby.

Because this decision didn't make sense.

That thought was all she could cling to, and she clung to it with all her might as she paced the kitchen floor, fighting the dizzy sickness in her stomach and waiting for the sound of Joe's car. It had to be a mistake. Rita had gotten the files mixed up. The phone wires were crossed. She must have dreamed the whole thing.

This couldn't really be happening.

But you thought the same thing when Paul called about Mom.

And when Dr. Larsen first suggested a fertility specialist.

She ought to start doing something, Meg realized through her haze of confusion, same as she'd done those other times. She ought to start throwing in a load of laundry, stirring up something for dinner, checking the rosebushes, turning this nervous energy into action. But she couldn't quite make herself move out of this mindless circuit from the phone to the table to the window and back. Phone. Table. Window. Phone.

It had to be a mistake, that's all.

Rita hadn't meant it. She'd been reading someone else's file. In an office that size, wires must get crossed all the time.

Back to the table. Still not set for a dinner she had yet to start, although Tony should be home shortly after Joe. On to the window. Over to the phone. Which she never should have answered. Back to the table.

This couldn't really be happening.

But she'd thought that about her mother, too.

Window. Phone. Table. Window—and there was Joe. The sight of him wasn't as reassuring as she'd hoped, but at least he didn't look upset. At least he hadn't heard that same news from Rita.

Which meant this could still be—*must* still be—a mistake.

She couldn't stop pacing, though. Not even to meet him at the garage door. If she stopped, she might fall or freeze or crack or collapse—although surely this was all a mistake—but the thing to do was to keep moving. Keep circling. Keep denying.

Even when Joe came into the kitchen, she couldn't make herself stop. She hunched her hands under her armpits, although the air that accompanied him wasn't especially cold, and continued her circle of motion. Of denial. Of hope.

"Megs?" she heard him ask through the fog that surrounded her. "What's going on?"

He didn't sound panicked, she realized with a tiny flicker of relief. He sounded concerned, cautious, but not like the earth had just shattered beneath him. Which meant he couldn't have heard from Rita. And if he hadn't heard anything, then the social worker must have just been confused.

Files got mixed up all the time.

"I got a call from Rita," she said, scrunching her arms even more tightly across her chest. "It was a mistake, though. Just a mistake."

Joe looked at her strangely, as if he hadn't quite understood her. She must be mumbling, Meg realized. She had to speak in a voice he could hear if she was ever going to reach him through this dense, swirling haze.

"The social worker said," she announced, forcing herself to stop moving so she could address him clearly, "that they couldn't place this baby with us, because she didn't think we were ready.''

This time the words must have come through, because Joe looked as stunned as she'd felt. ''Oh, God,'' he muttered.

No, that was the wrong reaction. He was supposed to dismiss the whole message with an easy shrug. Just an error. Nothing to worry about. A minor mix-up, that's all.

''But I think she was reading somebody else's file,'' Meg said hastily. ''I think it was just a mistake.''

Joe still didn't seem to have grasped that. ''She doesn't think,'' he repeated slowly, ''we're ready for a baby?''

That was what Rita had said, although it still didn't make any sense. ''She was reading somebody else's file, that's all!''

The desperation in her voice must have frightened him as much as it frightened her, because he crossed the kitchen to face her directly. ''Meg,'' he asked, ''what exactly did she say?''

If Joe was scared, too, then there was a reason for this nausea inside her. But there couldn't be. It couldn't be. If she just explained the whole conversation, he would see it had been a mistake. ''The baby?'' she whispered, watching his eyes for a glimmer of reassurance. ''They're not giving us this baby.''

His jaw dropped. ''They can't do that!''

''No,'' she agreed hopefully, although she knew they could refuse a baby to anyone. ''Of course they can't.''

As much as she wanted him to confirm that statement, his silence echoed with the realization that had already started nipping at her deepest fears. And when he finally spoke, she knew he'd accepted the truth she'd been dreading all along.

''I mean, they *can*,'' he acknowledged, ''but—did she actually say that? They think we're not ready for a baby?''

Meg closed her eyes. The words she'd tried to dismiss

were all too vivid, all too clear in her memory. "She was sorry about it. She said she hated to make this call, and she hoped we would understand…"

He responded with all the fury she had hoped for, but somehow it still didn't sound strong enough. *"Understand?"*

This was the part that hurt the most. The part she still couldn't quite comprehend, because how could anyone else love this daughter more? "That they have to do what's best for the baby. Well, of course they do! I know that! But—" If Rita was right, if the files hadn't gotten switched, someone honestly thought their daughter would be better off with other parents. And that hurt beyond belief, beyond measure, beyond bearing. "Joe…"

"They really think we're not ready?" he asked again, sounding even more upset than before.

"How could we *not* be ready?" The crib was waiting to be assembled, the wallpaper had been ordered—and yet Rita hadn't been talking about practicalities, Meg knew. She'd been talking about emotions, and it still didn't make sense. "We've been waiting forever."

He headed toward the phone, moving with grim determination. "I'm gonna call her."

"It won't do any good," she said numbly, feeling the nausea rise even higher as she faced the creeping awareness that this really was happening. That it couldn't be dismissed as a mistake. "They're closed."

Joe glanced at the clock, his body tense with outrage. "It's five-thirty! When did she call?"

"I don't know. Half an hour ago."

The dull despair in her voice must have touched a nerve, because he immediately turned back to her and then, in one swift move, crossed the room and drew her into his arms. "Aw, Meg," he muttered, gently stroking her hair as if to offer whatever solace he could. "Meg…"

"I keep hoping it's a mistake," she whispered, and felt his arms tighten around her.

"Yeah, I know what you mean." For a long moment he stayed silent, as if wishing he could shield her from the harsh impact of the realization that there was nothing either one of them could do. "I wish it was."

It took her a while to ask the daunting question, but she had to know. If this wasn't a mistake, the only place she could bear to hear that was in the shelter of Joe's embrace. "But...you don't think it *is* a mistake, do you?"

It took him even longer to answer, and when he finally did his voice was tight with compassion. "No, Meg. I don't think we're going to get this baby."

Somehow she'd known that ever since Rita called, but there was a strange bitterness in hearing the truth from Joe. If even her husband believed it, there was nowhere left to turn.

And yet the social worker's apologetic explanation still didn't make any sense. Meg straightened up, forcing herself to concentrate on movement. She had to do something. She had to start dinner. But she still couldn't quite comprehend what had happened. "I don't know how we could be any more ready," she protested, mechanically turning on the stove and extracting a package of lamb chops from the refrigerator.

"Well, maybe if we had a little more money set aside," Joe suggested, opening the china cabinet and taking out three plates. "Or if Tony was doing better in school."

He sounded so logical, so matter-of-fact, that she felt a flicker of uneasiness. He sounded as if he knew exactly what Rita was talking about. "Do *you* think we're not ready?" she asked him.

Joe faltered as he closed the cabinet door. "I—"

With a horrifying jolt, the realization struck her. "You don't think we can handle a baby, do you?"

"No, I do," he protested, but without quite meeting her gaze. "I'm just saying—"

"You don't think we're ready for a baby!" No sooner had she spoken the words than she recognized what they meant. He'd gone along with her plans for wallpaper, for a family portrait, for the countless joys of a child, but all this time her husband had been harboring doubts. What she'd blindly labeled a fear of getting his hopes up was something far darker than that. "I don't know why I didn't see it."

His stricken look confirmed her suspicion that this man hadn't truly wanted their baby. "Meg," he pleaded, reaching for her, and she backed away from him.

"Don't touch me."

Her voice didn't sound like her own, and it evidently startled him because he halted in mid-stride. "Meg, listen—"

"I mean it," she insisted, fighting down the tightness of tears in her throat and facing him with the package of lamb chops like a shield between them. "*You're* why we didn't get approved."

He flinched, and she saw his face turn pale except for the puckered scar at his hairline. "Come on," he protested, "I did everything right."

In terms of completing paperwork and keeping appointments and mouthing all the right phrases, he probably had. But the more she thought of it, the more certain she felt that his reluctance had somehow shown through the co-operative facade. "They don't go by what you *do*, Joe. Or what you say. They go by what you feel."

He closed his eyes for a moment, and when he opened them she could see in his gaze the damning combination of sorrow and guilt.

"And you don't really want a baby," she breathed, knowing even as she said it that nothing had ever hurt quite this deeply. Not her mother's death, nor the fertility specialist's recommendation that they consider adoption, nor even Rita's apologetic announcement about their daughter being better off with some other family had hurt as much as this shattering awareness that Joe simply didn't want a baby. "Not like I do."

"I want you to have a baby," he protested, but he didn't even try to deny the accusation.

"That's not like wanting one yourself!" And yet she would have sworn he'd wanted children when they first got married. Then, as a car pulled up outside and she heard Tony calling thanks, she felt the realization burst over her with agonizing force. "But you don't need a baby, do you? Because you've already got your son."

Joe shot a glance out the window and turned back to her with desperation in his eyes. "He's your son, too."

No, she knew better than that. "He's Elena's son. And that's all you care about." All the time she'd been dreaming of a family to bring them together, Joe had been perfectly satisfied with the child of his first love. "That's all you've *ever* cared about!"

She had to get away before she broke, and Tony's arrival was all the opportunity she needed. With a quick breath, she ducked past Joe and around the boy, who stared in obvious bewilderment, and before either of them could move to stop her she ran out the door Tony had just entered.

She had to get away. Somewhere, anywhere. It didn't matter that her coat was inside the house, that the stove was still on, that her body was racked with sobs so jarring it was hard to keep moving. She had to get away from Joe, who already had everything he wanted in Elena's son. Who would never share her dream of a family of their own.

"I *am* happy, Meggers," he'd told her only last week. "I've got a great son."

She could hear him calling out to her now as she fled,

but he'd already said everything that mattered. And by the time she heard their front door slam and realized Joe must be coming after her, she was already crossing the neighbors' side yard. She had enough of a head start to avoid him, and the Andersens' yard led directly into the tangle of bushes that lined the rest of their street.

All she had to do was keep moving. Crying wouldn't slow her down; she could duck through the hedges without even noticing whether they pricked her hands and face. Neighbors wouldn't slow her down, either; at this time of day everyone with any sense was heading inside for dinner. And as for the chill of twilight, she was so far beyond cold that even a blizzard wouldn't slow her down.

She had to get away. It didn't matter where, as long as she didn't have to face Joe and Tony. She had nothing to say to either one of them, those two who were so complete as a father and son that to them a new baby would be an utter waste of time.

No, they didn't need anyone else in their family. Because they'd had Elena.

Who would never lose her place in Joe's heart. She might as well admit that, now that she was finally confronting reality. He might insist for the rest of their lives that past was past, that Elena was dead and therefore no reason for jealousy, but all those reassuring words didn't make any difference. The truth was, Joe would never stop loving Elena.

He would never want any child but Elena's.

Which meant there was nothing left to hope for, Meg realized with another sob as she emerged from the prickly bushes and saw no sign of pursuit on the empty street. She'd spent too many years hoping, too many years waiting, too many years dreaming that a baby would somehow make a difference, but she had to face facts. There was nothing she could say or do or wish, no matter how intensely she wanted it, that would make Joe McConnell love her.

A water spaniel in the yard across the street set up an insistent barking, which made her aware she'd been standing in the same place for too long. Moving automatically, her arms still scrunched across her chest, she took off down Laurel Street. She could wander the neighborhood all night if she wanted, or make her way downtown or even back to her office if she felt like walking that far. It didn't much matter where she went, although sooner or later she'd have to return home—

But she wasn't going to think about that now.

All that mattered now was moving. Up Laurel Street and onto First. Past lit homes filled with families who *wanted* to be families, with husbands who wanted children from their wives, with mothers who rocked their babies to sleep every night and seldom recognized what a miracle had taken place under their roof.

Her face was stinging, probably from tears invading the scratches left by that hedge. She wiped her hands across her cheeks, blindly moving past the shuttered windows and closed doors that hid the families from anyone wandering First Street—which was just as well, Meg thought. If someone saw her this way they would likely ask what was wrong, and she was in no shape to deal with kindhearted sympathy right now.

She was in no shape to deal with anything right now. Especially not with her marriage.

And as she moved from First to Fifth and back across the side streets, her luck held. She saw cars arriving home and people hurrying inside for dinner, but no one called out to her. She doggedly avoided Main Street, where there would be too many people, but Oakville had plenty of residential sidewalks. Plenty of room to keep moving. Even plenty of light from the porches and corner streetlamps as the twilight faded into dusk, dusk into evening and evening into night.

It was getting harder to breathe, harder to keep up her pace. But she still wasn't ready to go home. Her legs hurt, yes, but she could put up with that kind of pain. And the nausea that had rolled through her ever since Rita's phone call seemed to have abated, but that still didn't mean she wanted any dinner. All she wanted was…was…

She didn't know what she wanted. Respite, maybe. Oblivion. If she could only lose herself in the rose garden, or in the majesty of the church organ—but she couldn't do that now. No, Meg realized as she drew a long, shuddering breath, all she could do now was face the truth she'd been fleeing for the past few hours.

Or rather, for the past four years.

Joe McConnell would never love her. She had to accept that. She had to face the fact that she'd been wrong, that not even a family would work the magic she'd been hoping for. He had warned her from the beginning that he couldn't give her all the love she deserved, but she had never truly believed him until now.

And now that she finally believed him, Meg realized through a wave of anguish, she would have to make some changes. She would have to quit hoping, quit fantasizing, quit believing that someday Joe would love her the way she wanted. She would have to give up on ever achieving the kind of marriage she'd dreamed of.

If she were Stacie or Roxanne or any of the women at the *Herald,* she suspected, she would already be planning a life without Joe. But walking out on a man she'd promised to love "until death do us part" felt completely wrong. There were plenty of people who could do that, she knew, and maybe they were wiser than she was. She couldn't claim that every woman who left a husband had made the wrong choice.

But neither could she justify making that choice herself.

Not when her only complaint was that he'd been right in his original warning that he could never love her the way she deserved. He'd given her every chance to walk out on him before reciting their wedding vows, and she'd chosen instead to spend the rest of her life with this man.

She'd made that commitment before God and half of Larkwood, and she wasn't going back on it now.

Which meant, Meg knew, that if she was going to salvage any kind of happiness in her marriage, she would have to forget what she'd gambled for and settle instead for what Joe *could* give. Respect. Affection. The outward trappings of a life together. A joint checking account, a dinner date every now and then, an escort to neighborhood potlucks and help with the storm windows every winter.

None of which was such a bad thing on the surface. On the surface, if you looked at it that way, she had almost everything a wife could want. Someone to care about, to call if she needed reassurance about her job or a response to the mortgage company or a ride home when her car wouldn't start. Someone with whom to share plans, a home, a life. Someone who, no matter what happened, would always stand up for her.

It wasn't everything she'd expected out of marriage, but there were probably plenty of women who would be glad of even that much.

So all she could do now, Meg told herself as she started for home, was to focus on what she *did* have, rather than on what she didn't. Start thinking of what she could do for herself instead of waiting for her husband to make her life complete. Settle for what Joe could give her, and quit hoping for anything more.

She must have cried out every last tear in her system, because that decision didn't produce so much as a single sniffle. A few hours ago, she knew, it would have devastated her...but she felt as if she'd somehow moved beyond devastation and into a curiously calm, bleak vacuum.

Which at least didn't hurt. Her side hurt, probably from all the walking, and her face still hurt from the scratches left by the hedge, but her heart felt strangely detached. And when she arrived home to find every light in the house on and Joe snapping orders into the phone, she felt only a distant sympathy for how upset he looked.

When he saw her in the doorway, he froze for a moment. "Never mind," he said into the phone, "she just walked in." Then, very slowly, without ever taking his gaze off her, he hung up the receiver and came to the door.

"Meg," he said softly. Almost as if he was afraid to raise his voice or come too close in case she might bolt. "God, I was worried about you."

He must have fed Tony something before putting him to bed, because the kitchen still looked disheveled. "I was just out walking," she told him, a little surprised by how her voice sounded. Detached, as if it belonged to someone else. "I'm fine."

Joe stared at her for a long moment. "Are you?"

He had no business looking so concerned, she thought, dropping into the chair nearest the door. Anyone seeing the worry in his eyes right now would swear this man loved his wife, and they would be wrong.

"You know what I figured out?" she offered as he closed the door behind her and returned to her side. "For the past four years, I've been waiting for something that's never going to happen. All this time I've been beating my head against a wall...and I'm not going to do it anymore." It was strange how free that knowledge left her. She was no longer anchored to an impossible hope. She was no longer anchored to anything at all, which must be why she felt so off balance.

Joe squatted beside her chair, looking her directly in the eye. "I promise you," he declared, "we'll get another baby."

As if that would make any difference. "You don't *want*

a baby," she reminded him, wondering how on earth he could have forgotten such a fundamental truth. "You've already got Elena's son, and that's all you care about."

He shook his head before she even finished speaking and took both her hands in his. "Meg, I care about you."

That, she realized with an unexpected stab of pain, was what hurt more than anything. He *did* care about her, at least as much as he was capable of caring about anyone....

It just wasn't enough.

"I know you do," she acknowledged over the sudden ache of heaviness in her chest. "I know you'll always remember my birthday and take care of the storm windows and say when I look nice. But that's not what I want, Joe." As soon as she heard the tightness in her voice, she pulled her hands away and stood up. She was getting too close to the edge of feeling again. "I finally realized tonight, I can't ever *have* what I want."

"You damn well can! Look," he offered with the same forceful determination she had always admired in this man, "we'll advertise for a baby. We can run ads out of state, do an adoption in Texas or someplace."

But unless he wanted her as the mother of his children, which he obviously didn't, it wouldn't really make any difference. "It won't help," she muttered, easing around him on her way to the stairs. There was nothing that would help, nothing left to hope for, and she might as well give up for tonight. "I'm tired. I'm going to bed."

"Meg, wait," he protested, catching up to her and gently touching one of the scratches on her cheek. "At least let me— Your face is all— Can I get you anything?"

A bandage? A husband who loved her? A life of her own?

"No," she answered, taking his hand and moving it away from her face. "Don't bother, Joe. Thank you, but there's nothing you can do."

Chapter Eight

There had to be something he could do.

Meg was hurting. He knew it, and it baffled him how she could go through the daily routine acting as if there was nothing wrong. All morning she'd been acting the same as if it were an ordinary Saturday—fixing waffles for breakfast, stripping the sheets off the beds and glancing over her music for the Sunday morning service while they finished a weekend-size pot of coffee.

On the surface, at least, everything seemed normal. But Joe sensed that she was only going through the motions of everyday life, that some vital part of her had slipped askew. Her movements were abrupt. Her smile was gone. And even though she kept telling him she was fine, anyone with half a brain could tell that this woman was hurting.

There had to be something he could do, he resolved as he watched her pour her coffee down the sink. He should have called Rita at home last night, even though Meg had insisted there was no reason for it. But he shouldn't have listened to her. She was in shock over the loss of a daughter--the baby she'd dreamed of, the child she'd kept beating her head against the wall for—and everyone knew that people in shock couldn't always make rational decisions, although she sounded pretty rational whenever she spoke.

She hadn't said a whole lot today, only answered Tony's questions about her disappearance with a simple statement that she'd gone out for a walk and lost track of time. Joe had been relieved when his son didn't press the issue—Tony must have noticed her crying when she fled the house, but apparently he understood it after hearing that their family wouldn't be adopting a baby after all.

Which Joe knew was his own damn fault. It was *his* inability to show the social worker enough eagerness that had cost Meg her dream. His lack of enthusiasm, no matter how carefully he'd tried to hide it, that had dashed her hope of a child. His son, if you came right down to it, who had first made him aware of the cost of parenting.

Right now Tony was sprawled in front of the TV set like any other kid who loved Saturday morning cartoons. And Meg was mechanically rinsing dishes to load into the dishwasher. Which meant, Joe decided as he gulped down the last of his coffee, this was the best opportunity he'd get to offer his wife whatever comfort he could.

He wasn't sure what to say, but he could at least show some support. Collecting the remaining juice glasses and silverware from the table, he silently stacked them on the counter.

With barely a nod of acknowledgment, she rinsed the glasses.

He opened the dishwasher and started filling it.

She stayed focused on rinsing silverware.

There had to be something he could do besides loading plates, Joe told himself. Meg was hurting, and it was his fault.

He slammed the dishwasher shut, noticing with another twinge of guilt that she jumped at the unexpected noise.

"Look," he said abruptly, "I want to help. I want to make you feel better."

She gave him a tight smile and went back to work without meeting his gaze. "I know you do. But this is *my* problem, not yours."

Since when had either of them refused to seek or accept help with a problem? "Come on, that's not how we operate," Joe protested before remembering his own belief last week that Tony was his son and therefore his responsibility. "Or at least it shouldn't be. You don't have to carry this all by yourself."

Meg hesitated for a moment, then returned to the silverware. It was as if, he realized, she was somehow beyond his reach. As if she honestly believed there was nothing he could do. And yet the stiffness of her shoulders, the shadows under her eyes told him she needed *something*—and he was damn well going to make sure she got it.

"I want to help!" he repeated, touching her arm and startling her into looking up at him. "Look, I'm gonna call Rita first thing on Monday."

"Don't do that," she insisted, reaching with her other hand to turn off the water. "It won't help."

All right, maybe they'd lost any chance of convincing Rita's office. "Or someplace else, if that won't work. There's gotta be agencies out of state where we—"

She interrupted him with a soft cry, and for the first time since she'd returned home the other night he felt a flicker of alarm at the sheer desperation in her voice. "Joe, please! I just can't deal with this, okay?"

"Okay," he said hastily. If she needed more time to recover from the loss of the hoped-for baby, the least he could do was respect her wishes. As long as she felt the weight of his support behind her, he would let her set the pace. "Sure. But...you know I'm here for you, right?"

It took her a moment to respond, and when she finally met his gaze he saw the sadness behind her faint smile. "Right."

Well, at least she understood that much. It didn't seem to cheer her up any, but he'd hate to think his wife felt like she had to endure anything alone. Or that all he cared about was Elena, who had given him a son he'd never expected. A son Meg had done her best to accommodate, with results that anyone would agree were completely unfair.

She hadn't shown any resentment toward Tony this morning—she was too innately good at mothering for that, Joe suspected—but if she truly believed Elena's child had cost her a baby, then Tony's presence had to be a strain. And yet they couldn't very well ship him off to summer camp or something, not with school still in session. All he could do was try and keep the boy out of her way for the next few days while she dealt with the loss of her long-awaited daughter.

And hope that would help a little.

"Whatever I can do to make things better," he told her, "I'll do. I mean it, Meggers. This isn't just *your* problem."

She took the last handful of silverware and deposited it in the dishwasher. "Thanks," she said abruptly, although he wasn't sure whether she meant for his reassurance or his help with the dishes. "Do you want any more coffee, or shall I get rid of it?"

He didn't want any more coffee. What he wanted was to correct whatever damage he'd done, to coax Meg into feeling better. To get that aching resignation out of her eyes. But maybe all he could do right now, Joe realized, was to let her grieve without the distraction of cartoons blaring from the TV set. "Get rid of it," he told her. "I'm gonna take Tony out for a while."

She didn't even ask where they were going, which he took as proof that Meg wasn't her usual self. Joe got Tony into the car before the boy could ask why Tía wasn't coming along and drove toward where he thought he remembered hearing about a miniature golf course.

"We need to be extra nice to Tía for a while, okay?" he instructed his son. "Because she feels really sad about not getting the baby."

The flicker of awareness in Tony's eyes showed that the nine-year-old had noticed something wrong with Meg. There was no good way to explain her belief that Elena's son was all he cared about, Joe knew, but he couldn't let the child aggravate that mistaken anguish with any curious questions of his own. He had to act like one of those fathers who always knew the right thing to say.

"She's still sad?" Tony asked. "Even this morning?"

She seemed more sad than he'd ever seen her, even more than when they learned they would never conceive a child. But it made sense if she had only now realized, like she'd said the other night, that she couldn't ever have what she wanted. He didn't see why another baby wouldn't fill the void, but Meg had obviously expected this particular daughter…and viewed her as irreplaceable.

"Yeah," Joe said slowly, hoping this was the right thing to tell his son. "When you feel really sad, it usually lasts for a while."

Tony stayed silent for a minute, evidently digesting that concept. Then he observed, "Like when my mother died."

The boy had spoken in Spanish without even realizing it, and Joe answered him the same way. *"Sí. Exactamente."*

"I cried a lot at first," Tony said, still in Spanish. Joe had always admired the boy's easy transitions from one language to the other, and over the past few weeks had finally regained enough fluency to keep up with him. "But Miguel said only little kids cry."

He could imagine all too clearly how an orphanage bully would take pride in putting down younger children, and it hurt to know that his son had been faced with such scorn. "Miguel's wrong," Joe said fiercely. "Everybody cries when they lose someone they love."

"Even grown-ups?"

Either the kid had been wondering about Meg's tears the other night, or he simply needed some reassurance that crying was nothing to be ashamed of. "Sure, even grown-ups cry when something hurts their heart."

There was another pause, as if Tony was trying to separate genial reassurance from actual fact. Then he asked very softly, "Did you cry when you heard Mamá died?"

Joe closed his eyes for a moment, caught without warning by the anguish that always accompanied any memory of the night he'd learned about Elena's death. "Yeah," he muttered. "It hurt my heart." Which was nothing he wanted to focus on now.

He had everything under control, and he kept his feelings where they belonged.

His heart would never hurt that way again. His emotions, his yearning, his entire *life* would never spin out of control again. After fifty months of absolutely no control, the last thing he needed was the tumult that accompanied any intense emotion.

"It hurt my heart, too," Tony said, jerking Joe's attention back to the present.

"Right. And that's how Tía is feeling now," he concluded hastily. "So you and I are going to make things easy on her."

He hadn't quite thought of how to accomplish that, but his son didn't seem to have any problem coming up with a plan. "I'll make my own lunch for school."

It might save Meg two minutes of work in the morning,

but the thought was what mattered. "Good for you, guy. That's the idea."

"What are *you* gonna do?"

There had to be something he could do. No matter how much he dreaded the financial, temporal and emotional cost of yet another child, he was going to make damn sure they wound up with a baby.

But while his automatic instinct was to take immediate action, he didn't think Meg was quite ready for him to line up another baby yet.

"Well," Joe said slowly, "I'm gonna give her some time to get over it." Meanwhile, though, he had to do whatever he could to make up for her loss. A new rosebush? A vacation? A grand piano? There had to be something he could offer.

"We could bring her some ice cream," Tony suggested, evidently warming to the idea of cheering up Tía. "And I could help her plant some more flowers."

If she honestly believed Elena's child had cost her a baby, though, the last thing she'd want right now was time alone with Tony. Not that he could tell his son that...but at least he could keep the boy out of Meg's way. "Well, let's see how it goes," Joe said before remembering the easier half of Tony's suggestion. "But, yeah, we'll bring her some ice cream."

Tony carried a carton of ice cream, Meg noticed when he and Joe came inside, exactly the same way his father had carried a bouquet of red and white flowers last week. The two of them looked so very much alike—the same posture, the same gestures, the same way of holding what must be a gift—that the boy's expression of excitement surprised her. Where Joe had handed her the flowers with dismissive nonchalance, his son fairly wriggled with anticipation as he presented her with a cold carton of strawberry ice cream.

"Papá and I wanted to make you feel better," he announced, and she saw Joe's jaw tighten as if he regretted Tony's candor. "He paid for it, but I picked it out."

"Thank you," she told them both. At least while they were gone she'd managed to work out some of her feelings at the piano, but she still couldn't bring herself to meet her husband's gaze. She was still too close to the ragged edge of anger, frustration and despair. "I'll put this in the freezer. Joe, Phil wants you to call him at the *Herald*."

"Ah." He glanced at Tony, then at her. "Okay, thanks. Tony, you need to get started on your chores."

The boy began to protest, but apparently remembered something before the words reached his lips. Without any argument he headed upstairs, and Joe watched him go before turning his attention to the phone.

They must have been discussing good behavior, Meg realized, feeling another surge of resentment that Joe had thought lecturing Tony would compensate for his own resistance to another child. Still, she had to give him credit for doing what he could. She needed to focus on what she *had*.

The task seemed immense, but she'd spent all morning reminding herself that plenty of women were worse off than herself. Joe might not love her, but he would never cheat on her. Never hit her. Never buy a house in Montana without consulting her, the way Stacie's husband had done.

Joe wanted to make things better, she knew. He'd said so a dozen times already, without ever realizing that he couldn't give her what she wanted most. He might go through all the motions, same as he'd done with the adoption agency caseworkers...but no amount of pretense could change the fact that he would never love anyone except Elena.

So instead of thinking about what she didn't have, Meg reminded herself, she was going to focus on what she did.

Like her garden. She'd started edging the borders before Joe and Tony came home, and she still needed to prune the roses.

Leaving Joe intent on his conversation with the *Herald* reporter, she returned to the roses in the center of the garden. She had just finished trimming the cluster beside the arbor bench when, to her surprise, Tony came outside with a dish of ice cream and handed it to her.

"I picked this kind," he explained, "because it's pink like your flowers. Only you have to eat it to feel better."

He seemed intent on making sure she complied, and Meg realized with a jolt of surprise that she'd completely forgotten about lunch.

"Thank you, Tony," she told him, taking a spoonful of ice cream and obediently swallowing it. "Don't you want some, too?"

He looked almost offended, as if she'd accused him of planning a theft. "It's for *you,*" he protested. "I'm not sad."

The ice cream felt suddenly too big for her throat. "Bless your heart," she whispered as she felt another swell of tears rising in her chest. Blinking furiously, she swallowed them back.

Tony eyed her uneasily, then sat down beside her as if to make sure she paid attention to his instructions. "You know," he said soberly, "it's okay for grown-ups to cry."

She'd already cried more than any sane person should cry, though, Meg knew, and she had to get herself back to normal. "Um," she murmured.

Which didn't seem to persuade Tony that she agreed with him. "Papá even cries," he announced.

That, she knew, was an exaggeration. Never once in all the years she'd known him had she seen Joe McConnell cry. "Well…"

"He *said* he did," Tony insisted, evidently sensing her

disbelief. "When he heard my mother died, it hurt his heart."

For a moment she felt as if her own heart had been wrenched yet again. It shouldn't surprise her, this new confirmation of how very much Joe had loved Elena, but she wondered how much longer it could possibly go on hurting. And even as she wondered it, she felt herself choking back a sob.

"So it's okay if you cry," Tony concluded, seeming to feel he'd convinced her, now that the first tears were welling in her eyes. "Because, like Papá said, it hurts when you lose someone you love."

Or when you lost the hope of them ever loving you. "I know," Meg whispered. "It does."

She couldn't let herself give way to a storm of tears in front of Joe and Elena's son. But it took all her strength to concentrate on swallowing another spoonful of ice cream, then another and another, while Tony watched with somber attention. He seemed to view it as a personal mission to make sure she ate the ice cream that supposedly would cheer her up, and she wondered whether such compassion was something he'd learned from his mother. Elena had been a doctor, after all, and—

"Meggins?" Joe's approach startled both her and Tony, who glanced at his bedroom window with such a guilty expression that she knew he must have left his chores unfinished.

"He was trying to cheer me up," she explained as Tony hurried back inside. But the catch in her voice evidently showed how unsuccessful the attempt had been, because Joe looked even more uneasy.

"You don't need anything else to deal with right now, I know, but…" He hesitated, as if trying to find the right words, then reached down to offer her a hand in rising from the bench. "But your dad's neighbor just called. Mrs. Emery?"

The Emerys had befriended her parents from the day they arrived in Arizona, and Meg had been glad that after her mother's death, her father would still enjoy home-cooked meals with friends. Joe's tone of voice, though, didn't sound like this had anything to do with friendship.

"She said her husband was driving him to the hospital," he continued awkwardly, "and that...you might want to come out there. Because they think he's had a stroke."

Although his heart might be forever out of reach, Joe had a definite knack for getting things done fast. By the time she'd packed a flight bag with a week's worth of summer clothes, he had located Paul and Fiona in Scotland, arranged for Meg's flight to Phoenix and booked a rental car so she and her sister could drive to the hospital together.

"It'll be kind of late," he warned, "but you're going west so you'll gain some time. Stacie's plane gets in first, so she'll pick up the car and meet you right outside the terminal."

He'd been wanting to help with whatever he could, Meg knew, and she should be grateful for his efficient assistance. But right now she couldn't seem to feel anything except a nameless, superstitious dread that losses always came in threes.

The baby girl. The hope of winning her husband's love. And now her father? It seemed like too many disasters for one person to endure.

But she knew that such things happened, and that they happened to real people. Joe had lost not only four years of his life, but also—after the announcement of his execution—his freelance career, his identity and all his worldly goods. Then a few years later, with virtually no time in between, he'd suffered the loss of Elena and his mother.

And yet here he was, looking very much in control as

he drove her to catch the three o'clock flight, as if surviving such horrendous losses hadn't hurt him at all.

Joe McConnell, she realized with a pang of admiration, was a lot stronger than she would ever be. Which was just one more reason she had wanted this man for so many years.

He must have sensed her silent scrutiny, because he turned to her with a look of determination. "It'll be okay, Megs. We'll get you there in time."

She hadn't doubted it. Nor had she doubted that Joe would carry out all the missions she'd listed in haphazard notes: alerting the music director to find someone for tomorrow's service, explaining her absence to the school, picking up the dry cleaning on Monday. "Not a problem," he'd told her in the midst of her worries about leaving him and Tony without much in the freezer. "We'll be fine."

They probably would, Meg thought as she watched Tony happily engrossed with his Lego in the back seat. It wasn't as if they really needed her, after all.

And right now, she reminded herself, that might be a good thing. Because, at least for the moment, someone else did.

Her father looked better than she'd expected, Meg saw with relief when she and Stacie finally arrived at the hospital. Visiting hours were long over, but the doctor had left word that everything was fine and that they could certainly see their father for a few minutes. Instead of the stroke Mrs. Emery had feared, he'd been diagnosed with diabetes.

"Dad's gonna hate that," Stacie predicted in a low voice as an intern with a haircut exactly like Joe's edged past them to draw a blood sample. "But as long as he's got another thirty years to live, I don't feel so bad."

She still felt a little dizzy. The dread that had surrounded her ever since Mrs. Emery's phone call had receded with the doctor's reassuring announcement, leaving her reeling with unsteady nerves. It was as if every last anchor, even the recent awareness of being needed, had been suddenly ripped away.

"Careful, there," she heard her father warn the intern. "You've got my daughters watching."

"Oh, right, like we know all *about* blood samples," Stacie teased, glancing at the man's name tag. "Don't listen to him, Jason. As long as you don't point any needles this way, we're fine."

The intern chuckled as he pocketed his equipment. "Glad to hear it."

Her sister gave him a speculative glance. "I'll bet he's the guy we need to be nice to," she told Meg in a voice meant to be overheard, "if we want Dad to get out early."

Jason raised his eyebrows and their father shook his head. "Watch out for my Stacie," he told the intern. "She's the charmer. And my Meghan is the sweetheart."

"Nice to meet you," the man told them both, but his eyes lingered on Stacie. "I'll see you around."

"You'll be sick of the sight of us in another few days," Stacie predicted with a cheerful wave before turning back to their father. "Dad, that is so *old*. Meg's still a sweetheart, sure, but I quit being a charmer years ago."

But no one could quit being what they were, Meg thought. Her sister would always be the kind of person everyone enjoyed meeting…and she would always be ordinary.

"Well, whatever you are, I'm glad you're both here," Dad said. "Ruth Emery tried to call each of you as soon as she heard it wasn't a stroke, only she was too late. But Joe phoned me after she reached him, Meg, and said for you to stay as long as you want."

She might as well stay for a few days, she realized through a tide of weariness, considering that the plane ticket was already paid for and that her parents' guest room was always kept ready for visitors. And that Joe was evidently in no hurry for her to return home.

"This'll be fun," Stacie said. "Becca's with Andy all week, so I'm totally free. Meg, whenever Dad's busy with those How To Manage Diabetes classes, you and I can go shopping."

Their father laughed. "Whole city's full of malls. Bet I won't see you girls again for another few days."

He saw them again the next morning, though, and Meg stayed throughout the day. Even while her dad was occupied with the nurses instructing him on sugar tests, glucose management and insulin levels, she occupied herself in the waiting room until Stacie dragged her out. "If you really want to be useful, let's go buy a bunch of healthy food we can leave in his freezer."

At least that way she could be of some use to someone. Meg spent the next four days alternating between the hospital and her father's kitchen, where she prepared a month's worth of dinners according to the diabetic cookbook Stacie had picked up at the mall. It was strangely poignant spending so much time with the utensils she remembered her mother using, and she wished again that her mom was still around to offer advice.

Not that there was much anyone could say, Meg knew. All she needed to do was to get used to the idea that no matter what she might have dreamed of, she could never measure up to Joe's first love.

The knowledge didn't hurt so much as long as she stayed busy, and she forced herself to keep moving from the kitchen to the hospital to the grocery store to the nursing station with such dogged efficiency that Stacie compared her to "The Little Engine That Could." "You can take a break, you know," her sister reminded her at three in the morning when she found Meg pasting recipes from the diabetic cookbook onto cards their father could keep handy. "It's not like the only thing keeping him alive is you going without sleep."

She wasn't sleeping in any case, though, which was probably why Joe's phone call the next morning sent her over the edge of despair. He sounded so cheerful, so re-assuring when he told her that he and Tony were doing fine and to take all the time she needed with her dad, that she hung up the phone and burst into tears.

It was frustration, that's all, Meg told herself. It was the aching confirmation that her husband honestly didn't need her. It was also a good reason to start chopping onions for chili, as long as she was crying, anyway.

But she had no sooner begun slicing the second onion than Stacie returned from her morning run, took one look at her and moved the cutting board out of her reach.

"Come on," her sister said as Meg blinked at her. "We're going shopping."

Shopping? At ten o'clock in the morning? "I've got to finish the chili."

"We'll buy chili," Stacie retorted, dumping the onions into a plastic bag and depositing it in the trash. "Come on. We need to get out."

She'd planned on stopping by the hospital after Dad's morning class, but right now she was in no shape to go anywhere. Meg rubbed her wrist against her eyes, catching another whiff of onions. "You can go if you want."

"Don't make me get nasty," her sister warned. "Be-cause I can, and you know it. We are going to the mall."

There was no use arguing with Stacie in a mood like this, and if she tried to protest that neither of them was dressed for shopping, her sister would only remind her that people wore jeans and running shorts even to the hospital chapel. "All right," she muttered, rinsing her knife in the sink. "But I'm at least going to wash my hands."

With clean hands and a last-minute change of clothes for Stacie, who admitted that nobody would let a sweaty runner try on dresses, they set off for Arrowhead Mall. It was a little strange seeing familiar stores transplanted to Arizona, Meg thought, although it was also a good excuse not to buy anything. If she realized later that she couldn't live without a copper recipe box, she told her sister, she could always get one in Minnesota.

Even so, she bought an inkwell for Joe and a race car for Tony, spending longer than necessary in the toy store while Stacie eyed the dress shop across the way. "I'm just gonna run over there for a look," her sister finally said, and Meg agreed to meet her in a few minutes.

But she got distracted on the way by the store window displaying a treasure trove of rag dolls, carousel horses and baby clothes. She stood staring at it, lost in yearning for so long that when Stacie tapped her on the shoulder, she realized her legs had gone numb.

"Let's get something for Becca," Meg suggested, gesturing toward the window.

Her sister evidently noticed the tremor in her voice, because she shook her head. "Beck's got more stuff than she knows what to do with. Come on."

But even though she knew it was pointless, she couldn't stop herself from wishing. Not yet. "I just want to look, all right?"

"We've got tons of other stores to look at," Stacie protested.

Only none of them meant as much as this one. "I know, but—" She had to struggle for a full breath, and it seemed like a losing battle. Already the persistent tears were rising in her throat. "But—"

"Meg," her sister ordered, "get off it." Taking her by the hand, Stacie almost dragged her away from the window and toward the food court, where she plopped their shopping bags beneath a vacant table. "Look," she said bluntly, "this isn't doing you any good. Just sit here a minute, will you, and I'll get us some nachos."

She didn't want nachos. She wanted a baby. But with a husband who didn't need any more children, she had no better chance of adopting a baby than she would if she'd been a single woman with a low-paying job.

Stacie was right, though, about staring at windows not doing her any good. "Okay," she agreed shakily. "Thanks."

Her sister returned with a cardboard tray of cheese-laden chips and two paper plates, which she filled with more nachos than Meg could possibly imagine eating. "I'm betting you didn't bother with breakfast," Stacie said. "You don't have to *like* eating, but you need to do it once in a while. Meg, you've got to get a grip!"

She knew that. She just didn't know how to go about it.

"Joe told me about what happened with the baby," her sister continued, surprising her. They must have talked more than she'd realized from Stacie's scribbled message yesterday. "And I'm really sorry you didn't get this one, but there'll be others."

It was a comforting thought, but she knew it wasn't true. "No, there won't," Meg said, easing a chip away from the puddle of cheese sauce and breaking off a dry corner. "Joe doesn't want another child."

Stacie gaped at her as if she'd mentioned green sky. "He what?"

"He's got Tony," she explained, swallowing the chip in spite of the tightness in her throat. "He's perfectly happy with Tony."

"But he said he was going to make sure you got a baby."

"It won't make any difference!" Joe still didn't understand that a baby was supposed to be for people who loved each other, who wanted to share a child. Not a consolation prize for a woman whose husband had all the family he wanted. "Stacie, he doesn't want a baby with *me*."

"That's silly," her sister protested, dunking another chip in the rapidly congealing sauce. "You're a better mom than anybody I know."

She knew what Stacie meant, even though she had never been a mom. "I always thought I would be," Meg admitted. "But if Joe doesn't want that…" He didn't, she knew, and with that knowledge had gone her last hope of ever winning his heart. She rested her face in her hands as another wave of anguish crashed over her. "That's all I've ever been any good at."

"Whoa," Stacie objected. "Come on, you're good at lots of things!"

Nothing extraordinary, though. Nothing that would ever lift her to Elena's level. "Okay, I grow roses and I play the piano. But those aren't anything special."

"You're plenty special," her sister argued, pushing the tray of nachos closer to Meg as if to drive home her point. "You've always been the one with the heart, remember?"

Only because that was all anyone could find to say about her. When Paul and Stacie had brought home their science awards and cheerleading trophies and student council victories and homecoming queen crowns, their parents had scrupulously searched for something to praise about their middle daughter. "That's just because Mom and Dad didn't want me feeling left out." And Dad still didn't, considering what he'd told the hospital intern. "Like maybe I'd never notice how ordinary I am."

"Meg!"

She had never admitted that to anyone before, but the ache in her chest confirmed it as truth. "Never mind," she said hastily, looking around for a place to dump the unwanted nachos. "I'm okay. Let's do some more shopping."

"No, wait a minute." Stacie grabbed her wrist before she could rise from her chair. "Hold on, this is important. You've got a problem with your self-esteem."

But she was well aware of her strengths—her music, her gardening, her nurturing skills. "I don't really."

"No, you do! Here you're thinking Joe doesn't want a baby with you because you're not special?"

The ache of truth grew even sharper. "Not special enough," she clarified. Although who would be, compared to a woman like Elena? "I don't know. I just kept hoping…" The hope sounded silly, now, but she had carried it for so long that it seemed to burst from her of its own volition. "If I could just give him a family, then he'd love me."

She knew even as she heard the statement that it was an utterly foolish hope, but Stacie didn't look horrified. Instead, she gazed at her with a look of compassion.

"And *that* would make you special?" she murmured. "Oh, Meg…you're asking too much."

It had taken her four years to realize what her sister had spotted in less than a minute. But then, it was probably easier for an outsider to identify an impossible hope. "I know that now."

Stacie moved the tray of nachos out of the way so she could rest her elbows on the table and fixed Meg with a lecturer's gaze. "First of all," she said, "Joe already loves you. But even if he didn't, you can't expect somebody else to make you feel okay about yourself."

That sounded vaguely familiar, like something she might have read in a newspaper advice column. "I know," she repeated.

But Stacie shook her head. "No, you don't. Because you won't listen to basic psychology stuff unless you think it'll help somebody else."

She was right about that, Meg had to admit. There were times when her sister could be remarkably insightful.

"Only this is important," Stacie continued. "This'll help you. Or, no—better yet, this'll help Joe. Will that make you listen?"

Even though she would have sworn Joe didn't need any help, she felt her interest quicken. "All right, I'm listening."

"You still love him, right?"

No matter how much it might hurt, she could never stop loving Joe McConnell. "Yes," she mumbled.

"Well, look at it this way," Stacie ordered. "If you're making him responsible for you feeling okay about yourself, that's just like using him."

A sudden hush seemed to descend over the food court. Meg caught her breath before realizing that no one else seemed to notice anything different.

"And you don't want to do that, do you?" her sister asked. "That'd be like using somebody for sex or for money."

But that, she thought as a slow chill of remorse reverberated through her, was what she'd been doing for the past four years. Using Joe to make her feel okay about herself. "I guess so," she admitted.

"So cut it out," Stacie said simply. "Because unless *you* believe you're special, Joe can keep saying he loves you until he's blue in the face and you'll never believe him."

Not that the problem would ever come up. "He's never said it, though."

"Bad puppy," her sister observed, shaking a finger at an imaginary husband before returning her attention to Meg. "He *should* say it, but that doesn't mean much one way or another. Andy said it all the time, and look what happened."

She didn't sound especially regretful, but Meg felt a stab of sympathy. "Even without Andy, though, you're still special."

Stacie beamed at her, as if she'd just passed an exam. "I know I am. And so are you."

It sounded logical, put that way, but no amount of logic

would ever make her as special as Elena. Would it? "Well..."

"You're special whether Joe loves you or not. And he does, even if he forgets to say so—but you've got to believe it for yourself."

That made sense, she supposed. After all, it wasn't fair to keep using Joe. "I guess so."

Stacie flagged down the only janitor in the food court and handed him the unwanted nachos, then turned back to Meg. "So repeat after me," she ordered, "'I am worthwhile even if Joe doesn't love me.'"

Acknowledging it was one thing, announcing it was something else. "I can't say that!"

"Yes, you can. Come on."

Meg took a deep breath. "I am worthwhile even if Joe doesn't love me," she repeated, trying not to listen to the second half of the sentence. "It feels so weird saying that."

"Only because you're not used to it," her sister explained. "Keep saying it to yourself."

Saying it to herself was like relinquishing all hope of Joe ever loving her, but in a way she had already done that. She might as well make it official. "Okay. I'll keep saying it."

"Until it sinks in," Stacie ordered. "I mean it. Because you need to realize you're worthwhile, or else you'll never believe Joe loves you."

She already knew he didn't, a fact which seemed to have escaped her sister. But she had to focus on what she had...starting with someone who cared enough to lecture her on self-esteem amidst a growing crowd of lunchtime shoppers. "And even if he doesn't love me," Meg recited, "I am worthwhile."

She was rewarded with a look of pure delight. "See? You got it!"

With a rush of gratitude momentarily diminishing the

ache in her chest, she reached across the table and squeezed her sister's hand. "I keep telling myself to think about everything I've *got*. And I've got a wonderful sister."

"You've got a hungry sister," Stacie corrected her, standing up and collecting their shopping bags from the nearest chair. "Come on, let's do something really worthwhile. Let's go get dessert."

Chapter Nine

"You can't eat dessert first," Joe told Tony. "Because if you get too full, then you won't eat the stuff that's good for you."

His son gave him a cheeky grin that hinted he'd known all along what the answer would be but felt it was worth asking, anyway. "Okay," Tony said, returning his attention to the plastic-coated menu. "Can I have a hamburger with cheese on it?"

"Sure." That was probably as healthy as anything he could have thrown together at home, although Joe knew that if Meg stayed in Arizona much longer he would have to attempt something for dinner besides the Grand Café. He and Tony had become regulars over the past few days, and he was beginning to enjoy the ritual of negotiating with his son about desserts.

Meg would probably be horrified if she saw what they'd been eating, but he made a point of assuring her in every phone call that they were getting along just fine. After all, she needed as much time as she could get to recover from the loss of the hoped-for baby…and he couldn't very well expect her to come racing home just because he missed her.

But he missed her more than he liked to admit, even to himself. With people from the *Herald* he made light of the situation, explaining that it was only fair for Meg to get some time on the road. When he was alone, though, he was uncomfortably aware of her absence. Not that he couldn't handle Tony alone, handle the household and the checkbook and the breakfast cereal alone, but…

He missed her.

And so did Tony. The kid asked at least once every day when Meg was coming back, and he asked it again about halfway through his hamburger with cheese.

"Is Tía coming back *tomorrow?*"

"I don't know," Joe answered, although he was still hoping she'd return the minute her father left the hospital. "Eat your lettuce."

Tony grudgingly replaced the lettuce leaf inside his hamburger bun. "If it's not till this weekend, she won't know I'm making my own lunch for school."

The kid had done a good job of keeping his promise to make things easier on Meg, apparently never considering that her absence relieved him of any lunch-making obligation. "Well, whenever she gets back, she'll appreciate it."

"And then she'll feel better," Tony predicted, as if his assistance at assembling peanut butter and jelly sandwiches was all she needed to regain her usual cheerful calm.

Joe wished that were true. Even more, he wished he knew some way of making things right. Some way to make up for the baby he'd lost her. "Yeah, we'll do what we can. *You* already are," he added in honor of his son's sandwich-making skills.

Tony looked exceptionally pleased by that. Almost relieved. "I'm really good at making people feel better.
Mamá used to say she didn't know what she'd do without
me."

He could almost hear Elena murmuring that endearment
to her child. "Yeah?" Joe acknowledged. "Neither do I."

The sudden rush of feeling that swept through him on
hearing that statement startled him. He didn't know when
his sense of parental obligation had turned into something
more primal, more vital, although the past few days of
single fatherhood probably had something to do with it.
He did know that his son mattered more fiercely, more
intensely than he'd once thought possible...and with a
surge of blind emotion he reached across the table and
ruffled Tony's hair.

The kid gave him a smile that Joe recognized as one
he'd used himself when making outrageous requests at his
own childhood dinner table. "So can I get two desserts?"

Joe grinned back at him, glad that at least some aspects
of parenting didn't take much experience. "Nice try,
buddy."

Tony took the refusal with his usual shrug of resignation, but it was a safe bet that he'd try another angle tomorrow. The kid was good at testing limits, which was
probably an inheritance from his father...no journalist
worth his salt would accept a refusal without some kind
of challenge.

No journalist worth his salt would neglect the *Herald*
the way he'd been doing lately, either, Joe knew. It wasn't
like his staff couldn't handle things, but he'd spent less
time at work over the past few days than he'd ever spent
in his life.

Well, unless you counted those months when he'd been
so wrapped up in the joy of loving Elena that he'd neglected to file any stories at all. Those months when he
had blithely abandoned everything that made him who he

was—the distance, the observation, the ability to keep moving—in order to follow music from the heart he'd ignored for twenty-five years.

A decision which still rattled him on the few occasions he couldn't manage to bury its memory in work.

"Are we going by the *Herald?*" Tony asked as he finished his milk. "I want to see the pictures."

He'd been taking his son with him whenever an assignment couldn't wait, and Tony seemed to enjoy the atmosphere. Yesterday the kid had spent almost half an hour with Randy, watching the photographer crop prints for the weekend edition that Gloria was laying out tonight.

"Sure," Joe agreed. He could use another couple of minutes to rework his editorial headline, and Charlee had asked for some background on the water rights story. It was nothing he couldn't save for tomorrow, but if Tony didn't mind another visit he'd be glad to look at Gloria's layout. "Let's go."

The office was busier than he'd expected, which sparked in him a mixture of pride and jealousy. His staff was well trained, Joe told himself firmly, so of course they could handle whatever challenges came up. But as soon as Meg came home, he'd be back in the thick of things. Back at the heart of the *Herald.*

"Tony, come see the photos you and Randy picked out," Gloria invited. "See how this fits along the top of the page?"

His son would be entertained for at least as long as it took to provide Charlee with the water rights background, Joe decided. And by the time he finished his summary, he found Tony pecking at the keyboard of Abby's typewriter.

"I'm spelling my name," the boy explained.

"In a newspaper, that's called a byline," Joe told him. "It's so people know who the story is by."

"Won't be long before he's got his own byline," Gloria predicted, and Joe felt a sudden surge of amazement. Another ten or fifteen years, and his son could very well be a journalist.

But I want more for him than that.

The thought came out of nowhere, startling him. How could he want more for Tony than a career in the field he loved? There was nothing more intriguing than news, nothing more challenging or seductive or exhilarating than the life of a reporter.

"Maybe he will," Joe answered Gloria. Tony had all the right traits for a journalist—the tenacity, the language skills, the ability to keep digging for answers.

But even so, he'd like his son to have the option of…of…belonging.

The word lingered in his mind as they left the *Herald* and headed back to the car. *Belonging*. It was a concept he'd never explored, never let himself covet, but it surprised him how acutely he wanted that for his son.

Although being half American and half Milaguan might make Tony's chances a lot less likely. He already stood apart from his classmates with their primarily Nordic heritage; he was the only kid at Oakville Elementary with a native language other than English. And in Milagua, with his unknown but obviously foreign father, he'd been equally different. It might not matter, he might fit in regardless of his background and he might never care about belonging…but Joe wished with an almost painful intensity that he could give his son that option.

It was a little frightening how much he wanted it, he realized as they drove home to see if Tía had left any messages on the answering machine. He had the feeling he might be getting in over his head. These surges of emotion—guilt and longing for his wife, affection and tenderness for Tony—seemed to be striking more and more often lately.

Still, wanting the best for his son was nothing to worry about.

You've got everything under control.

He had everything under control, certainly. But even so, it would be a relief when Meg came home and he could get back to real life. To the single-minded pursuit of news stories. To his calling as a journalist, as someone who stayed on the edges, observing but never feeling.

A political coup would come in handy right about now, Joe reflected as he parked the car and extracted Tony's backpack from the trunk. Or a flood, or a fire, or a hostage crisis…something that would let him walk the fine edge of danger, something that would prove he could still face fear and come out on top.

"Phone's ringing," Tony announced. "Maybe it's Tía."

His fingers felt clumsy as he fumbled to unlock the door, and as soon as he swung it open Tony raced to answer the phone.

"It's for you," he announced, looking so disappointed that Joe knew the caller wasn't Meg. "Somebody named Warren."

The editor of the *Journal,* right when he'd been wishing for a blockbuster story? "Thanks," he told his son. "Go get your pajamas on, and I'll be up in a minute."

It was more than a blockbuster story, Joe learned as soon as he and Warren finished the preliminary greetings. It was the job on Focus.

"Funny thing," the editor said. "Never thought we'd have an opening this fast, but I wanted to see if you could come in next week and get started meeting people."

Next week? He had envisioned something in the next year or so, after Tony was settled in. After the *Herald* could find a replacement. After he'd managed to persuade Meg that Chicago was a decent place to raise a family.

A family she'd been dreaming of ever since they were married. A family for which she'd already planned portraits and cupcakes and christening gowns.

A family she hadn't gotten, because of him.

He might yet be able to coax her into moving, Joe thought with an ache of recognition in his gut, but he wasn't going to try.

"Thanks," he told Warren, "but I can't do it. I appreciate your thinking of me, only…go ahead and take me off your list."

The second thoughts descended before he'd even hung up the phone, but he refused to listen. So what if he hurt? He could deal with hurt. What he couldn't deal with was hurting Meg. Seeing that despair in her eyes. Knowing it was his own damn fault.

"Papá," Tony called from upstairs, "I can't find the toothpaste."

"All right, I'm coming." He could deal with toothpaste, too. He could deal with whatever he had to, and there was no point in wondering whether he'd just made the right decision. He'd made it, and that was that.

"I thought that was Tía calling," his son said as Joe retrieved a new tube of toothpaste from under the bathroom sink. "Only it wasn't."

"No, it was an editor from Chicago." He might as well come out with the truth, considering that he'd effectively cut off his options. "They wanted me to come work for a newspaper there. But we're not going."

Tony accepted the tube, industriously covered his toothbrush with green gel and started brushing. "Mrs. O'Donoghue said there's millions of people in Chicago."

The teacher had identified exactly what made the city such a gold mine for news. "Yeah, there's a lot going on. All kinds of stories—trials, rallies, fires, gangs…"

His son's brushing halted for a moment. "I think," he mumbled through a mouthful of foam, "I'd be afraid to go there."

"Aw, Tony, no." Joe shifted his stance so he could address the boy's reflection in the mirror over the sink.

"You start being afraid of things and it's like—" He hesitated, looking for the right phrase. "You're crippled. You can't move."

Tony resumed his brushing, then nodded in recognition. "Like when they've got chains on you."

The kid had seen a lot in Milagua, he realized. Things that were merely graphic images for most people were everyday realities there. "Yeah, only it's more *inside* that you can't move. When you're afraid, it's like you can't do anything."

"Except feel scared," his son agreed, rinsing his mouth along with his toothbrush and returning it to the rack. "Like when Miguel and I heard the soldiers, I felt like my stomach was gonna blow up."

That was a great description, Joe thought. He remembered the sensation all too vividly from those nights of waiting for the torture to resume. "Yeah, exactly."

Tony looked at him curiously as they started toward his room. "Do *you* ever feel like that?"

He'd learned that the more often he faced down his fears of covering a fire, a helicopter rescue or anything else tinged with danger, the less he felt like his stomach was going to blow up. "That's why I keep doing news stories," he explained, "so I know I can handle it. I don't ever want to feel like that again."

His son seemed to accept such reasoning without question, climbing into bed and waiting for Joe to adjust the covers before kissing him good-night. Then, just before the bedroom light was extinguished, Tony threw down a challenge.

"Papá, if you *like* doing scary things, how come we aren't going to Chicago?"

Good question, Joe acknowledged as he turned off the light. "Because Tía wouldn't like living there, and I want to make things good for her."

"For Tía?"

"Yeah."

"Oh, I get it." In the darkness, the child's voice sounded very matter-of-fact. "You love her, don't you?"

For a fraction of a second he felt the familiar sensation of fear shoot through his veins. "Uh—I—" he stuttered, backing toward the door before his stomach could blow up. He had to get out of here. "Good night, Tony."

He needed a story, Joe thought, stumbling blindly out of the bedroom toward the stairs and trying to suck in a breath of air. A shot of whisky might work for some people, or a prayer, or a woman, but right now he badly needed a story.

Because he hadn't been this frightened in years.

You love her, don't you?

He should have seen this coming. That afternoon at the flower shop, when he'd felt so exhilarated just thinking about her. Or even before that, when he'd missed her so acutely at the Chicago hotel. Or that night watching her and Tony make bread…but he hadn't wanted to face it. He hadn't wanted to feel it.

You love her, don't you?

Loving Meg was more frightening than anything he could imagine. Snipers he could handle, guerrillas he could handle, even the prison guards of Milagua hadn't broken him in four years of trying. But giving his heart the way he'd done with Elena—out there, he knew, lay dangers beyond his capacity.

Out there lay insanity. Staggering, dizzying, mindless surrender. An utter loss of control.

Fine, maybe this time it wouldn't result in the kind of carelessness that landed foreign journalists in chains. But love was love, regardless of the circumstances. Love made you blind. Love made you crazy. Love made you forget things and care and need…and risk everything that mattered just to see a certain smile, to feel a particular touch, to hear a special laugh…

He didn't need this, Joe begged his heart with even more passion than he'd once begged the soldiers who blocked his third attempt at escape. But his heart wasn't listening any more than the soldiers had listened.

His heart was already somewhere in Arizona, tucked away in Meg's tender keeping, and completely beyond his reach.

How could he have let this happen? he wondered desperately as he turned on every light downstairs and double-checked all the locks. He had warned her from the very beginning that he couldn't love her the way she deserved, and she had accepted that, insisted it wasn't a problem. He had spent four years thinking he was safe, thinking he had everything under control, but somehow—

Somehow, he must have started loving Meg.

But it went beyond that, he suspected. Somehow, he must have loved her all along.

The way she scrunched up her face when she opened a window. Her excitement over the garden every spring. Her way of curling against him in bed, so warm and soft and welcoming, even when he got home past midnight. The fierce attention she devoted to reading his editorials. The way she hummed while putting away groceries. Her habit of ordering the same wine every time.

It was all of that and more, he knew. So much more. So much that it amazed him to realize he'd gone this long without ever once letting himself see that he loved his wife.

You love her, don't you?

"Yeah," Joe replied without even realizing he'd spoken aloud until he heard the soft statement thunder through the living room. "I do."

Meg, of course, had probably known that all along. She had said the other night that she knew he would always remember her birthday and help with the storm windows and tell her when she looked nice—but even so, he had the feeling that it was important to tell her he loved her. That, even if she already knew it, she deserved to hear the words.

"I love you, Meggins," he murmured, and felt another jolt of trepidation shoot up his spine. How the hell had he let this happen? And now that he'd admitted it, what the hell was he supposed to do about it?

Say it out loud?

She had to know it already, didn't she? But she'd said the other night that all he cared about was Elena…

No, he had to make sure she knew. He'd faced tougher challenges in his life, surely, although right at the moment he couldn't think of any more demanding than admitting he'd lost control of his heart.

So okay, he decided, over the growing swell of fear in his stomach. Regardless of how much it scared him, he was going to tell Meg he loved her.

The phone wasn't so good, though. He wanted to tell her in person, make sure she understood. Fly out to Sun City if he had to, although it might be awkward with Tony in tow….

No, better he should wait till she got home. Make an evening of it. This was the kind of thing that demanded candles and violins, or at least more than a brief acknowledgment across the kitchen table. As soon as he got word of her return, Joe resolved, he was going to set this up right.

He was going to arrange another evening at the Wayside Inn.

"The Wayside Inn?" Meg repeated, brushing back her newly feathered bangs. It seemed an extravagant welcome-home gesture, even though she'd been gone nearly a week. "Joe, you don't need to do that."

"I want to," he insisted, letting go of her hand so he could unlock the car. Ever since they'd met at the airfield gate, he'd been keeping his body in contact with hers. "I missed you. And Helen can stay with Tony."

"Well…okay. If you're sure." She could handle an intimate evening without falling into the same old false hopes, Meg reminded herself as she watched him deposit her flight bag in the trunk. She wasn't the same person she'd been a week ago, after all. She had a new haircut, a new attitude and a new determination to make her life work even without her husband's love.

An evening at the Wayside Inn would be fine as long as she didn't start hoping for anything more.

"We've got to celebrate your new look," he said, twisting one curl of her restyled hair between his fingers. "It's like getting a whole different Meg back. Although the old one was terrific, too."

She wished she *were* a whole different Meg. One who could change her old desires as swiftly as she'd changed her hairstyle. But the drive home would give her time to regroup, to remember what she could and couldn't expect from her husband.

"It really is good to have you back," he concluded, kissing her again before he started the ignition. "Tony and I both missed you a lot."

Of course Joe had better manners than to announce that he and his son had gotten along fine without her. "It sounded like you were doing okay, though."

He only shrugged, which she took as confirmation. "We spent some time at the *Herald.* Gloria let him help with the layout, so now he can't wait to show you the front page."

That was sweet, she acknowledged. One thing she'd begun to appreciate about herself was how well she got along with Tony…as well as anyone could possibly ask of a stepmother. And if the child wanted to share his accomplishment with her, he obviously felt the same way. "I can't wait to see it."

Joe gave her the crooked smile she had always loved. "He got kind of a charge out of the whole business. I'll let him tell you about it."

The look of affection in his eyes as he remembered Tony's achievement was new, Meg noticed, but it shouldn't surprise her. Naturally he would appreciate Elena's son more after having spent so much time together. In fact, considering that he'd managed the entire household for nearly a week, he had probably been learning as many new skills as she had.

Although what she'd been learning wasn't so much a set of skills as a new way of thinking. A new perspective on her marriage and her life. A new determination not to let her self-worth depend on her husband's love.

"So," Joe asked her as they started back toward town, "now that your dad's home, how's he doing?"

She filled him in during the drive to Oakville Elementary School, which let out for the weekend just as they arrived. Tony came racing toward the car, backpack bouncing in one hand, and broke into a wholehearted smile as he saw Meg.

"Hi, Tía!" he greeted her, clambering into the back seat with what looked like honest happiness at having her home. One more thing to appreciate when she focused on what she had. "Do you feel better now?"

Joe shot her a quick glance, as if wondering whether she minded such a question. He must still be feeling guilty over the loss of the baby, she realized with a twisting sensation in her chest. Which was a waste. There was nothing he could have done differently, not with his heart still lost to Elena.

"Yes, thank you, Tony." After a few days of repeating her sister's mantra, about being worthwhile, she could already feel a difference within herself. And on the plane coming back from Phoenix, she had come to one important decision. If having a child in her life mattered so much, she needed to do something about it on her own.

So as soon as she got home, Meg had resolved, she was going to join the Big Brothers/Big Sisters program. While having a Little Sister wouldn't be the same as having a daughter, she was already feeling a glimmer of pride in her self-esteem for having chosen such a positive course of action.

But the real test of her self-esteem, she suspected, would begin now that she was back with Joe. The real test would be whether she could keep from giving in to those false hopes that she'd dragged around for the past four years.

It was hard to keep the hopes from rising again that evening as they drove to the Wayside Inn, which was every bit as secluded and romantic and grand as she remembered from their anniversary dinner. But Meg forced herself to keep remembering Stacie's advice about not using her husband to make herself feel okay.

"I am special," she muttered to herself as she checked her hair in the ladies' room mirror while Joe waited by the fireplace, "whether or not he loves me." As long as she remembered that, everything would be fine.

And dinner *was* fine. Joe McConnell had always been an entertaining host, a delightful companion. She couldn't help enjoying his descriptions of the past week, his interest in the Big Sisters idea, his relief at hearing how well her father was doing. She couldn't help appreciating his skill at keeping the conversation going, even though her end of it sounded a little disjointed—probably because, for some reason, the past week had been more exhausting than she'd expected.

But Joe didn't seem to mind her lack of sparkling wit. He seemed almost enraptured by her stories about her dad and Stacie and the diabetic cookbook, which she realized must mean that he'd been craving another adult to talk to after six days alone with Tony. He admitted that he'd considered flying out to Phoenix a few nights ago, which she suspected was an exaggeration but accepted with a smile of thanks. And when she resolutely ordered her usual strawberry cheesecake for dessert, Joe gazed at her with an expression of indulgent tenderness before turning his attention to the waiter.

"I like how you always order the same thing," he told her as soon as the waiter had bustled away.

He must have remembered her attempt at trying something new the last time they were here, she realized, and wanted to reassure her. Which was a nice thought, and typical of Joe.

"It's kind of ordinary," Meg admitted, turning her wineglass between her fingers. But as long as she was going to believe herself worthwhile, she had to accept the fact that she *was* ordinary. "Stacie was telling me, though, there's nothing wrong with…well, with ordinary."

"Not when that's what you like," he agreed, smiling at her as he lifted his glass in agreement.

It wasn't what Joe liked, she knew. But at least he had never demanded that she change her style or attitude— maybe because he already knew she couldn't live up to his first love. Elena had been as far from ordinary as any woman could be.

No, she had to stop that line of thought. Thinking about Elena was the fastest way to shoot down whatever self-esteem she possessed. And she needed all the self-esteem she could muster right now, because she was getting dangerously close to falling right back into her old habit of longing for Joe's love.

Or actually, of longing for Joe.

Because he looked so good right now, especially after their week apart. Because he was paying such close attention to her, making a point of hanging on her every word as if she was the most fascinating dinner partner in the world. And because, since she was so tired already, it was even more appealing to imagine moving from her overstuffed chair into his lap.

But she wasn't going to do that, Meg told herself. It would be all too easy to lose herself in the rapture of his embrace…to forget that she didn't need his love to be worthwhile…to throw herself wholeheartedly, with all her hopes blazing, into an ecstatic night that wouldn't make one bit of difference in the morning.

Not that she intended to give up their sex life forever. It would be crazy, it would be wasteful not to enjoy what had always been a source of pleasure for them both. Once she knew she could keep her hopes detached, leave them safely buried and forgotten, she could make love with Joe every night of the week.

But on her first night back, it would be like throwing away every bit of hard-won growth she'd managed ever since that day at the mall with Stacie. To love him right now, to once again fool herself into believing that he loved her—no, she couldn't risk that yet.

"I'm glad you're back," Joe said, waiting until the busboy had delivered their coffee before directing his gaze at her. He reached for a spoon without looking at it and slowly stirred the coffee in his cup. "I'm really glad you're back. Partly because I missed you, and partly because…well, I've been wanting to tell you something."

In the flickering candlelight, she noticed, his expression looked a little shy. Almost nervous, but that had to be a trick of the light. A man like Joe, who faced down drug dealers without so much as a backward glance, would never be nervous in a setting like this.

"What's that?" she asked, pushing aside her untouched cheesecake.

He hesitated, almost as if searching for the right words. "It's…" he said slowly. "I…well—" Then in a rush the words came spilling out. "I love you, Meggers. I just wanted you to know that."

With a shock of recognition, it struck her. The whole evening had been leading up to this declaration, and she had never once suspected it. But her sister had obviously read Joe the riot act about saying the magic words. "Did Stacie call you?"

He looked startled. "Stacie?"

Of course he wouldn't admit it, Meg realized. He had more grace than to confess he was acting on her sister's orders, and it was impressive how he managed not to show the slightest flicker of acknowledgment. She shook her head, negating the question. "Never mind."

"Well, so, I just wanted to make sure I told you...I really love you."

Oh, if only he meant it! But there was no use wishing for what she could never have. No use dreaming that he would suddenly change his mind about preferring an ordinary woman to someone like Elena.

"And I'm sorry," he concluded, "that I never told you that before. I guess...I never wanted to admit it before."

"It's okay, Joe," she assured him. He'd done as good a job as he could do of making up for four years' omission, and this wasn't the time to tell him that his performance tonight had been unnecessary. That the mere words weren't what she wanted. "It doesn't matter."

"No, but it does. I should've told you a long time ago how—you know, you're always so comfortable to be with."

That part, she suspected, was true. She had no problem believing that Joe found her comfortable to be with. "Well, thank you."

"Like..." He hesitated, evidently searching for a better description. "I don't know, like—not like fireworks exactly, but more like the ocean."

Not like fireworks. No, that had been Elena.

"I was trying to think of what you're like," he explained, "and all I could come up with was the ocean. You know. Just really strong, and really relaxing."

The man had a gift for words, all right, with his ability to make those traits sound as desirable as the drama and sparkle and intensity of fireworks. "That's nice," Meg acknowledged.

He lifted his hands in a gesture of futility, almost as if he knew how hopeless the effort was. "I'm not saying this very well. It's just…last week, you were saying how I cared more about Elena than you?"

Meg groped for her fork and hastily dug it into the untouched cheesecake. "It's okay, Joe. We don't need to talk about Elena."

"No, but I didn't want you to think—" He broke off, looking faintly uncomfortable. "I'm not gonna say I didn't love her, but I didn't love *her* like I love *you*."

That much, she had guessed a long time ago. "I know," she said, concentrating on cutting a bite of cheesecake the right size.

"I mean, you're both—you're completely different people!"

Completely different, yes. She wished her fingers were steadier, but she managed to lift the fork to her mouth before realizing it was time to say something. "I know that."

"But loving her doesn't mean I don't love you," Joe concluded as she swallowed what felt like a brick of cheesecake. "Because I do, Meg. I do love you."

A few years ago she would have given anything to hear that declaration. But now she had to remember that it wasn't fair using Joe to make her feel worthwhile.

Still, it was nice of him to try. "Bless your heart," she said softly, relieved that her voice sounded close to normal. "Thanks for telling me."

He stayed silent for a moment, as if waiting for something more. Then, with an almost visible shake of his head, he reached for his coffee cup and gave her a quizzical look. "Are you tired from your trip?"

"I guess so." That must be why she wanted so badly to bury herself in a nest of blankets and shut out the entire world. Including Joe, whom she couldn't afford to risk wanting just yet...no matter how well he had responded to Stacie's order. "But it's been a lovely evening," she told him, realizing once again how much effort he must have put into this welcome home. "Thank you."

He dismissed that with a wave of his hand, exactly as the waiter arrived with their check. "I just wanted to do this right. I wanted to make sure you knew."

She had to focus on what she *had,* and not many husbands would go to this kind of trouble to make a second-choice wife feel loved. Right down to the spectacular setting, he had done a masterful job of delivering the right words. "I appreciate it."

"Well..." Joe left some money inside the leather folder and glanced at her uncertainly. "You want to call it a night?"

He wasn't going to suggest moving their homecoming celebration to one of the inn's guest rooms upstairs, she realized with a mixture of relief and regret. He seemed to know that all she wanted—or at least all she would allow herself—was to go straight to bed and fall asleep. "Yes," she told him.

He nodded in acknowledgment, but before rising from the table he reached for her hand and caught her gaze with his own. "Meg," he said softly, intensely, "I mean it, okay? I really do love you."

In spite of herself, she felt a shiver of yearning radiate through her. She knew better than to believe him, but she couldn't help loving him for such a valiant effort. "Okay," she answered with as convincing a smile as she could muster. "Thanks."

* * *

She didn't believe him. Over the next few days, he grew more and more certain of it. Somehow, Joe realized, he hadn't managed to make things clear enough.

Meg had listened to every word he'd said, but she still didn't believe he loved her.

She seemed cheerful enough on the surface. More relaxed than she'd been before she left for Arizona. She had never once referred to the loss of the baby, except when she'd refused his offer to resume the search, and she did seem excited about the Big Brothers/Big Sisters orientation date inscribed on her calendar. But there still seemed to be something missing from her life, although why he suspected that, Joe wasn't quite sure.

She just wasn't as happy as she should be. Not that being loved by Joe McConnell was supposed to send anyone into spasms of rapture, but he had the feeling that she ought to at least be pleased at hearing it. And she'd *said* she was, but even so...

Something wasn't right.

He'd hoped that their first night back together would give him the chance to show her how much he loved her. But she'd been practically drooping with exhaustion after her trip, and he didn't want to force her into a night of exuberant passion when all she wanted was sleep. Now he regretted it, because for the past few nights she'd gone to bed early...which meant he was still waiting for the magic of renewal.

Meanwhile, he was doing what he could to make things easy on her. Taking Tony with him when he returned to the *Herald* at night. Bringing home pizza with her favorite mushroom-and-bacon topping. Canceling the order for wallpaper they'd placed during the nursery decoration rush in case any reminder would start her grieving again.

But it wasn't enough.

Even Tony noticed something wrong. He waited until he and Joe set off for church Sunday morning before raising the subject, but it was obvious that in spite of Meg's cheerful wave when they left for Mass, she wasn't as happy as she pretended.

"Do you think," Tony asked, "Tía still feels sad? Even though I'm making my own lunch?"

There had to be something he could do, Joe thought for the fiftieth time. His declaration of love hadn't been enough to win her trust, but there had to be some way he could discover what his wife needed.

"Yeah," he admitted. "I've got to do something."

His son wrinkled his forehead in thought, evidently assuming the solution was something they could determine within the few minutes it took to reach St. Cecilia's. "Did you tell her we aren't going to Chicago?"

Joe had considered that, but it seemed like a thin offering. *Guess what, Meggers, I'm living up to my word!* "No," he explained, "because that was just keeping a promise I'd already made her. I promised we'd raise our kids in Oakville."

Tony gave him a questioning look. "I thought you said we weren't getting any more kids."

"Well, no, I guess we're not." Meg had flatly refused his offer to take the search out of state, which surprised him. He'd supposed that as soon as she recovered from the loss of the expected daughter, she would be clamoring to try again. But maybe the prospect of a Little Sister was more consolation than he'd realized. "Not now, anyway."

"That's good, because babies are a nuisance," his son announced matter-of-factly. "They cry all the time."

The boy was likely speaking from experience; he must have seen more than his share of babies at the orphanage. "Well," Joe repeated as he turned off Main Street into the church parking lot, "we're not getting any." Which ought to be a greater relief than it was, considering how he'd dreaded the financial and emotional cost of another child. It was probably his worry over Meg that had kept him from fully appreciating the reprieve.

"So is that why Tía's sad?" Tony asked as they parked the car and started toward the church.

"I don't know, Tony." He wished he could answer something more definite, but lately it felt as if Meg was farther away than she'd been last week in Arizona. "I wish I knew."

Chapter Ten

It was ironic that after their discussion about babies, Joe thought ten minutes later, today's church service should include a baby being baptized. This one wasn't crying—he wasn't sure if Tony noticed—and since the family sat a few rows ahead of them Joe spent most of the Mass watching the baby's parents.

They looked happy. The way he'd always assumed Meg would look once the adoption agency granted a baby. The way *he* might have looked during their own christening ceremony, if only he'd realized what it was like to care so intensely for a child.

But he hadn't. And now, in a way, he regretted it…even apart from the fact that his failure had hurt Meg so badly. Now they would never share the kind of union, the kind of connection shared by this couple with the baby. They might have another eight or ten years of raising Tony, but that wasn't the same thing as raising a baby from scratch.

Like this couple at the front of the church.

Still, Joe reminded himself as he watched the mother hand the infant to her husband, it was probably just as well that Meg had changed her mind about adopting a baby and was planning for a Little Sister instead. Nobody would expect him to love a kid who spent one afternoon a week with his wife.

There was nothing at which he could fail. Which meant that he ought to be feeling the light of relief, rather than this dark sense of regret.

It stuck with him, though, as he and Tony left St. Cecilia's and drove home by way of the park playground. Stopping there for a half hour on the monkey bars while waiting for Meg to finish her music at the Valley Cathedral had become a Sunday morning tradition, and Joe suspected that he enjoyed the roughhousing as much as his son did after an hour of circumspect behavior at church.

For some reason, though, today he was more aware than usual of other people at the park. It seemed like all of them had families—which he guessed made sense, since people without kids would have no reason to visit the monkey bars—but never before had he been so keenly aware of the intimacy between parents with children.

The couple coaxing their toddler to walk another step across the grass.

The wife clasping her husband's hand for an extra moment as he handed her a sweater for their baby.

The mom and dad smiling at each other as their daughter turned three clumsy somersaults in a row.

''Papá, look at this!'' Tony called from the top rung of the jungle gym before swinging himself down to the rings.

''Way to go!'' Joe responded, wishing Meg were there to help applaud. She seemed to know instinctively how much praise to offer, whereas he still had the feeling that he was flying blind. As much as he'd come to enjoy his son's company lately, he would never match Meg's intuitive skill at parenting.

Although there was no real reason to regret that, now that he knew there would be no more children. He wouldn't need much in the way of parenting skills with his son already half-grown.

He would never need to teach a kid to tie a shoelace, like that guy on the other side of the playground. He and Meg would never have to come up with plausible explanations of why Santa's reindeer hadn't left any footprints on the roof. They would never share the excitement of their child's first word or first tooth or first step, like that couple on the grass hugging the toddler between them.

They would do other things together, like buying Tony birthday presents and giving him driving lessons and attending his graduation, but they'd already missed out on the fundamental milestones of his life.

Which bothered Joe more than he wanted to admit.

It was his own fault, he reminded himself as he watched his son climb back to the top of the jungle gym. He could have shared all the joy and compassion and wonder and pride of raising a baby with Meg if he'd gotten his act together before now. After only a week of full-time parenting, he still couldn't qualify as an expert father—and maybe never would—but he had no business complaining about never getting the chance to try.

He'd had his chance, and the social worker had recognized he wasn't ready.

But damn it, he wanted to try again!

He wanted that so intensely, it startled him. Only a few weeks ago he'd been satisfied with the status quo, aware of how much time and money and emotional attention it took to raise one child, let alone two. And yet from the night he'd realized how much he loved his wife, it seemed as though something had shaken loose within him. Right now the cost of a child seemed insignificant compared to the vision of himself and Meg with a baby of their own.

"Papá, get ready!"

Joe hastily returned his attention to the monkey bars just as Tony performed another daring leap to the rings. The kid was good, he observed with a surge of pride. And if this was the only child he ever had, he should at least be glad for this chance at fatherhood.

He just wished he could have started from the beginning.

With a baby. Maybe a daughter this time, although either a boy or a girl would be fine. All that really mattered was sharing a child with Meg.

And maybe, he found himself thinking while he and Tony drove home, he could still make that happen. It might take a while to get back on Rita's list even after he acquired whatever skills she'd found missing, but they'd made it to the top once before. If Meg had the slightest interest in starting the adoption quest again, this time he would gladly throw his whole heart into the project.

This time he would do it right.

He waited to open the subject until Tony was in bed, after a day of virtually nonstop activity during which he wondered whether he would ever get ten minutes alone with his wife. She had a lot to catch up on after her week in Arizona, he knew, and it was silly to think she was trying to avoid him. That was what love did to you, Joe knew—it made you vulnerable to things you'd never worried about before.

He wasn't going to start down that path, though. Instead he got his son settled down for the night, finished locking up the house and joined Meg upstairs where she was already brushing out her hair the way she did every night before bed.

Her new haircut hadn't changed that practice, and he was glad of it. He had always enjoyed watching her run the brush through her thick, lustrous hair while he undressed in the bathroom to avoid any exposure of his scars.

Tonight he spent longer than usual watching her nightly ritual, and by the time she set down her brush and turned back the comforter on their bed he realized he was postponing the conversation. There was no reason to dread this, Joe told himself as he squared his shoulders and turned out the bathroom light. All he needed to do was find out whether Meg might want to consider adoption again.

"You know," he told her before she could pick up the book she kept on the bedside table, "this morning when I was watching the families at the park, I got to thinking about a baby. If you wanted to try again, this time—"

"No, that's okay," Meg interrupted before he could explain that this time he'd do whatever Rita thought necessary to be ready for a baby. "I'm getting a Little Sister, remember?"

He'd been pleased at her enthusiasm for the prospect, but it hadn't occurred to him that she might rather have a Little Sister than a baby. "That's not exactly the same thing, though," he protested. "I mean—"

She cut him off with a quick gesture, raising her hands as if to stop his words. "Joe, please. Let's not get into it."

Was this the same woman who had devoted rapturous days to planning what color wallpaper to install in the nursery, what kind of cupcakes to send for Tony's school celebration and what clothes the children should wear in their family portrait? This didn't make sense. "I thought you *wanted* a baby."

Meg reached for the book on her bedside table, turning her gaze away from him. "I can't go through it again," she said flatly. "I can't get all wrapped up in wanting a baby, and then—I just can't do it."

This time, though, he would be ready. This time he wouldn't let her be hurt. "But I want to make up for—"

"No. Stop," she protested with sudden, desperate energy. "You want to make up for it, then do this for me, all right? Don't start talking about babies!"

There was such passion, such ferocity in her voice that he realized Meg had suffered more over the first loss than he'd guessed. If she couldn't bear to think about another one, it didn't mean that her maternal heart had shut down. It meant that hoping for another baby would tear her apart from the inside out.

He couldn't put her through that. Not after what she'd already endured because of his delay in appreciating the wonders of another child.

"Okay," Joe said softly, and felt his heart twist with remorse as he saw her guarded expression. "I'm sorry, Megs. Forget I mentioned it."

But as long as he didn't raise her hopes unnecessarily, he decided after she turned off her reading lamp, there was nothing to keep him from talking to Rita again. He couldn't expect to get placed back on the waiting list yet, not when the social worker had so clearly noticed his lack of readiness for fatherhood. Still, he could at least ask about a class or something, find out what it would take to achieve the kind of parenting ability he needed.

He could master whatever it took to be a father, Joe resolved as he drifted toward sleep. He could learn. He *wanted* to learn. For Meg's sake, partly, but even more for his own.

He wanted to share a baby with his wife.

If he could just make himself clear to Rita—and somehow deal with Tony's distaste for crying infants—then sell enough freelance stories to ensure that money wasn't a problem…

He could do all that. He would have to do all that. His entire future, and that of the woman he loved, depended on how well he could carry out this specific set of tasks.

Which was exactly the same thing he used to tell himself back in the prison camp when he planned each successive attempt at escape.

The memories were still uncomfortably vivid: the weeks of preparation; the hoarding of what few moldy rations he could save; the secret calisthenics to hone his body for that desperate trek; the heartening focus on what waited for him if he made it; the dark memory of what awaited if he didn't....

God, if he didn't...

He'd endured the retaliation five times, and each time was worse than before. The searing awareness of failure, almost blotted out within the first few hours of punishment. The agonizing realization that he had cost himself another chance, dawning only over the next several days as his body screamed its way back to consciousness.

Right now, though, even the slow ordeal of recovery was still far beyond his reach. First he had to get through the next session, the next round of anguish, the crippling pain—

Hold on. Hold on.

Another wave of agony radiated through him, with another searing blaze consuming him in its teeth. Then another and yet another, sending him over the edge of reality, plummeting into madness, spinning out of control—

It was happening again, and this time he was on the verge of shattering.

Hold on. Hold on!

He couldn't let go, he couldn't let himself break. Teetering on the edge of the abyss, he grappled for the only fiber of sanity he could still reach and cried out with all the force he possessed. "El-e-e-e-na!"

"Joe," a voice pleaded, shaking his shoulder. "Wake up. It's okay."

He gave another hoarse cry and then gasped, cutting himself off in mid-shout, and felt his body jerk as every muscle seemed to tighten all at once.

"Joe," the voice repeated. "It's all right. You're okay. You're home."

He shuddered convulsively, then raised himself on his elbows and stared at her. This had to be Meg. It didn't seem possible, but maybe he was safe.

"You're home," she said gently, cradling his face between her palms. "You're okay now. It's all right."

God, had that been another nightmare? It must have been, he realized through a haze of confusion and still-too-vivid dread. He must have brought it on himself by thinking about Milagua when he fell asleep.

"You're okay," Meg repeated, wrapping her arms around him with such reassuring warmth that he felt the tightness in his chest ease a little. Already the room seemed surprisingly familiar...the faint moonlight behind the window shade, the glow of the clock radio on the table beyond her. "Everything's all right, Joe. You're home."

"Oh, God," he muttered. He'd done it again. He'd lost himself in the fears of the past—and in some part of his mind he could still hear the echo of his desperate cry. Meg had been right when she said it was the story of her life, that everyone woke up calling for Elena, but he'd never heard himself until now. "Meg, I'm sorry."

"It's all right. It's okay." She drew him closer to her, rocking him with the same sweet comfort that had saved him so many times before. "It was just a nightmare."

"Yeah, but..." She didn't sound upset, and yet he would have sworn he'd been crying Elena's name when Meg had pulled him back from the dark. "I really didn't mean to do that. If I was calling Elena—"

"Don't worry about it," she murmured, shifting so he could hold her against his chest. "It's nothing you can help, I know."

The faint tinge of resignation in her voice confirmed that he'd heard right, and he felt a sharp crack of guilt.

This was the woman he loved now, and it wasn't fair to keep reminding her of the woman he'd loved first.

"I've got to stop that," Joe told her hoarsely, pulling her closer to him. "It doesn't mean anything."

She didn't reply, only drew the blanket across them both. Maybe she believed him, he thought as she settled into his embrace. Because she didn't seem to be holding herself at a distance, for which he was profoundly grateful. There was nothing as reassuring as the feel of her against him, nothing as restoring as her soft warmth and the rhythm of her breathing gradually coaxing his rapid heartbeat into a gentler pace.

But still, he'd heard himself calling Elena…

"I promise I'll make it up to you," he pledged, and felt a sudden tightness in her muscles.

"It's okay," she whispered again. "I just wish…" Her voice trailed off, and it wasn't until he felt himself sliding over the edge of sleep that he heard what sounded like another whisper from her.

"I just wish I didn't still love you."

It was silly to keep remembering how he'd cried out for Elena. He'd done the same thing a hundred times before, and she ought to be used to it by now, Meg thought as she dealt with the work piled up in her office. It was silly that, after repeating Stacie's mantra over and over, she still couldn't quite seem to accept the fact that Joe would never forget his first love.

Everything else, she could deal with. She'd made her resolution to stick with this marriage, to continue nurturing Tony and Joe, to find a Little Sister on whom she could lavish her extra attention and to focus her thoughts on everything she *had*.

She'd been doing that all weekend, forcing herself to appreciate how well she'd played the recessional and how good her new haircut looked and how proudly Tony had shown her his book report. How skillfully she'd managed to keep from plunging back into false hopes that night at the Wayside Inn. How efficiently she'd registered for the Big Brothers/Big Sisters orientation her first morning back. How frequently over the past few days she'd remembered to stop and acknowledge, "Yes, I'm special."

Then one plea for Elena, and all her proud determination had gone skittering right down the drain.

It was stupid, Meg told herself as she slammed the yearbook receipts into a file drawer. She'd been doing so well, viewing herself as an independent person, as a woman who didn't need Joe McConnell's love to be worthwhile. She still knew that intellectually, of course, and she would surely come to know it in her heart soon enough.

But for some reason, the reminder of how much Joe had needed Elena hurt more than it should. It had always been a sore spot—Joe had recognized that himself, or he never would have made such a big deal of telling her he loved them both differently. Differently, right. As if they were both special. As if there were any room *left* in his heart for a woman who would never be, could never be, what his first love had been.

She had to get over this, Meg reminded herself as she swept the stack of phone messages into her drawer. She had to view herself as a person who was special in her own right. A marriage based on friendly companionship, flashes of passion and long-time affection ought to be enough. But holding him, nurturing him and falling asleep in his arms last night had reawakened all those old desires for a union that she had to accept would never come true.

Living with Joe McConnell would be so much easier if she could just stop loving him.

When she heard his voice in the reception area outside, it took her a moment to realize that it wasn't her own thoughts summoning up the image of her husband. Joe was actually at the school, and Roxanne was telling him to go on back to her office.

She had a fleeting memory of the morning when he showed up with a son they'd never envisioned, but this time when he burst in she saw none of the distress that had characterized his earlier visit. This time he looked exuberant, almost glowing with triumph.

In a few quick strides he crossed the room and swung her into his arms, spinning her around in an exultant hug. "Meg," he said, setting her down just before she had to gasp for a breath, "you're not gonna believe this. But believe it, okay? This is the honest-to-God truth."

It couldn't be bad news, not when he looked so radiant. Another award for the *Herald?* A lottery win? A Pulitzer prize?

"Okay," she said, forcing her thoughts away from Elena. "What is it?"

Joe rested his hands on her shoulders and looked straight into her eyes. "If you want," he said deliberately, the slowness of his words contrasting wildly with the heat crackling from his body, "the adoption agency's got a baby for us."

She felt herself sway, felt him steady her. "What?"

"A baby," he repeated, still watching her with a tinge of caution on his face. "I know you said to forget the whole thing. But I couldn't just—"

"A baby?" Her voice didn't sound quite like her own, and in some corner of her awareness she wondered whether this was all an elaborate fantasy. "Of our own?"

"Yeah. Not the *same* baby," Joe amended hastily. "Another one, but Rita said it's already born."

This was too much to take in. A baby? From the same agency who had refused them before?

"You went back there?" Meg stammered, seizing the first coherent thought she could voice in a whirlpool of disbelief. "Just now?"

He must have sensed the dizziness coursing through her, because he slid one arm around her waist and guided her to a resting place against the edge of her desk. "I had to," he said simply. "Look, I know now what you were going through, wanting a baby. I've been—"

This still didn't seem possible. But he'd said when he came in here that she wouldn't believe him, and that this was the honest-to-God truth. She dropped her head toward her hands, gasped and looked up at him again. "You got us a *baby?*"

"Yeah. A girl."

A daughter. He'd promised last night after crying out for his lost love that he would make it up to her, but she'd never expected anything like this. "How on earth?" she began, and he swung into an explanation as if he couldn't quite yet believe it himself.

"I went and asked Rita what I could to do to be ready for a baby. Told her what was going on. And—"

"And we're getting a daughter," Meg breathed. Saying the words out loud made them seem, for the first time, within the realm of possibility. "For real."

"For real. That's what she said."

It shouldn't surprise her that Joe had managed to talk Rita into such a dramatic change of heart; with his editorial skills he could probably talk anyone into anything. But that he had done it so quickly after his pledge last night.... "Joe, I can't believe this!"

"I know," he said, crossing the room to swing her door shut as if he had to put feelings into motion somehow. "All the way over here, I kept thinking the same thing. Only it's for real, I swear. I wouldn't be telling you any of this if I hadn't seen the papers."

Papers. Yes. Adoption certificates. Baby announcements. Wallpaper for the nursery. Her mother's christening gown...

"We can take her home in about three weeks," Joe said,

returning to the desk and sitting down beside Meg, then giving her a questioning smile. "If you want."

"If I *want?*" she repeated incredulously before remembering how she'd begged him not to talk about babies. But talking about another search was completely different from actually getting a daughter. "Of course I want! It's what I've *always* wanted."

"Yeah, that's what I thought."

It was ironic, in a way, that she had wanted a baby to make them into a real family—a family where Joe would love her as much as she loved him—and that instead this baby was being offered as a gesture of atonement. But she needed to focus on what she had, and a daughter was a treasure she'd dreamed of for years. "Joe, honestly, this is wonderful!"

"I'm excited myself," he said, which she knew was true. He'd come in here practically shooting off sparks of elation. No matter what his motivation, the man deserved to feel excited about having single-handedly reversed the decision of an entire adoption agency.

"I don't know how you managed it," Meg told him. Telling Rita what was going on seemed like the last way to convince anyone he was ready for a child, but he'd sworn this would really happen. "This is—you're sure? We're definitely getting a baby?"

"Not the same one as before," he said, standing up again as if he couldn't quite contain himself in one spot and taking her hands in his. "I guess they already found parents for her. But the people who were waiting for this girl just found out they're getting transferred to the Philippines, and Rita hadn't found anyone else yet."

And just like that, he had changed the social worker's mind about not being ready for a baby. "So you talked her into—Joe, you are incredible!"

He shrugged as if dismissing the tribute, with his eyes

still fixed on her. "It's just…I want you to be happy. And I want us to have a baby."

For a moment, against her better judgment, she felt a sudden, radiant surge of hope. Even though she knew it was wrong to fall back into the old habit, the expression on his face was almost enough to make her believe he loved her. "Joe," she began.

With a sudden rush of words, almost as if he was embarrassed, he hurried into speech. "And I was thinking," he said, "a daughter is the way to go, because that way you won't be the only girl. I mean, when Tony and I are doing guy stuff, you can do…girl stuff."

That, she realized with a tug of disappointment at her heart, made more sense. That fit with what she'd finally come to accept about Joe—both the fact that he was satisfied with the child he already had, and that he would always offer her whatever compensation he could. If he was going to enjoy Elena's son, he would at least make sure that Meg had a daughter.

So she might as well appreciate what she had, Meg reminded herself. She might as well concentrate on the fun of preparing for a baby—the pink wallpaper, the flowered blankets, the soft robes and all the other painfully sweet details she hadn't let herself remember since that first, devastating loss.

"Sure," she agreed. "This weekend I'll get—" Then, without warning, a wave of uncertainty broke over her. "Do you really think it'll happen?"

Joe didn't look at all surprised by her question. Instead, he reached forward and gently took her hands in his.

"This time, yeah." With a look of resolve, he met her gaze directly and delivered a confirming promise. "This time, Meggers, I'm not going to screw it up."

Chapter Eleven

This time, Joe vowed, he was going to do everything right. Rita had already said after barely ten minutes of conversation that it was obvious he could handle another child—a pronouncement that still amazed him, considering that all he had going for him was the desire to love a family—but he still felt keenly aware of his inexperience when it came to acting like a dad.

Telling Tony about the new baby, though, would be a good test. He left the *Herald* a few minutes earlier than usual so he could practice his speech on the way to Oakville Elementary, and wondered why addressing a nine-year-old boy should frighten him far more than addressing a convention of eight hundred journalists.

It would be a little easier to get started, though, without the encumbrances of a moderator and a podium in the way. He opted to have this talk at the downtown diner he and Tony had frequented for most of last week, just because the place had some good memories, and waited until they were well into their chocolate chip ice cream before launching into what he hoped would be the right announcement.

"Hey, guy. You remember how we were talking about babies yesterday?"

His son glanced up from the cone that seemed to drip unevenly no matter how many times he licked its edges. "Uh-huh."

"Well," Joe said, "it turns out our family is going to get a baby after all. A daughter, which is great because you're already our son."

He'd been proud of that line, figuring Tony could appreciate the distinction of being the only boy in the family, but he hadn't expected the child's immediate correction.

"I'm *your* son," Tony informed him. "And Mamá's."

"Well, yeah, you'll always be her son." He could never expect the boy to forget his mother, no matter how much he wanted to view the McConnells as a unit of four. "But you're Tía's, too. We're all in the same family."

It took a minute, but finally Tony nodded and Joe felt a surge of relief. "All three of us," the kid said.

"Right, only in another few weeks there'll be four of us. And you'll be the baby's big brother."

He could almost see the impact of the news on his son. Tony stopped licking his ice-cream cone, stared into the distance for a moment and then fixed Joe with a challenging gaze.

"Babies cry all the time."

"Sometimes, sure." There was no use denying that, and he didn't want to paint any false pictures. "But remember when you used to hear babies crying all the time? That was a lot of babies. This is only one."

Evidently Tony could grasp the implications of that, as well, because a cautious look of relief stole across his face.

"Yeah," he said, then returned his attention to his ice

cream. "One baby can't cry all the time or else it'd suffocate."

It would be entertaining, Joe thought, to watch this whole experience through his son's perspective. If ever he and Meg worried that their baby wouldn't stop crying, he would have to remember Tony's words.

"Right," he agreed with a straight face, but Tony wasn't finished.

"But if there's any stinky diapers, I'm not gonna touch 'em."

Joe swallowed a smile. Of all the comments he'd anticipated, that one hadn't been on the list. "No, you won't have to."

"Promise?"

Tony must be exceptionally worried about diapers if he felt this point demanded the wholehearted commitment of an official promise. "Yeah, I promise. That's Tía's and my job."

His son looked startled. "*Your* job?"

In Milagua, Joe realized, men would butcher livestock without shrinking from the blood, carry their wounded through muddy jungles for endless miles and matter-of-factly dig graves for fallen comrades, but they would never change a diaper...if, in fact, there were any to be changed.

"Yeah, in this country fathers help with babies whenever they're at home," he explained. "I'll still go to the *Herald* every day like I do now, but Tía will stay home instead of going to her school. She wants to take care of this baby herself."

Tony nodded thoughtfully, looking as if he was trying to figure something out. Finally he swallowed the last of his ice cream and looked up at Joe. "So is Tía happy?"

Another question he hadn't expected, but it was nice of his son to wonder. And it was easy to answer after seeing Meg's joy this morning. "Yeah, she is. She's wanted a baby for a long time."

"Years and years?"

"Probably," Joe said, reaching for his wallet as he picked up the check. For as long as he'd known her, she'd been gifted with the ability to nurture. Even before he came back from Milagua, he remembered Paul's sister as the kind of girl who would always take in stray kittens and offer lemonade at the end of any football scrimmages on their lawn. Meg was a natural caretaker, a born nurturer. "I guess for her whole life."

He couldn't think of anything he'd wanted for his whole life, he realized as he and Tony drove home by way of the Baby Emporium a few blocks from the diner. There had been a series of goals set and achieved, and the passion for news that had sustained him over the past fifteen years, but nothing that compared to Meg's vocation for motherhood.

She showed it again when she came home and found him and Tony assembling the baby car seat they'd picked up.

"Tony," she said, giving them both a quick hug, "thank you for helping Papá with that. You're going to be a wonderful big brother."

She was practically shining with happiness, Joe realized, and in spite of that she was still concerned about making sure the boy felt included.

"You're welcome," his son said solemnly. "But I'm not changing any skunky diapers. Papá promised."

Meg treated that with the gravity it deserved. "Big brothers don't change diapers, Tony, but they do other things. You can show her how to walk when she's older."

Joe could almost see the boy standing a little taller. "Okay," Tony agreed.

"And how to make sandwiches for school in the mornings, like you've been doing," Meg continued, moving the car seat box to the kitchen counter. "She'll be too little to do anything like that for a while, but she'll be glad to have a brother who can show her things.''

''I'm good at showing people things,'' Tony announced. ''One time Sister Ana asked us to help her with the juice, and I showed Miguel how to use the can opener because he'd never opened any cans.''

''I'll bet you were a big help,'' Meg observed, including Joe in her smile of commendation. ''Sister Ana was lucky you were there.''

Already he could see his son's pride growing. ''She said she and Sister Maria were glad to have me.''

Meg took a stack of plates from the cupboard and nodded in agreement. ''I'll bet they were. I'll bet they miss you.''

How did she do that? Joe wondered. How did she always know exactly the right thing to say? It never would have occurred to him to reassure Tony that Sister Ana missed him, but his son seemed pleased at the thought. It made sense, the kid had spent six months of his life in the orphanage, and of course he must have some good memories of the people there, but Joe never would have thought to offer such a comment.

Megs was born to be a mom, no question, and he was glad she was finally getting her chance.

''I called my dad and Stacie,'' she told him as she started dinner, ''and they're both thrilled. Stacie said she's expecting thirteen rolls of pictures the first week. And Paul and Fiona get back Friday. I can't wait to tell them.''

It was fun watching her excitement, especially when he imagined the implications. Next time he made love to her, this bubbling joy would likely engulf them both like a wave of champagne. Meanwhile, he enjoyed the rapture in her eyes, in her voice and in her gestures as she made lists of friends to share the news with, put a new roll of film in the camera and began unpacking all the baby clothes he never realized she'd set aside in the attic.

His only regret was that she didn't seem to view this as a shared venture. Admittedly, he couldn't offer much in the way of knitted bibs and satin-rimmed blankets and all the other paraphernalia she seemed to have acquired over the years. He didn't have any family to add to her list of exultant phone calls, and he'd already told everyone at the *Herald*. But still he wished Meg would say she was glad they were starting a family *together*.

Still, there was no denying that she was happier than he'd seen her in a while. And the next time they made love, which would happen by tomorrow night even if he had to unplug the phone, he could show his wife he loved her without guarding his heart the way he'd always done before.

The thought stayed with him as he wrote his editorial the next morning, called the lawyer about the adoption papers and phoned a few other editors in search of potential sales down the road. He would have to be more aggressive about marketing his freelance stories, Joe knew, if he was going to spend less time at the *Herald* and more time at home with his family. But he could manage that. He'd already won a baby from Rita and convinced Tony that a sister wouldn't be so bad...so a couple more freelance assignments should be a piece of cake.

His calls paid off faster than he expected. In fact, no sooner had he and Tony and Meg sat down to dinner that night than a Minneapolis contact phoned to offer him a freelance contract covering a rapidly spreading fire near the Canadian border.

"We just got word of it half an hour ago, but it sounds like a big one," the editor told him, "and you're as close as anyone we can get. Can you take it?"

His first response was an instinctive rush of excitement, a surge of exhilaration in his veins. This was his kind of story! But just as that jolt of recognition set his pulse at a higher speed, he realized what the assignment would mean.

He would have to leave Meg right now.

"Tell you what," Joe said, "I'll either cover it myself, or I'll send the guy who worked with me on the drug dealer story last month. You bought that one, remember? Either Phil or I will get you something by midnight."

He confirmed the background on the fire, hung up the phone and saw Meg staring at him in amazement. "You'd send Phil to cover a story that big?"

It went against every instinct, but he couldn't take off for Canada now. Not when Meg had been home only four days. Not with all the baby preparations barely underway.

"Well," he said, "Phil can use some experience selling freelance, too. And I figure, with the baby and everything…"

"Bless your heart!" She sounded genuinely touched, genuinely surprised. "But you don't need to stay home yet. The baby won't be here for another few weeks."

He knew that. For the first time in four years, though, he wished his wife would complain about him leaving home too often. "Even so," Joe reminded her, "we've got to get all the furniture moved in."

"That's what delivery men are for," she answered with a smile, taking his untouched dinner plate to the microwave and pushing the Reheat button. "It's sweet of you, really, but Tony and I can handle things. And you love doing big, scary stories."

She was right, and this one sounded like a winner. The suspicion of arson following the drought, a thousand acres of timber at risk and the wind playing hell with the firefighters' strategy were the kind of elements on which career-shaping articles were built. But it would take him away from home for at least two or three days.

"I don't mind missing this story," he said.

That was half true and half false, and she seemed to

read the falsehood more easily than the truth. "Joe, don't be silly," she protested, sliding the salt shaker across the table to Tony. "Once the baby's here, who knows how often you'll get the chance for an article like this? But right now I can still take care of getting Tony to school and everything. So go on, do your story. I'll fix you some coffee to take on the road."

With an order like that, how could he do anything but agree? He threw a few days' worth of clothes and his cell phone into the car, left a terse set of instructions with Mark at the *Herald* and headed north with Meg's flask of coffee as his only source of warmth. It was pretty battered from the past few years of knocking around in his car whenever he spent time on the road, but for some reason he wanted it close to him now.

This wasn't like his usual experience setting off in pursuit of a breaking story—the thrill of anticipation was tempered, somehow, with the awareness of Meg still at home. Probably getting Tony's dessert right around now… finishing the dishes…checking his homework…tucking him into bed…sitting alone at the mirror and brushing her hair…

How long could this story take, anyway? A day, maybe two? If the wind changed and the firefighters won their battle tomorrow, he could probably make it home by Thursday morning.

This wasn't like him, Joe admitted as he drove the last fifty miles with the orange glow lighting the horizon ahead of him. Normally he'd be figuring every angle, looking forward to finding his lead, feeling the rush of adrenaline that accompanied the first sight of a story. Here he was, on a trek he would have gloried in two weeks ago, and all he could think about was how soon he could get back to Meg?

Once he started the story, surely, the old magic would come back. Once he got to work, found some people to talk to and took notes and then found someplace quiet to phone in his first report to Minneapolis, then he'd be back in the thick of things. Back to his calling as a journalist.

He managed two incisive reports before dawn and collapsed in the car for a few hours' sleep, relieved that his skill hadn't deserted him. He could still hold his own on a story like this, still get the quotes and the facts and the color that would make this scene come alive for readers all over the state. But when he encountered the fire chief that afternoon and learned that the battle was barely beginning, he felt as much dismayed as he felt intrigued. The longer this fire lasted, the better coverage he could generate…but the longer it would take him to get home.

This was wrong, he knew. He was at the front of the action, he was getting material most reporters would kill for, and why the hell couldn't he just stay focused on the job? Since when did anything in the world matter more than a great story?

This was what happened when you listened to your heart, Joe reminded himself. This was why he'd been afraid of loving Meg.

But it was Meg who had told him to do this story.

Had it cost her? he wondered the next morning as he banged out another report on the laptop computer he'd borrowed from a TV reporter. Had she hesitated for even a moment before telling him she and Tony could manage just fine? Maybe this was just wishful thinking, but had she guessed he needed the reassurance of knowing he could love a woman without sacrificing his career?

Because after thirty-six hours on the front lines, he now knew that he could. And he was glad of it. But that was small comfort during the unexpected moments with no mission to accomplish, when all he could do was stand around missing Meg.

As soon as he got the chance, Joe resolved, he was going to phone her. He'd have to find a phone with better range than his own, which barely reached Minneapolis, and it might take some effort now that the fire was spreading far enough to attract reporters from all over the Midwest...but he'd give a lot to hear her voice.

He had to stand in line for a phone at one of the satellite trucks that afternoon, yet any amount of waiting would be worth it. The timing was right on target, he knew with a glance at his smoke-smeared watch, because she and Tony would have just gotten home from school.

It took him twenty-five minutes to reach the head of the line, but his call went through without delay. He found himself tensing every muscle in his body as he waited for her to pick up the phone, and when he heard her familiar "Hello?" he felt a rush of pleasure so strong it nearly sent him reeling.

"Meg," he said softly, basking in the sensation of her voice as close as the phone in his hand. "It's good to hear you."

"Joe, is that you?" Her end of the line must be as crackly as his, but still he could hear the excitement in her voice. "Oh, this is perfect, I'm so glad you called. Guess what? Tony and I are on our way to see the baby!"

"Right now?" He felt a pang of alarm on realizing that with any more people in line, he would have missed them. Next time he left home on a story, Joe resolved, he was going to bring one of those cell phones that worked no matter where you took it. "They're letting you see her?"

"We can't take her home yet," Meg explained, "but one of the caseworkers needs a signature on some paperwork, and she said if we came right away we could take a peek in the well-baby clinic. There's only a few people coming in this afternoon, and our baby is one of them."

Our baby. She had definitely said *our* baby, Joe thought with another rush of happiness. "I wish I could be there."

"I wish you could, too," she said fervently amidst another burst of static. "Joe, really, I'm so glad you called. I've been wanting to tell you…"

I love you. He closed his eyes, feeling the impact of the awareness even before she spoke.

"I really, really appreciate what you did," she concluded. "Getting the baby, I mean. I wasn't going to make a fuss about Elena, honestly, but when you said you'd make it up to me—"

He felt a sudden coldness in his chest.

"Meg, that wasn't what—"

The static crackled so sharply that he could barely hear his own words, but when he shook the phone again he realized she still hadn't finished.

"It's the nicest thing anybody's ever done for me, and I never even said thank you."

She honestly thought he'd meant the baby as an apology? That he'd simply been doing her a favor?

"That's not what I was doing!" he shouted into the static. "I was—"

Another burst of crackling exploded in his ear, followed by a muted buzz.

"Meg? Are you there? Meg, damn it!" He shook the phone desperately, hoping to restore the connection and swearing until the cameraman behind him in line took the phone from his hand.

"Sorry, pal. You lost her."

"I don't know what happened," Meg told Tony, hanging up the phone that had suddenly gone dead. "Papá sounded fine, but it was hard to hear him. I guess the phones don't work too well up there by the fire."

"Is he gonna call back?"

She hoped so, even though it was embarrassing how much she enjoyed hearing his voice. She still wanted Joe too much for comfort, and in a way it had been a relief to know she'd have a few more days to steel herself against the wishful thinking that would inevitably accompany a night of lovemaking. But no matter how much she appreciated the sound of his voice, there was no reason for Joe to call back now that he'd performed his obligatory check-in.

"Maybe tomorrow," she said. There was no sense raising false hopes in Tony as well as herself. "I don't think he has much free time. But when he does, we'll tell him about your new sister."

At least she'd gotten the chance to thank him for having arranged the baby before the static cut off their conversation. She owed him that for having kept his pledge of atonement so much more decisively than she had ever expected. And today's preview would be an extra miracle, thanks to the caseworker who didn't believe in scrupulous observation of the rule separating parents from their babies for the first six weeks of life.

One more thing to appreciate when she focused on what she had.

The appreciation stayed with her as they found the adoption office, where Meg signed all the papers bearing Joe's signature without even reading them. He was always careful about technicalities, and anything he'd signed would be fine with her. All she wanted was to get the paperwork finished and hurry off to the clinic, where her daughter—her daughter!—was waiting.

When she and Tony peeked in the waiting room and saw a grandmotherly woman holding a baby in a pink blanket, Meg felt as if her heart had leaped into her throat. After so many years of fantasy, it didn't seem possible that her daughter could really be within reach. And when the woman asked, "Mrs. McConnell?" and lifted the blanket to reveal the baby's face, she would have sworn she heard angels in their midst.

The child was beautiful. So tiny, so wrinkled, with a faint dust of hair on her soft, shiny head and with gnarled little fingers clutched into red fists. Such an astonishing mixture, with all the staggering impact of a lifetime of dreams contained in a bundle so small.

"Oh," Meg whispered, sitting down beside the foster mother, "can I hold her?"

The moment the baby was placed in her arms, she felt a soaring sense of rightness unlike anything she'd ever known. This, *this* was her child. This warm little armful of blanket and breath and bone was her destiny, the daughter she would cherish for the rest of her life, the culmination of so many years of waiting, imagining, hoping and planning.

If only Joe were here! But he couldn't possibly understand what this meant, this sweet promise of immortality. He might appreciate the concept of a baby—after all, he'd managed to convince Rita he was ready for a child—but he would never see this daughter as a lodestone to draw their marriage into new and closer bonds.

And that was asking too much of anyone, Meg reminded herself. This baby was already a treasure in her own right, a perfect little miracle of soft skin and wrinkly eyes and a chin so endearing that merely to look at it was to smile.

"Aren't you precious?" she whispered, holding the baby even closer to her and feeling with a thrill of certainty how very rightly the child fit against the curve of her breast. Oh, this baby belonged with her! Maybe not legally, not for another few weeks, but already this child was hers.

Next time she held her in the nursery at home, surely her daughter would feel this same sweet tug of recognition, the same heady awareness that *this* was where she belonged.

"She's a little angel," the foster mother told Meg. "Doesn't eat much at a time, but when she burps, you'd swear she was a linebacker. Cutest thing you've ever heard.''

Meg laughed and felt her eyes filling with tears at the same time. Never once had she envisioned a daughter who would burp like a linebacker. But from now on her whole life would be this way, one astonishing and blessed surprise after another, and she couldn't wait to watch them unfold.

It took all the willpower she possessed to leave her daughter with the clinic nurse half an hour later, even though the foster mother seemed reassuringly kind. But in only three more weeks, she reminded herself, she and Joe and Tony would be back here with their new car seat…and they would walk outside into the sunshine with their baby as part of the family.

Oh, God, thank you. Thank you! Thank you.

Her eyes began filling with tears again and she stopped to wipe them before turning on the car ignition. She couldn't drive home in a cloud of tears, although dry eyes still wouldn't do much for her overall stability. She felt as if she'd just spent half an hour on a trampoline, or several hours in bed with Joe—her heart was racing, her skin flushed with warmth, and everything around her seemed more vivid, more beautiful and more intense than it normally did.

"Wasn't that wonderful?" Meg asked Tony, forcing herself to take deep breaths as she backed out of the parking lot. "Did you see how she smiled? Almost like she knew who we were."

"Maybe somebody told her," Tony offered.

She felt another crazy laugh bubbling up inside her. "Maybe so. Or maybe we've got a baby genius on our hands. She woke up this morning knowing that today she was going to meet her mother and brother." The vision felt almost possible, both so fantastic and so realistic that she felt her throat tightening. "Oh, Tony, it's going to be so wonderful having a baby in the house!"

The nine-year-old obviously hadn't experienced the same rapture Meg had, but at least he didn't seem bored. "What's her name?"

"We haven't picked one yet." That had been her suggestion when they first discussed adoption a few years ago—a way to preserve some element of surprise in the legally scheduled arrival of a child—and Joe had agreed that it made sense to wait until they actually saw the baby before selecting a name. "Now you and I have seen her, but Papá still hasn't."

"I guess he will when he comes back."

Oh, once Joe saw her, he would surely feel this same sense of awe. Even if he didn't appreciate the joy of sharing a family, he would have to feel some spark of excitement. "He'll be amazed," she predicted. "He doesn't realize yet how…how *wonderful* a baby is."

"Uh-huh."

She probably sounded dippy, Meg thought as another wave of pleasure crested over her. Like an adolescent girl who couldn't stop gushing about a new boyfriend. But the wonder was so intense, so astonishing, that she couldn't keep it from bubbling over. "I just…oh, Tony, the way she *felt!* So perfect."

He gave her a disapproving look. "Nobody's perfect."

Whoever coined that phrase must never have held a new baby. "And holding her! I wish Papá could have been there. Once he sees her…"

She didn't even have to finish the sentence. "He'll love her, too," Tony concluded.

"This is so—" There was no way to describe the sensation without sounding light-headed, she decided through another surge of elation. "It's like when you were excited about building a snowman, only then it was even better than you expected, remember?" It was a good thing they were barely two minutes from home, because all this joy-ful energy had to go someplace. "I've got to start calling people."

Tony hunched his shoulders, a somber look on his face. "I've got stuff to do, too."

"Oh, that's right, you've got homework. Do you need any help?"

"No," he said flatly, which relieved her. All she wanted now was to exult with Stacie, with Susan, with everyone who had ever held a baby and experienced this overpow-ering sense of truth and fantasy mingled into a staggering, breathtaking awe.

It took her a good hour to finish the first rush of calls, and when she looked at the clock she realized it would be silly to start dinner this late. She might as well take Tony out for pizza, especially since they had so much to cele-brate. And he'd been so engrossed in his homework that he was surely ready for a break.

"Tony," she called upstairs. "Let's go get some pizza for dinner."

He didn't reply, which made her realize that he might want a little coaxing. He'd been terrific this afternoon, not showing any sign of jealousy over the new baby, but lis-tening to her rhapsodize for the past hour probably hadn't done much for him. Bless his heart! She would have to make a point of giving him some extra attention, just to make sure he knew he still mattered.

"Tony," she called again. "What kind of pizza shall we order? I'll let you pick it out."

Still no answer. Meg grabbed the pizza menu from be-side the phone, took it upstairs and stopped at the door of his room.

His school books were piled neatly on the desk, but the lamp was dark. His dresser drawers were tipped open, with a few handfuls of clothes spilling out. His desk chair was propped against the wall beneath the window, as if offering a foothold.

The window was open.

And Tony was gone.

Chapter Twelve

"Tony," she called again with mounting panic. "Tony!"

There was no sign of him in the yard. Nor up and down the street. Where on earth would he go with a backpack full of clothes? Not to a classmate's, not when any child's mother would have phoned her. Not to the park, not with such calculated packing.

No, Tony was intent on leaving home.

And it was all her fault, Meg realized with a rising sense of guilt as she stared up at his open window. She never should have chattered so blithely about the joys of a baby in front of a boy who until now had been the only child in the house. She should have made sure that Tony knew he was special in his own right before she started oohing and ahhing over a daughter.

But this was no time for wondering how she could have failed him so badly in the midst of her enthusiasm. She

could—and would—do that later. What mattered now was
finding him.

"To-o-ony! Tony, where are you?"

He wasn't anywhere within earshot, Meg admitted two
minutes later as she emerged from the bushes behind the
Andersens' house. Dear God, was this anything like what
Joe had gone through that night she walked out on him?
The utter horror, disbelief and desperation of how it felt
to see someone vanish had never struck her with such
impact until now.

But she couldn't think about that yet, either. Right now
she would have to think like a purposeful nine-year-old
rather than a guilt-stricken adult. If Tony was serious about
leaving home, where could he possibly—

Then it struck her.

Sister Ana said they were glad to have me.

There weren't many nine-year-olds who could conceive
of setting off for an orphanage in Milagua, but Tony had
both the background and the determination to come up
with such a plan. He might not know exactly how to get
there, but he obviously had enough confidence to embark
on the journey.

Which meant, she realized as she forced herself to keep
thinking logically, he must have some kind of transpor-
tation already in mind. There wasn't enough money in his
piggy bank to get very far, but he wouldn't know that until
he tried to buy a ticket south. And the obvious choice was
by air. He'd come from Milagua to the Twin Cities on a
plane, he knew where the local airfield was, and if he had
even half his father's grit he wouldn't be the least bit
daunted by a five-mile trek.

Meg raced inside and grabbed her purse. She wasn't
going to call the police to retrieve him, not when she knew
exactly where Tony must be heading. The last thing any
child needed was someone like Sergeant Sanders coming

after him with flashing lights, especially if he already felt rejected by his family.

No, she had to find him herself, somewhere along the highway to Aviation Field, and make sure Tony knew how much he mattered. How very much he mattered, regardless of the new baby who had occupied every scrap of her attention for the past three days.

She drove with excruciating slowness, peering at every late-afternoon shadow that might obscure a child and wondering how far he could have gone in the past hour. Surely no one would have picked up a boy toting all his worldly goods without phoning his mother, would they? Not in Oakville.

This, after all, was where she'd convinced Joe they should raise their children.

But after covering two miles with no sign of Tony's yellow shirt, she began to wonder whether she should have phoned the police. At least that way there would be someone else looking, someone else watching every tree, every fence post, every inch of the road. Could he have made it this far? Or had she passed by him already and not even seen him?

It seemed possible. Because she'd been blind today, Meg knew. She'd been so wrapped up in the baby that she hadn't even spotted Tony's worry over losing his place in the family…but she should have.

He must have been worried before they ever set out for the clinic, and she'd made things even worse on the way home. Raving about her daughter, exulting over how wonderful this child was and how thrilled Joe would be to have a baby. Then spending a good hour crowing to all her friends about the miracle of a child—

Tony wasn't dull. He was as keenly observant as his father. He noticed what went on around him, and he knew perfectly well that she'd never once phoned all her friends to exult over the arrival of a nine-year-old boy.

And here you'd kept saying you wanted a child...

But she knew painfully well why she hadn't welcomed Tony with the same joy as her daughter. He was a reminder of the woman who would always outshine her, who would always hold first place in Joe's heart.

Stop it, Meg ordered herself. This was no time to think about Elena. It was envy that had drawn her—and an innocent child!—into this situation in the first place, and she had to focus on what she could do now.

Find him. Just find him.

A flash of movement caught her eye and she slammed on the brakes before realizing it was a teenage girl walking her dog. Not a boy lugging his backpack...but still, maybe the girl had seen something.

"Excuse me," Meg called to her. "Have you seen a little boy heading this same direction?"

The ponytailed teenager looked at her curiously, probably wondering what kind of mother would have to search for a runaway child.

"No, sorry."

It would have been too easy, Meg admitted as she continued on her way, if the girl had reported passing Tony near that last fieldstone house and sending him inside for lemonade. Tony wouldn't have gone, anyway, not when he was intent on a mission. Even so, the disappointment thickened in her throat, pressing against the mixture of guilt and worry that rose steadily with every passing minute.

God, please just let me find him.

The intensity of her plea felt almost as fierce as the intensity of her thanks, only a little while ago, for the arrival of the baby. Yet that shouldn't surprise her, Meg realized with another pang of desperation. Tony mattered every bit as much as the baby, only she hadn't seen it until now.

Oh, but she should have. She should have paid more

attention to those familiar stirrings of affection, those sweet moments of worry and those heady moments of pride. She should have been appreciating him all along, rather than waiting until he took off.

From now on, she vowed as she scanned both sides of the road through a growing haze of tears, she would treasure Tony the way he deserved. Not just as a way to show Joe she'd be a great mother, not as a substitute for the daughter she wanted, but for himself.

A boy who loved exploring the basement.

Who paid such careful attention to the spacing between sweet peas.

Who insisted on her eating every last spoonful of strawberry ice cream—

Dear God, let me find my son!

No sooner had the prayer burst from her soul than she saw a familiar figure in the distance. That had to be Tony, she could tell from his walk—so much like Joe's—and the last rays of sunlight glinting off his dark hair. That had to be Tony, and she had to make him see how much he was wanted.

How much he was loved.

He didn't even glance her way when she stopped the car at the side of the road and got out. Instead he plodded on, looking straight ahead as if it had never entered his mind that someone might come looking for him.

"Tony!" she called.

Without breaking stride, he darted a quick look over his shoulder. Then, when he saw Meg, he hesitated.

"I missed you," she told him, hurrying to his side and matching her pace to his. He shouldn't have to face the choice of whether to turn back just yet, and they could walk another ten miles together if that would let him save face. "I don't want to lose you, Tony."

It took another minute before he answered, still without looking her way. "You've got the baby," he said flatly.

She did, but right now Tony needed her more. Her mother had been right, Meg realized, when she used to explain that the child you loved best at any given moment was the one who needed you most.

"I've got the baby," she agreed, walking beside him, "but I want you, too. If you want to go back and visit Milagua someday, that's fine, but right now Papá and I want you with us."

He didn't seem convinced. Instead he continued his dogged pace, making her wonder whether they might have to return to the car after dark. It was another few miles to the airfield, and surely the car would be safe where she'd left it, but she wished she'd brought jackets for them both.

"I should have brought along some pizza," Meg observed after several minutes of silent trudging. "I was thinking we'd go out for pizza tonight, only I didn't know which kind you wanted."

Tony slowed his steps.

"Because I remember how you liked pepperoni that time, but I wasn't sure if you wanted that again or if you'd rather try something new."

"I don't care," he muttered, still without meeting her gaze. "I don't want any pizza."

All right, at least he was talking. "That's okay. Would you rather have hamburgers?"

Still no answer. It was as if, she realized, he couldn't let himself accept any offer that might involve returning home. Dear God, how could she have hurt him so badly?

"Oh, Tony," Meg exclaimed, coming to a halt, "I'm so sorry!"

He hunched his shoulders and scuffed his foot at the dirt, and with a swell of compassion she drew him into her arms. He stayed stiff at first, but when she felt his body shaking she knew he was trying not to cry.

"It's okay," she whispered. "Sweetheart, I didn't mean

to make you feel bad when I got so excited about the baby. It was just because I'd never met her before.''

Tony pulled away and kicked at the dirt again. ''Everybody loves babies.''

He was right, and there was no use in denying that. ''But just because I love the baby,'' Meg said desperately, ''doesn't mean I don't love *you*.'' The words sounded vaguely familiar, but right now her only thought was for the boy in front of her. ''You have the Tony place in my heart and she'll have the baby place, but I love you both.''

The headlights of a car swept toward them from the distance, and Tony automatically stepped back. ''But you love her better.''

''No, sweetheart. Just different.'' The same sensation of familiarity nudged her again, and this time she recognized the words as Joe's from that night at the Wayside Inn.

The night she hadn't believed him.

Any more than Tony believed her now, she realized with a pang of dismay as he shoved his hands in his pockets and stared at the passing car. ''But babies are special,'' he muttered.

''So are nine-year-old boys!'' She felt a tide of tears rising in her throat at the realization that Joe must have meant every word of his declaration…as fiercely, as wholeheartedly as she meant hers now. ''Tony, *everybody's* special. You and the baby are both different, and I love you both.''

He didn't believe her, she could see when he kicked at another clump of dirt before turning to face her again with defiance in his eyes. ''Sister Ana would be happy if I came back.''

Her heart twisted. When she'd told him that, trying to boost his self-confidence, she had never envisioned it coming back to haunt her this way. But if Tony truly felt so unwanted at home that he needed the memory of the orphanage to sustain him, she couldn't very well rip it away.

"Of course she would," Meg said over the tightness in her chest, "but Papá and I want you even more. Tony, I love you. I want you to come home."

With a sigh of resignation, he shifted his backpack and started toward the car. "Okay," he muttered.

From his grim look, though, it was obvious that the agreement wasn't voluntary. He might be giving in because he felt there was no other choice, but not because he felt wanted or loved.

How on earth, she wondered as they walked back down the road, could she convince Tony she loved him? It was her own fault he didn't believe it, she knew, but that didn't make his disbelief hurt any less. She could try saying she loved him every chance she got, and yet until Tony recognized it was true, there would be no alleviating this curious, forlorn pain.

All she could do, Meg decided, was keep telling him—
The way Joe kept telling me.

It hit her with such impact that she nearly lost her balance. She gasped, felt herself miss a step and saw Tony glance at her, startled, as she caught her breath and continued on her way.

The way Joe had told her, over and over, and she hadn't believed him.

I love you, Meggers. I just wanted you to know that.
I don't mind missing this story.
I didn't love her like I love you.
It's just...I want you to be happy.
I mean it, okay? I really do love you.

How could she have ignored all that? How could she have kept believing he only loved Elena? Why hadn't she *listened?*

And if it hurt this much for her to know that Tony didn't believe her, what on earth had she done to Joe?

She had to call him, Meg knew. But she couldn't do

that from the airfield highway, and she couldn't postpone getting Tony his pizza—because even though she couldn't make amends to Joe right this minute, she could at least do something about their son.

Tony was looking more tired with every step, and when she stopped him to transfer his backpack onto her shoulders he made only a token protest. She had to get him home, get him fed and comforted and tucked into bed with whatever reassurance she could give him. Not the assurance that he would be a terrific big brother, which implied he was worthwhile only in relation to the baby. Besides, all he'd really cared about big-brother status was the issue of changing diapers, even after Joe's promise—

A promise, she remembered with a sudden flash of hope, meant something special. To Tony, a promise was a pledge that could never be changed.

Meg halted. "Tony, listen," she said. "This is important, okay?"

He stopped his dogged trudging and looked at her warily in the fading twilight. "Okay."

She bent toward him so he could see the truth in her eyes as she delivered the commitment. "I promise," she said deliberately, "I love you as much as the baby."

The light of awareness on his face told her that he understood the impact of such a vow. Even though he held himself straight, she could see the yearning in his body. "Yeah?" he whispered.

"I promise," Meg repeated, opening her arms, and with one quick lunge he threw himself into her welcoming embrace.

"Okay. I'm coming home."

Their homecoming was delayed only for as long as it took to stop at the pizza place on Aspen Street and order a double pepperoni special that Meg feared would keep Tony up with heartburn all night. But after only two slices, he began nodding off—probably in response to the stresses of the day, she decided—and he offered no resistance when she coaxed him through his bath and tooth brushing and into bed an hour before his usual bedtime.

Only after he was comfortably asleep did she let herself return to the question of how to reach Joe.

The fire had been on the TV news every night, she reasoned as she made herself a cup of coffee in hopes that it would help her think. Maybe if she called one of the stations they could give her their reporter's phone number, although why would a TV reporter's cell phone work that far away when Joe's wouldn't? And no one would deliver a telegram to the middle of a fire zone, she felt pretty sure. But there had to be some way she could tell him that finally—finally!—she believed what Paul and Stacie had said all along.

Joe McConnell loved her.

The knowledge was wonderful, but she couldn't take pleasure in it with Joe still hurting over her disbelief. Because it *did* hurt, she knew firsthand, to tell someone wholeheartedly that you loved them and see that they didn't believe you.

Which was exactly what she'd been doing to Joe.

She had to find him. She had to reach him. She had to accept his declaration the way she should have accepted it from the start, if only she hadn't been so convinced that nobody could truly love two people.

But she'd been wrong about that, Meg knew as she choked down a swallow of coffee. If she could love both Tony and the baby with such fierce, consuming passion, then Joe could certainly love her that way. Just because he'd also loved Elena didn't mean his heart was permanently closed.

She had to tell him she believed him, and she had to tell him now. Only then could she let herself accept what she'd dreamed of for so long. Only then could she celebrate the glorious awareness that the man she'd loved for half a lifetime loved her just as much.

But how could she find him at some widespread fire near the Canadian border?

The only way, Meg decided, was to drive there in person. She'd have to bring Tony along, but he could sleep in the back seat. And if they were both late to school tomorrow, she could justify it.

After all, her husband was on the front lines of a fire.

She dumped her coffee down the sink and got their heavy coats from the closet, remembering how Joe's report had described the unseasonal cold up there. She loaded an extra pillow and blanket into the back seat of the car, figuring she would let Tony stay in bed as long as she could before moving him. She turned off all the upstairs lights except the one outside his room, braced herself to rouse the sleeping child, then remembered she'd left the coffeemaker on.

One more trip downstairs, then, and—

And there was Joe. Just coming in from the garage, looking so disheveled and sooty and downright furious that she stared in shock.

"Joe?"

Slamming the door behind him, he strode across the room and pulled her roughly into his arms. "Meg, I gotta tell you—"

"You're home," she gasped, startled by the odor of smoke that seemed to rise from his very skin. "The fire—"

"Forget the fire," he snapped, cupping her face in his hands and tilting her head to meet his determined gaze. "This business about the baby—"

"I know," she whispered. "I understand."

He didn't even seem to hear her, he was so intent on his point. So grimly focused. So intensely aroused that she could almost feel the heat pulsing from his body. "I wasn't doing it as a favor, damn it! I was doing it for us."

"I know," she repeated, but she might as well not have spoken.

"You and me, you got that?" he demanded, pressing her closer to him as if nothing but physical contact could make her listen. "*Us.* Not some—"

"Joe," she interrupted him, "I believe you. You love me."

"Yeah!" Only after he shouted the word did he stop, take a breath and look at her with amazement in his eyes. Then, as the realization stole across his face, she could feel the tension in his muscles begin to ease. "Yeah," he said softly.

Oh, he meant it. She could feel the truth of it in the way he held her, with such fierce desperation that she wanted to melt into his arms, soot and smoke and all. "You love me," Meg repeated with soaring certainty. "I don't know why it took me so long to believe you. But I *do* believe you, Joe. I do."

"It's about time," he muttered, and she could hear the rasp of relief in his voice. With an edge of challenge in his gaze, he rested his hands on her shoulders and looked at her straight, as if he wanted to see her reaction to his commitment. "I love you, Meggles."

She felt a shiver of joy. "Say it again."

A faint smile crossed his lips. "I love you," he repeated.

"I love you," she told him at the same moment, and saw his smile deepen.

"I could get used to this," he murmured, then bent to kiss her.

Even his kiss felt different, knowing that he loved her. She buried her hands in his hair, glorying in the feel of his body against hers, and gave herself up to the sheer, staggering pleasure of believing that Joe McConnell loved her.

That they both felt the same way.

She felt a little dizzy by the time he let her go, and she had the impression he was none too steady himself. The man must have been driving nonstop for hours, if he'd come all this way since they talked on the phone—

Which he'd done because she hadn't believed him. Meg took a long, sustaining breath and launched into the apology she'd been on her way to deliver.

"I'm so sorry," she told him, "that I didn't believe you before. Today I was trying to tell Tony I love him and the baby both differently, and it kind of hit me for the first time, you've been saying that all along."

Joe's eyes darkened. "Not long enough," he said, yanking off his coat and dropping it over the back of a kitchen chair. "I should've figured it out a lot sooner."

"Everybody else knew already," Meg admitted, taking another chair for herself. She hadn't just covered three hundred miles on the road, but even so she felt glad to sit down. "Paul and Stacie kept telling me, 'Of course he loves you.' But I was just too jealous of Elena—"

He cut her off with a quick gesture as he sat down beside her. "It was my fault for not telling you I love you. *Love* you!" he muttered, as if wondering how those words could ever be enough. "It's like…I need you and I like you and I want you and—"

"All of that, I know," she agreed with the same thrill of rightness she'd felt at holding the baby this afternoon. "Oh, I know. I was coming to tell you…everything I just told you."

He looked at her incredulously. "This time of night? It's a five-hour drive."

"That didn't stop *you*."

Joe felt a twinge of embarrassment, remembering how frustrated he'd been when he'd departed from the fire site. He'd taken barely three minutes to work out a note-sharing deal with one of the TV reporters before burning up the road home to confront Meg...and yet it turned out she'd already grasped what he wanted her to know. "When you said thanks for the baby, like it was some kind of favor—"

"It wasn't, I know," she interrupted. "You really want us to share a family, don't you?"

"Yeah," he confirmed, feeling a sudden thickness in his throat. "I really do."

She blinked a few times, and with a rush of wonder he saw that her eyes glistened with unshed tears. "Joe, I feel like I'm dreaming. I've never been this happy in my life."

Just because he wanted to share a family? Or was that wishful thinking? "You mean," he asked, "because we're finally getting a baby?"

"That's wonderful, too," Meg agreed, propping her chin in her hands as her lips curved into a smile of reminiscence. "But this afternoon, holding her, I kept thinking how much better it would be if we were both in this together."

So that *was* what she wanted, he thought with a rush of gladness. And he could confirm it with all his heart.

"We are, Meggers." Even if he didn't know squat about babies, he could learn. With this woman at his side, he could be the kind of dad he'd always wanted for himself. "We're in this together."

"And Tony is, too," she reminded him.

That was nice of her, but he knew she'd had a hard time coming to terms with Elena's son. "I wish he didn't make you feel like—"

"He doesn't anymore," she protested before he could even finish the sentence. "I never realized until today how much I love him...but I do. That's a whole other story."

Any stories she wanted to tell him, he'd be glad to enjoy. And with the coffeemaker still lit on the counter, it was obvious she'd been in no hurry for bed. "We've got all the time in the world," Joe told her, filling two mugs with the remaining coffee and bringing them back to the table.

She wrapped her fingers around her mug, watching him with a mixture of wistfulness and caution. "Don't you have to go back to the fire?"

He needed to exchange notes with the TV reporter, but that could wait until later. "I can do it tomorrow. You're more important than any story."

Again he saw the faint shimmer of moisture in her eyes, and again it swelled his heart. "Ah, Joe... I wish I'd listened to you sooner."

"I wish I'd *told* you sooner," he admitted. She'd spent four days ignoring his profession of love, but he'd wasted four years pursuing the crippling illusion of control. "All this time I loved you, only I was scared to admit it. And then when you were in Arizona..."

A glimmer of curiosity lit her face. "What happened?"

He took a gulp of coffee and closed his eyes, remembering the revelation. "Tony spotted it, when I turned down that job in Chicago—"

"You got another job offer?" Meg interrupted.

"The *Journal*. I told you about that after the convention." Although he hadn't mentioned the Focus section, he realized. He'd been waiting for the right opportunity, then rejected Warren's offer before it ever arose. "But that's old news."

Moving very slowly, she set down her mug. "Joe," she said softly, "if you'd still like that job...we could live in Chicago."

His first impression was that he hadn't heard her right. But when he saw the gritty resolve in her eyes, he knew she'd meant the offer seriously.

"Because," she continued as she met his gaze, "I know how much it means to you. And now it's like—I've got everything I ever wanted. You ought to get what you want, too.''

He felt as if she'd just offered him a magic carpet ride, as if his bearings had suddenly shifted under him. As much as he'd wanted the Focus section, this didn't make sense. ''What about raising our kids in Oakville?''

Meg twisted the mug between her fingers again, then gave him a faint smile. ''Well, millions of people raise kids in Chicago.''

But there was something missing here, he realized when she averted her eyes. How could she have changed her mind so abruptly, after insisting all these years that Oakville was the ideal place for a happy, healthy childhood? ''Megs...''

''All right!'' she cried, and he saw a flush of embarrassment on her cheeks. ''I wanted to stay here because I thought if we lived in the city, I'd never *see* you. It was stupid, okay?''

''No, it wasn't,'' he protested. Knowing how he drove himself on the big stories, she was more than likely correct. But she wasn't finished with her stammered explanation.

''I was always afraid I'd lose you. Only now...it's different.''

It sure was. Joe reached across the table, removed the mug from her fingers and took her hands in his. ''You're never gonna lose me. Never.''

''That's what I'm counting on,'' she said, her face still tinged with color even while she resolutely met his gaze. ''Honestly, Joe. We'd have to stay here long enough to finish the adoption, but if you want to take the job in Chicago, I could handle that.''

She meant it, he realized. Somehow, the core of strength he'd always admired in his wife had grown beyond anything he'd seen before, and he was staggered at the impact of her gift. ''You'd do that for me?''

"Well, I know how much you love reporting news," she explained, withdrawing her hands from his grasp as if she needed movement to illustrate his passion for journalism. "That's you, that's who you are." She lifted both hands in a gesture of acknowledgment, then gave him a smile that combined shyness with certainty. "That's who I love."

"Aw, Meg..." He couldn't keep from touching her, not when she touched his heart that way. Moving behind her chair, he wrapped his arms around her shoulders and let her clasp his hands in hers. "I do love news, you're right. But that's because news is all I'd ever *let* myself love."

She twisted around to face him, looking ready to protest, but he knew he hadn't explained himself right. "It always let me stay on the edge, you know?" he continued. "It gave me an excuse for not belonging."

Meg stood up and slid her arms around his waist. "You've always belonged," she said softly.

"Only with you." And that, Joe realized as he drew her closer to him, was why he loved this woman. "I didn't even let myself admit *that* for a long time. But now..." Now, with her in his arms, he could face the truth he'd avoided for so many years. "I'll always love news, yeah. But I love you more."

She didn't say a word, only buried her face against his chest, and as he held her close he could feel himself growing warmer. Ah, Meg...

"The whole time I was doing this fire story," he murmured, "I kept thinking about how fast I could get home to you."

Meg drew back and looked up at him, her eyes bright with pleasure. "Really?"

Could she honestly not know, even now, how much he wanted her? "Damn right I wanted to stay with you. Only you were telling me to go and do the story...."

"Not because I wanted to get rid of you!" she protested, then blushed again as she lowered her gaze. "Well, maybe a little."

Joe stared at her.

She wriggled in his grasp, still not meeting his eyes, and he realized she was embarrassed. "I just... I was trying not to *want* you. I thought if I could just get over wanting you—"

The very thought was appalling, but he knew from the quickness of her breathing that no matter what her words might indicate, her body was speaking the truth. "Do you still want me?" he interrupted, and when she finally met his gaze with a wholehearted smile he felt as if his blood had just caught fire.

"I always will," she said simply.

Joe pulled her back against him, exulting in the warmth that leaped between them. This woman belonged with him, and he belonged to her. "I'll always want you, too."

She raised her face, her lips parted, and he saw in her eyes the same radiant joy he felt within himself. "That's good."

"That's love, Meggers," he told her, and felt the same tremor of happiness surge through them both as they shared their first, promising kiss. "That's us."

Epilogue

"That's why," Meg told Joe three weeks later, "I think we ought to let Tony name her. So he'll know he's as important as everyone else in the family."

"You think he can handle it?" Her husband looked at the baby in his arms with the same expression of wonder he'd worn ever since they brought her home yesterday afternoon. "Picking a name's a big responsibility."

"So is being a brother," she answered, handing Joe the bottle she'd just warmed in the microwave. "Tony deserves to feel important, especially now."

He gave her the crooked smile she had loved for half a lifetime and offered their daughter her first bottle of the morning. "Anybody who lives with you is always gonna feel important. But if you want to let Tony pick the name, that's okay with me."

She was determined that Tony would never again feel left out, and had made a point of including him in as many decisions as possible over the past few weeks. This one, though, was special. The naming of their daughter was the greatest gift she could offer their son.

''I'll mention it to him,'' she said, letting her gaze linger on Joe and the baby for another heartwarming moment before seeking out Tony in the garden. He had taken it upon himself to pick flowers for his sister's room, and Meg had equipped him with a white ceramic vase to fill however he liked.

She found him with a gathering of pink flowers that showed more enthusiasm than artistic skill, but she knew he would take pride in presenting the baby with a gift of his own.

''That's nice of you,'' she told Tony as he held up the vase for her review. ''Now, if you'd like to do something very important for your sister, Papá and I think you should be the one to choose her name.''

''Me?'' He looked astonished, and yet mingled with the amazement she could see a tinge of pride. ''I get to name the baby?''

''If you want.'' Her instinct told her that he would appreciate the importance of the task, which meant he might find it too intimidating. ''Now that we've all seen her, you can pick a name just as well as Papá and I could.''

Tony set down his vase on the same bench where he'd made her eat strawberry ice cream a month ago and stared thoughtfully into the distance. ''It ought to be a special name,'' he announced.

''Good idea,'' Meg agreed. ''You can take your time thinking about it. I just wanted to see if you'd like to do that.''

''Yeah,'' he said immediately. ''I'm gonna think of the very best name for her. Only…I'm not sure how to pick.''

Oh, he definitely understood the magnitude of this choice. ''Well,'' she suggested, sitting down beside the vase of pink flowers, ''sometimes people choose a name they liked in a book or a song. Or a name that means something, like Faith or Charity. Or a name that belonged to someone special.''

''Like George Washington.''

She bit back a smile, imagining the tiny girl resting in Joe's arms with a name like George Washington. ''Well, that's a man's name. But there are special women, too.''

Tony frowned in concentration. ''I never heard of any.''

His third-grade history lessons had probably focused solely on the founding fathers, Meg realized as she saw her husband bringing the baby outside. ''Special women aren't necessarily famous,'' she explained, moving the vase so Joe could sit down beside her. ''But they can be just as important as—well, like your mother. She might not be in any books, but she was still special.''

The child nodded soberly. ''I know. Her name was Elena.''

Almost instinctively, Meg braced herself for the flash of jealousy. And realized, with a rush of wonder, that she felt nothing except a heartening sense of calm.

''A lot of people pick names from their family,'' she told Tony. ''So if you'd like to, that's fine.''

Joe looked from her to their son and back again, and she could almost see the protest forming on his lips. Before he could voice it, she reached to touch Tony's shoulder.

''Sweetheart,'' she asked, ''do you want to name the baby for your mother? I think Elena is a pretty name.''

Still holding their baby in one arm, Joe drew Meg closer to him with his free hand. ''You're amazing,'' he murmured. ''Every time I think I can't possibly love you any more, you make my heart bigger.''

''I like using a family name as long as it's a special one,'' Tony said, gazing at his sister. ''Are you sure that's okay?''

''I promise,'' Meg answered, leaning closer into her husband's embrace.

Tony looked up at them both with a mixture of pride and pleasure on his face. "I know!" he said. "Let's call her Baby Meg."

* * * * * *

▼ SILHOUETTE
SPECIAL EDITION®

AVAILABLE FROM 24TH DECEMBER 1999

BABY LOVE Victoria Pade

That's My Baby!

Rugged Ry McDermot is in trouble; named legal guardian to an
adorable toddler, he is out of his depth. Tallie Shanahan is the solution
to his problem. But playing house with Tallie is proving more tempting
than this sworn bachelor would like!

JUST THE THREE OF US Jennifer Mikels

As a businesswoman, Taylor Elmhurst is a success, but as a guardian
she has a lot to learn. Help unexpectedly comes in the form of sexy
Matt Duran. A natural with her nephew, his interest soon extends to
Taylor…

A WEDDING FOR MAGGIE Allison Leigh

Daniel Clay left town rather than watch Maggie wed another. Now
she's a widow, and one stolen night of passion leads to an unplanned
pregnancy; so will *he* be marrying Maggie after all?

THE COWBOY AND HIS WAYWARD BRIDE
Sherryl Woods

And Baby Makes Three

Harlan Adams has just discovered he's a father and he's furious! His
childhood sweetheart, Laurie Jensen, has secretly given birth to their
daughter. Now this determined dad won't take no for an answer—
starting with his proposal!

HOMETOWN GIRL Robin Lee Hatcher

Monica Fletcher had cut Daniel Rourke out of her life forever, never
dreaming that one day their daughter would need him. But now Daniel
is back and determined to be a part of both of their lives!

THE SECRET MILLIONAIRE Patricia Thayer

Jill Morgan has accepted that to Rick Covelli she was just a fling. But
he's back, and he says he's changed. Money's no object, but can Jill be
wooed, given that she has to think of her child?

AVAILABLE FROM 24TH DECEMBER 1999

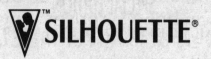

Intrigue
Danger, deception and desire

RYAN'S RESCUE Karen Leabo
A COWBOY'S HONOUR Laura Gordon
JACKSON'S WOMAN Judi Lind
REDHAWK'S RETURN Aimée Thurlo

Desire
Provocative, sensual love stories

SHEIKH'S RANSOM Alexandra Sellers
A MATCH FOR MORGAN Marie Ferrarella
THE MILLIONAIRE AND THE PREGNANT PAUPER
Christie Ridgway
THE STARDUST COWBOY Anne McAllister
SECRET DAD Raye Morgan
THE SCANDALOUS HEIRESS Kathryn Taylor

Sensation
A thrilling mix of passion, adventure and drama

THE TOUGH GUY AND THE TODDLER
Diane Pershing
LIKE FATHER, LIKE DAUGHTER Margaret Watson
THE MIRACLE MAN Sharon Sala
ONCE MORE A FAMILY Paula Detmer Riggs

9912

Sometimes bringing up baby
can bring surprises —and
showers of love! For the cutest
and cuddliest heroes and
heroines, choose the Special
Edition™ book marked

That's my
baby!

SILHOUETTE
SPECIAL EDITION®

MONTANA
...where passions run deep and mystery lingers

NEW from Silhouette®, a sizzling twelve book continuity series set against the majestic backdrop of the Montana mountains.

The stories from Whitehorn, Montana capture the excitement of living, with a mix of romance, mystery and suspense.

Unforgettable, the Montana legends will live on, long after you have finished the final story.

Montana is a compelling series of books from your favourite Silhouette authors.

Available Now

Available at branches of WH Smith, Tesco, Martins, RS McCall, Forbuoys, Borders, Easons, Volume One/James Thin and most good paperback bookshops

S H A R O N

Sala

He knows more than any innocent
man should…

Gabriel Donner has been experiencing
disturbing dreams of horrible murders, dreams
that mean he knows details of the murders
the police don't yet know.
Will they believe he is innocent
or does he know too much?

R e u n i o n

Available from 19th November

FREE
4 BOOKS
AND A SURPRISE GIFT!

We would like to take this opportunity to thank you for reading this Silhouette® book by offering you the chance to take FOUR more specially selected titles from the Special Edition™ series absolutely FREE! We're also making this offer to introduce you to the benefits of the Reader Service™ —

★ FREE home delivery
★ FREE monthly Newsletter
★ FREE gifts and competitions
★ Exclusive Reader Service discounts
★ Books available before they're in the shops

Accepting these FREE books and gift places you under no obligation to buy; you may cancel at any time, even after receiving your free shipment. Simply complete your details below and return the entire page to the address below. **You don't even need a stamp!**

YES! Please send me 4 free Special Edition books and a surprise gift. I understand that unless you hear from me, I will receive 6 superb new titles every month for just £2.70 each, postage and packing free. I am under no obligation to purchase any books and may cancel my subscription at any time. The free books and gift will be mine to keep in any case.

E9EC

Ms/Mrs/Miss/Mr ....Initials............................
BLOCK CAPITALS PLEASE

Surname..

Address...

....

....Postcode ....

Send this whole page to:
UK: FREEPOST CN81, Croydon, CR9 3WZ
EIRE: PO Box 4546, Kilcock, County Kildare (stamp required)

Offer valid in UK and Eire only and not available to current Reader Service subscribers to this series. We reserve the right to refuse an application and applicants must be aged 18 years or over. Only one application per household. Terms and prices subject to change without notice. Offer expires 30th June 2000. As a result of this application, you may receive further offers from Harlequin Mills & Boon Limited and other carefully selected companies. If you would prefer not to share in this opportunity please write to The Data Manager at the address above.

Silhouette is a registered trademark used under license.
Special Edition is being used as a trademark.

Revisit the MacGregor family in

NORA ROBERTS

new blockbuster

The MacGregor *Grooms*

Daniel MacGregor is using his matchmaking powers once again. This time, he has his sights set on getting his three handsome, eligible grandsons to the altar. And he knows just the right women to tempt them...

On sale 17th September 1999

Available at most branches of
WH Smith, Tesco, Asda, Martins, RS McCall, Forbuoys,
Borders, Easons, Volume One/James Thin
and most good paperback bookshops